DEEP 6

A SECOND CHANCE REVERSE HAREM ROMANCE

STEPHANIE BROTHER

DEEP 6 Copyright © 2021 STEPHANIE BROTHER

All Rights Reserved. This book or any portion thereof may not be reproduced or used in any manner whatsoever without the express permission of the publisher except for the use of brief quotations in a book review.

This book is a work of fiction. Any resemblance to persons, living or dead, or places, events or locations is purely coincidental. The characters are all productions of the author's imagination.

Please note that this work is intended only for adults over the age of 18 and all characters represented as 18 or over.

ISBN: 9798486898419

1

SANDY

The road stretches in front of me, empty except for a huge truck in the distance. It's hot, but the air-conditioning is keeping me cool. I'm thankful because I want to arrive at Connie's wedding looking fresh, not a sweaty crumpled mess.

I have a small suitcase in the trunk just in case I need to stay over. I haven't booked anything, which is stupid, but money is about to get tight. I figure there'll be a room available somewhere if I need one.

The music blasting on the stereo makes me tap my fingers on the wheel. I've always loved 1970s disco. The classics make me want to get up and dance, but it's been a long time since I hit a club. My friends are all settled down now with job responsibilities, boyfriends, or husbands. Now the only time I get to dance is at weddings, and each one that passes makes me feel more and more of a failure.

My mind wanders where I don't want it to venture, back to the last night I spent with Tyler. He's the last man

I allowed into my bed and the last man I trusted with my heart. It didn't end well, and even just a fleeting thought about what happened four years ago sets off an ache in my chest that is hard to push away.

I focus on the song lyrics, starting to sing along even though I know I sound loud and tuneless. There's no one here to listen to my awful voice, and singing lifts my spirits. At least it lifts my spirits until the car fills with smoke, and I'm forced to pull over in a panic. As I scramble out of my old Lexus, I have the sense to grab my purse from the passenger seat. If it's going to go up in flames, I need my phone.

On the side of the road, I glance back the way I came, hoping a friendly person might be coming up behind me, and then reconsider. It could be dangerous. So many true-crime stories start this way, with a woman in a vulnerable position. I grab my phone from my bag, walking a little further from the car. There are no signs of flames, so I'm wondering if it's the car's cooling system that has ruptured. What I thought was smoke must have been steam.

Running a quick search, I find a local garage that's only two miles away. Deep Repairs. It seems like an odd name, but I couldn't care less what it's called so long as they can come and rescue me and the car and fix it up quickly.

A deep husky voice says, "Deep Repairs, how can I help you?" and I quickly explain what's happened. The guy tells me they'll be with me in twenty minutes, and when I hang up, I breathe a sigh of relief.

Twenty minutes feels like twenty hours standing in my silver heels and strapless dusky pink dress by the side of this dusty road. People drive past, but thankfully no one stops. I guess the good Samaritan is a concept relegated to the past. When the repair truck is visible in the distance, I practically sing again with happiness.

The driver pulls over in front of my vehicle, emerging from the cab of the truck hidden behind a baseball cap and sunglasses. The gray shirt he's wearing hugs his broad chest and muscular arms, leaving nothing to the imagination. There's grease on his forearms and a tattoo too.

A tattoo that looks familiar.

When he focuses on me, he stops dead like someone shot him in the chest, the ready smile on his lips falling away as he recognizes me at the same time that I recognize him.

"Sandy?"

His rich, deep voice sends a shiver through my whole body, not of fear but of awareness. It's like every molecule of my body knows this man and is drawn to him.

"Tyler?" It comes out as a question too, even though I know it's him. Tears burn behind my eyes and in my throat. Tears of anger, of betrayal, of disappointment so deep it cut me open so wide that I've never been able to fully repair myself.

This man was responsible for my happiest days and my most blissful moments. He filled me with light and laughter and hope, and then he disappeared, and all I was left with was the ghost of what we were when we were together and a million unanswered questions.

How could he leave me? How could he not tell me he was going? Did he ever love me? Was it real or all just a cleverly crafted lie?

My hands tremble at my sides, and I clasp them in front of me, not wanting to give anything away. Our days of sharing everything are so deep in the past that they feel like something I watched at the movies, not something that actually happened to me.

Tyler's hand goes to his jaw, and he rubs his stubble in the way he always used to when he was thinking. I guess he's as lost about how to be as I am. "So, you've broken down?"

My eyebrows draw up, and my eyes widen. Is he seriously going to ignore the giant elephant sitting between us and pretend everything is fine?

He rounds my car, opening the driver's-side door and popping the hood before I can reply. I totter in my ridiculous shoes, watching as he ducks his head over my frazzled engine, taking comfort as he always did in the simple mechanics of metal and grease, pushing emotions aside.

"I'm going to have to tow you?" Tyler says, dropping the hood so that it clanks noisily back into place.

"Okay."

"Jump into the truck while I hook it up."

I stand for a moment, gawking at this man who, apart from the initial shock of seeing me, seems totally unaffected by my presence. How can he be so cool, calm, and collected when I feel like my skin is going to peel away at the sight of him?

Then I remember it was his decision to leave me. He must have known for a while what he was going to do. Maybe on the last night that we slept together, when I thought that I was feeling real love in his fingertips, in his mind, he was already gone.

Pulling myself together, I turn and stride to the front of his truck, pulling the door open and climbing up with as much grace as I can manage. When the door is closed, I sink into the seat, clutching my purse on my knee like I would cradle a child.

How is this happening? I thought about him, and then he was there—there in all his overwhelmingly gorgeous glory. The years have been good to Tyler. He's grown into his manhood in a way that calls to the primal, animal part of my brain, filling me with self-loathing. There's not a hair on his head that deserves any response from me, let alone a sexual one.

The trouble is that Tyler was always good at setting me on fire. He could make me come with just his dick and his words, and I know from talking to my friends that it's an unusual skill. I reckon I could have come just from looking at his naked body and listening to all of the filthy things he would whisper in my ear.

He's broader and thicker now. The muscles I used to trace with my fingertips while he slept are rounder and stronger. There's more of a swagger to the way he walks and an extra gruffness to his voice. Any boyishness that remained when we were together is long gone.

This man I knew more intimately than I've ever known another human being is a stranger to me, and it devastates me all over again.

I watch in the mirror as he attaches my car to the truck and lifts it onto the flatbed. He's precise in his movements, so we're ready to leave more quickly than I was anticipating. As he rounds the side of the truck, I smooth my hair and fasten my seatbelt, inhaling and holding a deep breath.

When he throws open the door, my heart skitters, and when he hauls himself into the cab next to me, his scent floods me with memories.

Memories I thought I'd left behind but still feel as raw as they did in the past.

Memories that I wish I could forget. Except I can't. They're as etched onto my skin and into my life as deeply as they are in my mind. There's no forgetting Tyler Evans. There never was, and there never will be.

"So…" He turns the key in the ignition, and the radio bursts to life. Except it isn't just the radio. He's playing 70s disco, which he always used to tease me about liking in the past. Our eyes meet through the dark of his glasses, and it's like a bolt of electricity running through me. Then he flicks the music off, puts the truck into gear, and pulls onto the road.

DEEP 6

I guess I'm not the only one still thinking about the past.

2

TYLER

Fuck.

The word has been the only thing pounding in my head since I caught sight of the beautiful woman broken down at the side of the road and then realized it was Sandy.

Sandy, the girl I left in bed, kissing her pretty lips while she slept, and never returned to.

I feel the anger radiating from her. Coiled and powerful, I know if she wasn't clutching her purse so tightly, she'd lash out at me. I deserve a slap round the face—even a punch in the mouth. I deserve harsh words and cutting glances. I deserve her hate.

The atmosphere between us crackles like the air before a powerful storm. I don't know what to say or how to be. I don't want to make things more awkward between us than they are already. I glance at her out of the corner of my eye, and her pretty profile catches at my heart like a hook in a fish's mouth.

She smells different too, of a fragrance womanlier than

she used to wear.

"What are you doing out here?" I ask.

She turns, staring at the side of my face as I keep my eyes on the road. "I'm on my way to a wedding."

"The car's not looking good," I tell her. It's an understatement, but I don't want to stress her out before I know one hundred percent what all the issues are.

"Shit," she mutters, rooting around in her purse.

Pulling out her phone, she flicks through her contacts and dials a number. Almost immediately, my gut contracts at the thought that she's dialing her boyfriend to tell him what's going on. There's no ring on her finger so I'm taking it there's no husband.

"Hey," she says, then I catch a woman's voice replying, and I exhale. "I've broken down…I don't think so…I know, I'm so gutted…can you send Connie, Karter, Kane, Holden, and Harris my best wishes…sure. Okay…bye."

"Carmella's sister's getting married?"

Sandy nods, sliding her phone back into her purse and zipping it back up.

"That's nice."

We ride together in silence as a million conversations play out in my head. A million conversations that I'll never be able to have with her in real life because it just wouldn't be fair, and she probably wouldn't want to hear any of it.

Too much time has passed.

Too much water under the bridge.

I'm a different man than I was when we were together. A man too splintered to ever be able to make things right.

When we pull into the repair shop that I started with my friends, and that saved my life, I feel such a sense of relief that the tension constricting my throat relaxes enough for me to swallow. Damien is the first to emerge, lumbering as he always does on his huge feet. He's looking especially rough today, as though he's spent the morning tearing up trees from their roots and chopping them into pieces with just a butter knife. He doesn't wait for us to open the doors to the vehicle. He just strolls past and begins to unhook Sandy's car, ready for inspection. He has no idea that the woman sitting next to me is anything more than a stranded client. He has no idea that I feel like my heart is tearing in two just from being near and not being able to touch her.

Sandy puts her hand on the door handle and then turns to me. "What's going to happen?"

"We'll take a look and give you a rundown of what's gone wrong." She nods and pushes open the door. "Where can I wait?"

"Inside. There's a waiting area and a coffee machine."

Sandy slides out of my truck, slamming the door before hitching her purse onto her shoulder. I sense that she's not used to wearing heels because she walks slowly into Deep Repairs and my eyes trail her, hungry and reluctant at the same time.

She's like a magnet, and my heart is a piece of shrapnel left over from another time and place. A time when I had peace in my soul. A time where I could sleep without waking from the same nightmare that comes to me over and over, no matter how much time passes.

"She's a piece of ass," Damien whistles as I finally throw open my door.

"Say that again, and I'll rip out your heart," I say, then feel fucking awful when Damien's face drops like a wounded puppy.

He might be big, but he's got a heart as soft as the center of a cream donut. "Who is she?" he asks. "Someone special?"

"The most special," I say, shoving my hands into my pockets.

"Sandy?" His bushy eyebrows shoot up when I nod. "Shit, dude. How'd that happen?"

"I don't know. Fate. The universe conspiring. Who knows?"

"What are you gonna do?"

"I don't know, man. Let's take a look at this car and see what we're dealing with."

"Sure, Tyler," he says, patting me on the shoulder, telling me he's with me. All my boys know about Sandy. They were the ones to pick me up when my life spiraled. They were the ones who put me back together.

The music inside Deep Repairs is blaring. Greg is in charge of the tunes today, so it's rock that's keeping the mechanics focused. We push Sandy's car inside, and Greg slides out from the blue truck he's been working on. "Whatcha got there?"

"Cooling system's shot somewhere. Looks like it's losing oil too."

"Shit." He's on his feet and looming into the car before I have the opportunity to tell him I've got it. At six-foot-four, Greg isn't a man you tell to mind his own business easily. Plus, he's the best at diagnosing fast, and that's what Sandy needs.

I watch him fiddle with the engine, touching grease and smelling his fingers. He's a tactile mechanic in a way, using all his senses to feel out the problem. "We're gonna need to order parts," he says eventually.

"How long?"

"Maybe seventy-two hours," he says. "Weekend delays."

"Shit." Sandy's going to be devastated to miss Connie's wedding. Then I have an idea.

"You guys okay if I duck out for the rest of the day?"

Damien and Greg glance at each other, and then Greg

nods. He's not in charge here, but as the oldest, he's taken the role of organizer.

The click of heels alerts me to Sandy's presence behind me. "Is it bad?"

Greg and Damien stand straight, and I turn to face the woman who is in my blood so deep I've never managed to bleed her out.

"It's bad," Greg says, shaking his head.

"Can you fix it today?"

"We need to get parts. They won't get here for at least forty-eight hours. Then we need time to fit them."

"Three days." Sandy's face falls, and so does my stomach. Seeing her disappointed is like a kick in the gut. "The wedding…" She shakes her head, blowing out a steadying breath, her eyes focused on a grease stain on the ground.

"Wedding?" a voice pipes up from the other side of the shop. It's Andrew, his bright blue eyes peering at us with interest.

"She has a wedding she's going to miss," I explain.

"Is that why she's dressed up so pretty?" Damien asks innocently, then blushes almost immediately.

"Yes." I shoot him a look, and he has the decency to shrug.

"Why don't you drive her?" Andrew asks, oblivious to all the history bubbling between us but an answer to my prayers. He's suggested it before I could get a word in, and that makes this situation way easier.

All eyes land on me, and I shift on my feet. "I could drive you…if you wanted me to?"

Sandy clutches her purse in front of her body like a shield against me. "It's too far."

"Where?"

"An hour away."

Is that it? "I can do that."

She bites her lip, and I know she's torn. Saying no means that she misses her friend's special day but saying yes will put us in close confines for at least two hours in the car. "You better go home to change first," she says eventually, shocking me so much I take a step back.

"What?"

"Well, you can't go to a party dressed like that."

I gaze down at my stained overalls tied at my waist and the tight gray shirt I pulled on this morning. She's right, but I wasn't thinking I'd be attending with her. I'd imagined driving her and waiting outside.

I should have known she wouldn't have liked that. Sandy never was okay with people putting themselves out for her. She's fair and considerate, from her pretty little toes to the last hair on her head.

"Looks like you just got yourself a free meal," Arden says, grinning next to his brother. He rubs his beard, the only obvious thing that sets him apart from his triplets.

A free meal with an awkwardness chaser.

Shit. I guess I better go scrub up.

3

SANDY

As I sit waiting outside the colossal house where Tyler is currently changing, I pick at the skin around my nail, still reeling at the strange circumstances. In a million years, I never would have predicted something like this, and now I'm here, living in this peculiar reality with the very solid version of my ghost-ex-boyfriend, I don't know how to be.

I'm on a raft, lost at sea, adrift and floundering.

My initial anger has settled into something curious. Something hurt—something worn down and filled with questions.

When the door slams, my eyes are drawn to the shape of the man who wrecked me so badly I've never found the courage to trust again. He's swapped his mechanic's uniform for navy dress pants and a white button-down shirt that he's left open at the collar. He's rolled up the sleeves, too, probably for the heat but maybe because he always loved to show off his ink. The baseball cap has been ditched and now I see the dark curls that I used to run my fingers through, sometimes when we were relaxing on the couch in front of the TV, and sometimes when Tyler was moving inside me, like he was always going to exist between my thighs.

My cheeks flush, and a feeling stirs between my legs that's been absent for a long time.

Arousal.

It's not that I haven't wanted sex in the years after Tyler. It's more that I haven't felt *this*.

What is it? Attraction that's more than the physical? I knew this man and believed he was good in every way.

"Hey." He slides in next to me, smelling like an alpine forest at dawn, taking up way more space in the truck than is decent. When his hand finds the stick, the memory of his palm gripping my ass hits me full force. The whimper that leaves my lips is shameful.

I'm better than this. Stronger than this. He doesn't deserve to know that his presence still affects me in any way other than drawing contempt.

"Do you want to type the zip code in?"

He hands me his phone, and I punch the address into his app. We're on our way in no time, with only the noise of the air-conditioning and engine for company.

The awkwardness feels terrible.

"Thanks for doing this," I say to break the silence. "I'm sure that you have better things to be doing…working…"

"It's okay. The boys have all the jobs at the shop under control."

"Still. This is…it's a lot."

He turns to me, taking his eyes from the road for a few seconds. "It's nothing, Sandy." He nods as though I'm supposed to take more from those three words, and I do. He means it's nothing compared to leaving me without saying goodbye—nothing for going without explanation.

And it is nothing in comparison to all that we've been and all that we lost.

"Connie will be happy," I say.

"Who's the lucky guy? Is it someone I know?"

I pause for a moment, thinking how to answer his question, but there's no softening the answer when we'll be there soon, and he'll see for himself.

"Guys," I say. "She's marrying four men."

"FOUR?" He turns to me again, and I point at the road.

"Four brothers. They're in a polyamorous relationship. A reverse harem."

"Reverse harem?"

"Yeah, you know. Like a king with lots of concubines, except she's a queen with lots of kings."

I grin as he whistles long and low. "Connie?"

The disbelief in his voice is too funny. "I felt the same when I heard about her situation. She was even suggesting I should meet her boyfriends' cousins to see if I wanted the same kind of relationship."

"Oh yeah," Tyler says, all bright and breezy, but I know him well enough to know he's taking my bait.

"Yeah… They're ranchers, five of them."

"Five?"

"Yeah." I leave that hanging for a while, watching Tyler's jaw ticking out of the corner of my eye. When I think he's stewed long enough, I put him out of his misery. "It didn't work out, though."

"Connie didn't seem the type," he mutters uncomfortably.

"And what's that supposed to mean?"

"Well, she…I don't know." He stumbles over the last words as though he's regretting his statement.

"Who would seem the type?"

"Someone with looser morals, I guess." Looser morals. Is that what he's insinuating that I have? Well, fuck him. He lost the right to think anything about my morals or lack of them a long time ago.

"It isn't just about sex," I tell him, with a bite in my tone. "It's about love. Love between five people that transcends societal constructs. Love that battles every day against prejudice."

Tyler nods, his hands clutching the wheel just a little tighter. "I get that," he says. "Love isn't always easy."

I grit my teeth and purse my lips, his comment slicing at my skin. It takes a few deep breaths to steady myself enough to reply because what I say next is important. "Love is very simple, Tyler. Love is honest and kind. It's selfless and sacrificing. It's believing that someone is as important as you are and always treating them as you would like to be treated. It's everything."

His head droops, and his eyes drift closed, then he shakes his head and refocuses on the road. His knuckles whiten as he grips even harder. "I'm sorry."

A sound leaves my throat that I haven't made for three years. I promised myself that crying over Tyler was in my past. I promised that I'd never give him that power again. But when I made that promise, I thought he was always going to be a ghost. I never believed I'd hear those two words that have torn my heart out all over again and left it pulsing and bloody in my palms.

"Shit," Tyler mutters, glancing at me as bitter tears spill over my cheeks.

"I can't do this now," I gasp, swiping at my face. There will be no point in Tyler driving me to Connie's wedding if I weep my makeup off and am too emotionally wrecked to put on a brave face. "Can we just pretend that we're two old friends...just pretend that none of it happened?"

Tyler's jaw ticks again as he grits his teeth. My eyes drift down, finding a date tattooed into his skin. It's the date three months after he left me—three months into my sadness. "Of course," Tyler finally says. "Whatever you need."

I turn my body away from him, twisting so my knees are resting against the door of the truck and my line of vision is fixed through the window. I stay that way until I've swallowed down all my emotions and pressed them into the box that I made to keep them safely away from my heart.

When we pull into the lot of the hall where Connie's wedding is in full swing, I straighten up, smoothing my skirt and patting my hair into place. I run my finger beneath my eyes to pick up any mascara smudges and inhale a deep, steadying breath.

"It looks like it's buzzing," Tyler says as he pulls into a vacant space and flicks off the ignition.

"Let's go and have a good time." I throw open the door and shake my head at my own flippancy. Who would have thought that I'd be this way? Not me. The thousands of conversations I had with Tyler in my head were never anything like this. But real life is often so different from imagination.

Tyler follows me into the hall as I scan the crowd for Carmella or Connie or another familiar face.

Carmella spots me first, though, barreling toward me with a plate filled with dessert. "Sandy." Her arms go around my chest, and I sink into my best friend's hug, so grateful to see her. I know the moment she spots Tyler because her whole body goes rigid. "What the fuck…?"

"It's a long story," I say quickly. "Don't make a scene. He drove me from the repair shop. I've told him I don't want to talk about anything…that we're just going to have a good time. When this celebration is done, I'll say what I need to say and walk away, okay?"

With her free hand, Carmella tucks a lock of my hair behind my ear with the tenderness of someone with love in their heart. "Protect that heart of yours, San San." Her use of my nickname brings back the burning sensation in my throat.

I nod firmly. "I will. I've gotten to be an expert at that."

Turning, I usher Tyler forward. "Tyler, you remember Carmella." He nods and has the decency to do it with shame on his handsome face. It's so weird to see him standing amongst my friends, as though I've portalled in Tyler's imaginary older brother.

"Tyler." Carmella nods once, telling Tyler with every fiber of her being that he's treading on thin ice.

"There you are." Derek appears next to his wife, handing her a long-stemmed glass of what looks like champagne.

There's a moment of awkwardness as we all stand in silence. Then Carmella springs to life. "Derek, this is Tyler."

Both men reach out politely to shake hands. "*The* Tyler?" he asks, glancing at his wife, and she nods. Derek's eyes open a little wider, then he smiles politely. "So you guys are back together?"

Trust a man to put his foot into it.

"Err, no darling," Carmella says, trying to rescue him. "Sandy's car broke down, and Tyler kindly offered to escort her."

"Well, that's good of you," Derek says, glancing between us as though he's hoping he'll be able to read our minds and find out what's really going on.

"Let's get something to eat," I say to Tyler. "And a drink. You must be starving."

I grab his hand out of instinct, and the feel of his big rough palm in mine is overwhelming to me. We used to measure our hands, mine so small against his capable strength. He holds me gently as though he's frightened that I might break, and it's true. I might. I could if I keep drifting backward.

"Sandy," Connie's voice calls over the chatter of other guests. "I didn't think you were going to make it…" Her eyes fix onto our joined hands, then run up Tyler's muscular arm to his muscular shoulder and across his insanely ripped chest before drifting up to his face. "Whoa," she says. "Well…Tyler, I was not expecting it to be you."

"Congratulations," he says, sliding his hand out of mine. "You look beautiful."

"Thanks," Connie beams. "I just tossed this outfit together. There was absolutely no planning involved at all." Her eyes roll and then find mine, wide and searching. "I'm so glad you came."

"Me too." I pull her into a hug, remembering how kind she was to Carmella during her wedding breakdown. "Now, where are those sexy husbands of yours?"

"Well, to be honest, I have absolutely no idea. There are too many of them to keep track of, so I've just had to accept that they're out there somewhere." She waves her hand around theatrically. "One of them has Brett, of that I'm certain."

"I can't wait to see him. He must have grown so much."

"His voice is practically breaking," Connie laughs. She's exaggerating excessively, but I get her point. Out of the corner of my eye, I see Natalie with her twin sons, and they seem to have shot up inches since the last time we were in the same room.

Time is passing for everyone, but my life has been standing still.

"Connie." A woman waves from across the room, and Connie shrugs apologetically.

"Please help yourself to some food. It's all come from an organic farm owned by those ranchers I was telling you about." Connie winks and I have to stifle a smile.

"Thanks."

She touches my arm before disappearing into the crowd.

Tyler moves closer, the heat of his body and his looming height stealing my breath. "She hasn't changed," he says.

"No," I say. "All the best people remain true to themselves." It's a dig for sure, and I regret it as soon as the words leave my lips. "Let's fix a plate."

"Sure." I wait for Tyler to set off toward the buffet first and follow him, chastising myself with every step. I don't want to stoop low. I need to maintain the high ground because that's where I've always stood in this situation.

Tyler hands me a plate before taking his own, and we heap on salads and cold meats, delicious cheeses, and soft bread. Everything looks and smells awesome. There are tables around the edge of the hall, and we make our way to a vacant one. Tyler passes me silverware and waits until I'm ready to eat before starting himself. In all of the sadness, I'd forgotten what a gentleman he is. His size and strength, masculinity, and gruffness are what you see first, but beneath the exterior is a whole world.

"What are you doing these days?" he asks me, eyes flicking up to mine as though he's scared about what to say.

"I'm a literature teacher," I say. "For a local high school."

"Wow...that's great."

"It is." I nod, chewing a mouthful of the most delicious savory pastry slice. "The kids are so awesome, and my colleagues are supportive. I'm lucky to have found such a fantastic school." I don't tell him that the principal has managed to fire me on a technicality in my contract after he tried to grope me in the teachers lounge, and I pushed him away. That is something I'm going to keep to myself, along with the depressing fact that I'm going to have to move out of my apartment and back into my sister Suzanne's basement. At least I'll get to spend more quality time with Sophie. It's absolutely the only good thing about the situation.

"So you have some vacation time right now?"

"Yeah. It's one of the perks. And you...you're working at Deep Repairs?"

"I'm a partner with the other guys you met. There are six of us."

"Six! And that's your house?"

"We all live there," Tyler says. "Workmates and roommates"

"Don't you get sick of each other?"

Tyler shakes his head. "Never. They're like my brothers."

I smile at the certainty in his voice. I always thought that guy friendships are so much less complicated than girl friendships. "And what about your family. How's Luna? How's Jake?"

The change in Tyler's face makes my whole body run cold. His mouth drops open, and his eyes widen, his fists clutching the silverware like they're weapons he's ready to use at any moment. The silence stretches between us, slick and sour before someone in the crowd begins to clink a glass.

"SPEECH!" A man who has definitely had too much to drink struggles to climb onto a chair, trying to get a view over the crowd. "Kane, Karter, Holden, Harris, get your butts over here." The room erupts into cheers, and I'm drawn to look at the crowd, where I start to see movement. Whatever I said that just spooked Tyler is better left alone for both our sakes.

Connie's husbands begin to make their way across the room, smiling and embarrassed. The man who yelled has procured a microphone from the DJ and is waving it around like it's a weapon. Kane is the first to reach him and he quickly takes the mic as though he's worried the guy is going to injure someone.

Kane waits until his brothers surround him, then he brings the mic to his lips. "Connie, where are you, baby?"

He scans the crowd as Karter adjusts little Brett on his hip, little Brett, who really has grown so much. "I'm here," Connie shouts, waving as she makes her way into the center of the crowd. Holden pulls her into a hug, and Harris joins her on the other side. She grins broadly, looking around at all of her towering, gorgeous husbands.

"There she is," Kane says softly. "We haven't prepared anything. This is supposed to be a relaxed event, but I guess some traditions stick no matter how much you try to be different."

There's a rumble of laughter in the crowd, which Kane waits to subside. "What we want to say is that we couldn't be happier that this day is finally here. We wanted to marry Connie a long time ago, but she's been making us wait."

"Playing hard to get," Harris shouts, and the crowd laughs.

"But then we went to Carmella and Derek's wedding, and something clicked," Kane continues.

I turn, searching for Carmella in the crowd, finding her beaming happily. Derek throws his arm over her shoulder, and he pulls her close. They're the picture of a happy couple that should only inspire good thoughts but instead sends a shiver of jealousy through me that I hate. She's my best friend and I'm so happy that she's found her one, but I'm not less deserving than her, am I?

"And here we are," Kane says. "Connie has made us

the happiest men on earth today. She's the strongest person we know, battling for our family, standing up when people judge our love. We know it isn't always easy to live a life that's different to the majority, but we promise we'll be by your side in every way…for as long as we're breathing, we are yours."

Connie's hand covers her mouth, and her eyes brim with tears. Holden kisses the top of her head, and the Banbury men gather around their bride, taking it in turns to hug and kiss her. They are the picture of unity, the very image of happiness and contentment, and amongst them, Brett, their son, squeals happily.

I hate the label, but they really are "couple goals" except they're not a couple. They're not even a throuple! What the hell are they? A pentuple? I don't think that's a thing. In fact, I think I just made up a new term!

The crowd cheers, and the DJ flicks the switch so the music fills the room again, and in a flash, everyone is up and dancing.

Tyler's focus is back on his plate, the haunted look has almost gone from his expression, but I can't forget it. Something bad happened in his family. Something that made Tyler look like I ripped out his heart and incinerated it with just the mention of his brother and sister.

He's not going to tell me. I know enough about this man to know that his vulnerabilities are kept under armor plating. So if he won't tell me, I'm going to have to find out another way.

4

TYLER

Connie drags Sandy up to dance, and I watch them from my seat at the edge of the dancefloor. Sandy's movements are stilted at first, but soon, she's dancing like they're listening to Spotify in their bedroom at home.

She always loved dancing, and I always loved watching the light spill from her when she was happy. I see some light now, but not like when we were younger. Not like before.

People begin to leave, and the caterers clear the food and tableware until it's obvious that the party is almost over. I catch Sandy looking at her watch, and then she finds where I'm sitting, and our eyes meet. As she whispers something to Carmella, they both look in my direction, then kiss as though they're saying goodbye.

I don't mind waiting for Sandy. Today has been strange and challenging in some ways, but like a glimpse into a past life too.

It's hard to admit I'd do anything to go back there, to

when there was nothing bad between Sandy and me, only laughter and love and a connection so deep and intense it was as though we were bolted together with steel.

"Hey," she says, reaching for her purse. "We should go. I've kept you here long enough."

"It's okay. I don't mind," I say, but Sandy shakes her head.

"I'm ready. And to be honest, I need to get back to try and find a hotel for the night. I'd stay here, but I left my suitcase in my trunk."

We start to drift out of the hall, searching for Connie and her husbands but not finding them. Maybe they snuck off earlier, or maybe they're putting Brett to bed. In the parking lot, I open the door of the truck for Sandy and wait for her to slide in demurely, making sure the door is safely shut. When I round the back of the truck, my mind is torn as to what to do.

I don't want Sandy to stay in a hotel. To be honest, there's only a trashy motel near Deep Repairs, and there is no way that I'm planning on dropping her there. I want to tell her that she can stay with me. I'll give up my room and take the sofa. But will that be weird for her?

Probably.

But I know I won't sleep at night with her in a nasty place like Green's Motel.

Fastening my belt, I start the car. "I think you should stay at mine," I say. "The motel isn't nice or safe. You can have my room, and I'll take the couch."

"I can't," she says.

"You can and you will," I state firmly but softly. "The house is big. We'll all be up early for work. You'll hardly know we're there, and you can make yourself at home. Just…you know…as friends."

"Friends?"

I know it's a stupid label to give us. We were so much more, and now we're so much less. It's not an honest descriptor of the past or the present. "No strings is what I mean." I'm bumbling like a fool and cringing at the words tumble out of my mouth. I haven't been this nervous around a woman since I was fourteen and fumbling for a first kiss.

As I throw the truck into reverse, Sandy goes back to gripping her purse like she's drowning and it's a life preserver. "It's okay. I know you're just trying to be polite, but honestly, today is enough. You've put yourself out a lot, and none of this was supposed to happen. I'll be okay at the motel."

"If something happened to you, I'd never forgive myself." I put my foot on the gas a little too hard, and the wheels spin out, revealing my frustration.

"A lot has happened to me in four years, Tyler. You weren't worried about that."

My jaw hurts as I grit my teeth hard. What does she want from me? Can't she see that I was wrecked too? There's no way she thinks I'm the same man I was. Sometimes, I look in the mirror, and I don't even recognize the green eyes that look back at me emptily. "I was worried every day, Sandy. Every fucking day."

"Not worried enough to come back, though. Not worried enough to explain why you disappeared and give me some peace."

"It was too late," I say, repeating the words I've told myself a million times. Too late. Too much water under the bridge.

"Too late...exactly," she whispers as though I've proved her point for her.

"Your suitcase is in your trunk. I'm going to call Greg and tell him to take it home with him. I'm bringing you to our place, fixing my bed with clean linens and that's it. If you decide you want to walk out into the dark and find someplace else to stay, then that's on you, Sandy. I'll have done my best to keep you safe."

She doesn't reply, maybe seething inside like I am. Four years apart and look how we are with each other. Seeing her has been amazing but fucking gut-wrenching too. And now I've got another two days of this to get through without spilling my guts and undoing everything it's taken me to make myself whole again.

We don't speak on the journey, and that's okay with me. I put on the radio, and we listen to country music. I don't dare play the disco classics that I know she loves. I don't want to bring more of the past into the present than is lurking between us already.

When we're at the house, Sandy follows me up the steps to the front door. Inside, the TV is blaring a football game, and my boys are yelling at each other about something. We're not united on our choice for the best team, so maybe it's an argument about that, or maybe they're just ripping on each other like they usually do. Whatever it is, I feel grateful to be home.

This is my turf.

These are my people, who know every dark and terrible thing about me and love me anyway.

"We're back," I shout, and a head appears around the door from the den. "Hi honey," Arden says. "I made you dinner, and then I ate it." He laughs at his own pathetic attempt at humor, and I cringe.

"We went to a wedding, you douchebag. I've eaten better food than you could ever make."

"Hey, don't diss the only chef in this place," he says, bringing his hand to his heart as though I physically wounded him.

I turn to Sandy, who's watching everything with interest. "Come in. I'll show you around."

Another triplet appears next to Arden. It's Able, the only one who didn't meet Sandy at the shop earlier. "Able, this is Sandy."

"There are three of you," Sandy says, her voice light and singsong.

"Three's a charm," Able says in a faux Irish accent. I mean, his family does hail from Cork, apparently, but it's too many generations back for anyone to still have a language connection with the place. Ignoring him, I wave at the doorway.

"This is the den. Over here is the kitchen." I lead Sandy to my favorite room in the house. It's an open-plan kitchen diner, with a couple of couches in the corner. We hang out here most of the time, reserving the den for watching TV.

"Wow. It's really nice." Sandy swivels on her heels, taking in the modern white gloss cabinets and the marble countertops. We did all of the work ourselves, and I'm damn proud of the effect. I'm even prouder that my boys have kept the place tidy. Some nights, the dirty dishes spill out of the sink.

"It opens onto the yard. You can't see right now, but I'll show you tomorrow when it's light."

Sandy nods, then spies her suitcase against the wall and strides toward it.

"Don't worry about that. I'll take it up for you. I'm just going to head upstairs and deal with the linens. I'll come back when I'm done."

"Uh...sure."

"You can wait here if you like."

"Okay." She decides to perch on the edge of the dark blue couch in the corner, and I dash for the door, knowing that my room needs a little more than a change of bedding to make it a nice place for her to stay.

Racing up the stairs, I root around for clean sheets and

pillow covers in the hallway closet. Heavy footsteps sound on the stairs, and Andrew comes into view. "What's going on, man?"

"Sandy's gonna stay in my room. I'm taking the couch."

"Yeah. I got that part. I mean, what's going on with you guys?"

Shrugging, I force an even expression onto my face, relaxing my clenched jaw and lowered brows. "Nothing. I mean, I'm just helping out while her car is in the shop."

"Yeah? Just helping out?"

"Just come out and say what you mean," I bark.

Andrew leans against the wall, his hand sliding into his pocket as though he's trying to make himself appear relaxed and easygoing. "This is Sandy." He emphasizes her name, and my stomach clenches.

"Yeah."

"This is you and Sandy," he repeats, even though I got his meaning the first time.

"I know, man. What do you want me to do?"

Andrew cocks his head, and his ice-blue eyes fix on mine. With his pale blond hair and tan skin, he looks like a Disney prince just waiting for his princess. A prince with lots of tattoos. "I want you to be careful, okay. You're in a good place. This…we've all worked for this. I don't want you risking the progress you made, okay?"

"I'm good. You don't have to worry about me."

Andrew shakes his head. "We're brothers from another mother," he says. "I'll always worry about you, the same way I worry about Arden and Able and Greg and Damien. This is who we are. We've got each other's backs, no matter what."

"I know," I say. "And I've got yours."

"So, just listen when I tell you to be careful."

My fist balls the soft fabric of the bedcovers in my

palm. "Sometimes it's impossible to be careful, Andrew. Sometimes, your heart rests in someone else's hands even though you don't want it to."

"I get it," he says. "Sandy...she's special."

"Special?"

"The whole package. Pretty, smart, a good person, funny...don't forget you've told us all about her, and now we get to see her in the flesh."

"And you agree?" I ask.

"She's just about perfect," Andrew says, and although a sliver of jealousy runs through me, it's also a big relief. These guys are important to me, and so is Sandy. If they could like each other, it would mean a lot.

"She is."

"But she's going to leave," Andrew says softly, and the pain I feel at those words is seismic. I turn away, heading to my room, pushing away the truth in his words, as though if I ignore him, it won't be the case. He follows me, lingering in the doorway.

"She doesn't have to," I tell him.

"Are you ready to open up to her? Are you ready to tell her what happened?"

I shake my head, using the distraction of pulling the covers from my pillows to avoid looking at him. "Until you can be honest about that, she won't understand, and she won't be able to forgive."

His words freeze me. "I know," I say softly. "Even if she knew, it doesn't automatically mean she'd be able to forgive me or to trust me again."

"Nothing you ever told me about her would make me believe she'd hold a grudge like that."

"But forgiving someone and trusting them again are two very different things. Sometimes, the trust part is impossible."

"If I thought you were ready…" Andrew trails off, and I know what he's trying to say. It's my boys that pulled me back from the darkness. They don't want me to slip into that place again, and I don't want to go there either. My throat burns, and any more of this conversation is just going to make it worse. I need to change the subject.

"The wedding was good," I tell him. "Sandy's friend Connie married four guys. They're all brothers."

"Four guys?"

When I turn to Andrew, his face is a picture. "Yeah. Four. They already have a kid together."

"Imagine growing up with four dads," Andrew says, shaking his head.

"It'd be better than growing up without," I say. When he nods, I know it's coming from a deep place of understanding. Every man in this house knows what it's like to need a father and be disappointed.

"Very true."

"There were two other groups like that at the wedding too. Connie's best friend Natalie is with three dudes, and another girl, Melanie, is with five."

"Is it catching?" Andrew jokes. "I mean, how do people even get into that situation?"

"I guess it starts with the men. There has got to be a lot of love and trust there to want to share a woman."

"And a woman who can divide herself between multiple men."

"That's just it. I watched these groups while Sandy was dancing. They work as a team. Better than any true couple I ever saw."

Andrew nods, his hand moving to his chin. He rubs at his day's growth of stubble. "I can see how it could simplify things. Like, have you ever thought about what it will be like in this house if we all had girlfriends?"

"Six women living here, you mean?"

He shrugs and shakes his head. "That would never fucking work. We'd have to sell the place and buy our own apartments."

"Fuck that," I say. "Bros come first."

"So maybe the group idea isn't such a bad one."

A look passes between us that feels heavy with intention, but before I ask Andrew if he really means what I think he means, he's turned and walked away. His feet thud on the stairs as he goes back to the game, and I'm left alone in my room, with sheets to deal with and a whole heap of confusion too.

5

ANDREW

Sandy is waiting by herself in the kitchen, so I head there, wanting to make the most of the time I have while Tyler is busy upstairs.

She's perched on the edge of the couch as though she doesn't feel comfortable enough to rest back and relax. In her pretty dress, she looks like an angel who fell from the heavens. The skin on her bare shoulder's glistens. Maybe it's a cream that she's used, or maybe she just radiates from within. I'm not an expert. I just know that if I could, I'd kiss her right there and watch her shiver.

But that's not what I'm here for. I'd never go there unless Tyler was cool with it. Sandy was his girl. He might have left her, but it wasn't because he didn't want to be with her or because he didn't love her. Sometimes life deals us a shitty hand, and we lose the advantages we accumulated before.

"Hey," I say softly as soon as she notices me. "I'm Andrew. I just wanted to come and make sure you're okay."

"I'm great," she says. "Just waiting for Tyler. I told him I'd stay in a motel. To be honest, I would have preferred it, but he wouldn't agree. I just don't want to put you all out."

I wave my hand, then rest it on the table, leaning just a little, so I appear more relaxed. "It's no trouble. There's plenty of space."

"That's what Tyler said." She smiles, but it's with restraint. "Can I ask you something?" She glances at the door as though she's worried that Tyler might appear at any moment.

"Sure."

"Has something happened in Tyler's family? I mentioned his brother and sister, and he looked like he'd seen a ghost."

Shit. I can't believe she's asking this outright. All I wanted to do was to tell her to be cautious with Tyler, not to spill all his secrets, but what do I say now? If I tell her that I can't say, she'll probably end up asking Tyler. I don't think he'd be able to deal with that question without breaking down, and no dude ever wants to break down in front of the girl they love. I close my eyes, torn over how to respond, and Sandy waits without pressing harder.

"Yes," I say eventually. "Four years ago. It wouldn't be fair of me to tell you, though. Do you understand that? It's Tyler's family. Tyler's story."

"Four years ago?"

That's enough information for her to realize that there's a link between Tyler leaving her and what happened. Maybe that'll be enough for her to treat my buddy with some care.

"Yeah. Four years."

"The date on his arm. The tattoo?"

Fuck. I didn't even think about that. She must have

noticed it's new. I nod, but I don't elaborate.

"Please? Can you tell me? Was it Luna or Jake?"

"I'm sorry," I say softly, putting my hand up, palm facing her. "Please don't ask me anymore."

Even as the words leave my lips, Sandy is resting her face in her hands. Her shoulders shake with a suppressed sob, and I'm across the room in a second, driven by instinct rather than sense. I never was good at watching women cry. My momma did enough of it. I spent half my childhood trying to make up for my douchebag father's absence, to be the man she needed to keep her strong.

When I'm next to Sandy, I smell her sweet scent. I put my arm around her small frame and try not to let myself feel the attraction that I know is wrong, but it's impossible. This woman is everything I ever wanted. I fell in love with the version of her that Tyler created with rambling stories he'd tell when he was drunk, and now she's here in the flesh, and everything has gone from fantasy to reality.

"I'm sorry," I say. "I shouldn't have told you even that. Please don't be upset. Please. If Tyler finds out I said something…"

Sandy stiffens, then uses her hands to clear the tears from her cheeks. She inhales a deep fortifying breath, holding it to stop her body's physical reaction to the news. She gazes up at me, her hazel eyes almost cat-like, filled with questions and mystery. My hands itch to slide into her brown wavy hair and pull her closer. Her pouty lips are so near it would take nothing to kiss them.

Nothing and everything.

"Tyler's good now. He's in a good place. I just want to make sure it stays that way."

"I would never hurt him," she says. "Not like he hurt me."

"Sometimes things happen…sometimes we do things we never thought we'd be capable of and regret them forever."

"He regrets leaving me?" she asks.

"He never left you," I tell her. "He just couldn't find a way back."

She frowns, and her head moves quickly from side to side as though she doesn't understand what I'm trying to say. I wish that I could talk openly, but none of this is mine to share. I've spilled enough.

Seconds tick past and Sandy seems to be wrestling with what to ask next but in the end we're interrupted. Arden appears at the door, and I snatch my hand from Sandy's shoulders too late. My brother's eyebrows practically hit his hairline. "There you are."

Sandy stands, smoothing her hands over the silky fabric of her dress, still clutching her purse like it's filled with gold bullion. "Is Tyler done?" she asks.

"I don't know," Arden says. "I was looking for Andrew."

Standing, I make sure to put some distance between this woman, who is effectively a stranger, and me. A stranger that my friend has loved for most of his adult life. "Why don't you come and hang out in the den?" I ask her. "I'm sure Tyler will be tidying his mess, and believe me, that will take a while."

Sandy snorts lightly. "I remember he had a preference for storing his clothes in a pile on the floor."

"Not much has changed," I laugh. "But at least he's learned to keep his mess in his room. He's housetrained in the communal areas."

We follow Arden into the den, and when Greg, Damien, and Able see Sandy, they all scramble to sit up straighter, turning the TV volume down from its usual epic level.

"It's okay," Sandy says, perching on the couch next to Damien. "Don't worry about me."

"You like football?" Damien asks hopefully.

Sandy shakes her head. "I'm more a baseball girl. It's what my dad liked to watch."

"Baseball is cool," Greg says. "But there's nothing like the sheer brute force of football to get a man's blood racing."

"I can think of something else that gets a man's blood racing," Arden says.

"Not in the presence of a lady," I say in a warning tone that has my brother chuckling.

"And who are you, Prince Andrew?" He tosses a pillow at me, which I catch and return with way more speed. We've been playing this game since we were kids. There were times, when we were in the group home where we met, that tossing pillows was our only entertainment. It's hard to think back to those times without getting a knot in my stomach. They were painful and we were all filled with the anxiousness of kids whose adults were failing to be there for them. But there were happy times too, which I don't want to banish from my memory.

I would never have met these guys if it wasn't for that set of circumstances. I wouldn't have this stable life with these men who are more than friends to me. Sometimes, out of the darkest time, we find light.

Sandy watches our back-and-forth with a small smile on her face.

"Do you have brothers, Sandy?" Greg asks her.

"No. Just a sister."

"Chill out, boys," Greg barks. "Sandy's not used to this shit."

"It's okay. I used to get into it with my sister sometimes, too, although she is nine years older than me."

"Nine?" Greg says.

"He's an only child." Damien points his thumb in

Greg's direction. "He still can't hack all the sibling behavior shit in this house."

"I'm used to it now," Greg says, cutting his friends a dark stare.

"Used to what?" Tyler appears in the doorway, surveying the scene of comfortable domesticity in front of him. Sandy stands immediately, turning to face Tyler. The change in his expression when his eyes meet hers is like nothing I've ever seen from my friend before. It's like he goes from ice to melted butter in a second.

Shit.

This is bad.

I hate always being the one who sees disaster coming. I know my boys think of me as too responsible. They don't realize that I wish I could shrug off my sensible nature sometimes, but I just can't. It's too deep-rooted—a childhood response born out of needing to grow up too soon. Feeling in control keeps me safe, but it's as though Tyler is teetering at the top of a rollercoaster that is only heading down.

I like Sandy, but she has no idea what trouble she could cause if she makes a wrong move. Tyler's heart is in her hands, and she's completely unaware of the power she has.

I think back to what he said upstairs about the polyamorous relationships he witnessed today.

Maybe that's the solution here.

Of course, part of my thinking is selfish. I'd love Sandy to be mine, too, even if I had to share her.

But part of it is knowing that Tyler just can't handle the pressure of an intense relationship again. The weight of Sandy's expectations and needs would be too heavy. But shared amongst six of us, they might just be comfortable enough for him to bear.

6

SANDY

"The room's ready," Tyler says, his eyes scanning my face. It's sweet that he's checking that I'm okay after being left in a room with five of his friends.

Despite appearances, they all actually seem like good guys. Really good guys built like houses with enough tattoos to open an art gallery. It's hard to know where to look when confronted by so much *man*.

I guess this is something that Connie has to deal with every day. And Natalie. And Melanie, who got with the cousins that Connie intended for me.

She actually thought I'd be able to handle five ranchers.

I think Connie has a much-inflated opinion of my capabilities.

The feel of Andrew's arm around my shoulder and his soft whispered words of sympathy flash through my memory, and I flush. He's the first man to touch me that way for a very long time. Maybe that's the reason that such a simple touch stirred something inside me.

That and he looks like Paul Walker's younger brother.

"Okay. Shall I come up?" I ask.

"Sure. I'll get you settled in."

"Yeah, he will," Arden says with a wink.

"Are you starting again?" Andrew says in a warning tone that only amuses his brother even more.

"Come on." Tyler leads me out of the room, and I follow him up the stairs, which curve around, ending in a wide and open hallway. Seven doors are arranged around, but only one is open. "Here, let me show you," Tyler says, holding out his arm to steer me into what I guess is his bedroom.

There is something so personal about being in this space. The air holds Tyler's scent, and all around are the things that he uses every day. I used to know all of his clothes. I used to know what shower products he used and what toothpaste. Now, everything is unfamiliar.

Except…

"You still have the bear?" It was stupid of me to buy him a teddy bear, but we were young, and I loved him, and somehow, at the time, it seemed right. I flush with embarrassment, and he stuffs his hands into his pockets as though he feels the same.

"Yeah."

The room is tidy, although I'm pretty sure that if I threw open the doors to the closet, I'd get smothered in his hastily stored clothes. The bed is big, dressed in fresh white linens and draped with a large gray blanket. "It sometimes gets cold at night," he says, noticing where I'm looking.

"Okay, thanks…" I scan the walls, and there are plenty of photographs but just of Tyler and the men downstairs. None of his family. That tells me a lot. "You know, I really don't mind taking the sofa. You should stay here, and I'll take a sheet and comforter…I just hate to put you out."

"Honestly. It's no trouble."

We stand awkwardly for a moment while all of the unsaid questions spin through my mind like a hamster on a wheel. In the end, I remember Andrew's words and stuff everything back down where it will have to remain.

My sister always says that it's best to leave the past in the past. When I bring up my mom and dad's selfishness, she tells me that it's pointless dwelling on it because they're never going to change. Holding onto past hurt only hurts me more. I was doing okay at trying to forget, but now, being surrounded by everything Tyler, it's all come flooding back.

But I can squash it down again for a night or two. I can be this version of myself that puts Tyler first because that's what he needs. Lashing out won't make me feel better, and it won't undo what happened to me either. Best to just get on with it.

"Thanks," I say softly.

Tyler smiles then grabs a pile of clothes from the dresser. "I'll be downstairs if you need anything." Nodding, he leaves, and I take a deep breath before closing the door. I slowly lower myself onto the bed, feeling weary. The buckles on my shoes are tight, but I manage to unhook them, relishing my feet being freed onto the cool wood floor. The zip at the back of my dress is awkward, but I succeed in lowering it and end up standing in Tyler's room in just my panties and a strapless bra.

So many times, Tyler undressed me after we'd been to a party, unwrapping me until I was left just like this. He loved to drop to his knees in front of me and kiss the soft line of skin above the fabric of my panties. He'd tongue my clit through the lace before baring me to his eyes and mouth. His mouth on my nipples was so hot and wet, teeth nipping, hands gripping, everything so frantic.

I cup my own pussy as the intense feelings spill

through me all over again. The ache of the absence of his touch is just as painful now as it has ever been. It's like a part of me was hacked away, but the memory of it is still fresh, maybe something like the way the body remembers an amputated limb.

Biting my lip, I close my eyes and try to focus on the here and now and what I need to do to get through; find my nightwear, clean my teeth, and wash my face. Get into bed and sleep. Wake up tomorrow and put one step in front of the other. Once I've listed it out, I start to tick off each task until I'm sliding into Tyler's bed and inhaling the fresh lavender scent of his sheets. Staring up at the ceiling in the darkness, my mind wanders again. How many times has he lain here thinking about me? How many times has he touched himself in this bed, stroking the cock that used to be mine?

Has he had other women in this bed? Did he like them better than me?

Those last thoughts make me feel sick to my stomach.

Rolling onto my side, I pull out my cellphone and text Suzanne. I'm sure she'll be asleep, but I know my sister will worry if she doesn't hear from me after a long journey.

Wedding was good. All fine. Staying away for a couple of nights. Be back Tuesday. Kiss Sophie for me.

Then I set my phone to play the meditation music that soothes my mind into sleep on nights when I'm thinking too much.

It's silent in the house when I wake and still very dark. Reaching for my phone, I see that the time reads 2:30 am. There's a distant thud, and I wonder if that's what woke me. My mouth is dry, and I have the beginnings of a headache coming, which is dangerous. The prospect of experiencing a full-blown migraine while I'm staying here isn't a pleasant one.

I should get some water and take my pills. It's the only way I have a chance of being okay in the morning.

Sliding out of Tyler's bed feels strange. Opening the door into the corridor feels even stranger. There are six men sleeping in this house, and here I am, tiptoeing around like a thief in the night.

At the bottom of the stairs, I hear another thud and a low deep growl that quickly switches to something high-pitched and frantic. My feet carry me toward the sound that's coming from the kitchen. Even in the dark, I see Tyler's limbs writhing. His blanket is tangled around his legs and arms, and he seems to be struggling.

"NO," he groans. "NO…JAKE."

His face contorts, his eyes still tightly closed. It's a nightmare…the kind that tortures from the inside out. I stand paralyzed, watching him fight, but the sounds he makes become pitiful, and I can't take it anymore.

I drop to my knees beside him and rest my hand on his face. "Tyler," I say firmly. "Tyler. It's okay. It's just a dream."

His hand grabs my arm in the fastest reflex I've ever seen, and his eyes bolt open, flashing the color of a green tree snake in the darkness.

"It's just a dream," I say again, believing he's awake, but he looks right through me. "JAKE," he says again. "I'm sorry."

"TYLER." I'm firmer this time, using my other hand to touch his face. "Tyler. Wake up."

He blinks, still holding me tightly enough to bring tears to my eyes. It takes him a few seconds to come to, and when he does, the first thing he does is to focus on the place we're touching. My hand is released like it was molten against his skin, and then he closes his eyes, his jaw ticking as he grits his teeth.

"Tyler, it's okay. It was just a dream."

"Not a fucking dream," he says, and a tear leaks from his eye, running into the shell of his ear. It's a crazy instinct to brush it away with my finger, the heat of his skin so intense against me that I let out a puff of air. His eyes find mine, and I'm locked in place. He seems to stare into me and through me all at the same time, searching for something intangible. At least, that's what it feels like. My heart races like it always did in the moments before we kissed, with anticipation and desperation and a deep, deep connection. Before I say anything, his hand is in my hair, the brute force of him pulling my mouth to his.

The kiss is rough and unchoreographed, a clash of lips, teeth, and unfamiliarity. My heart pounds as my body primes for more. Tyler's hands hold me firm, and I brace myself on his muscular chest, palms feeling the pounding of his heart beneath. His tongue forces its way into my mouth, and I whimper as a flash of our past passion blasts into my mind.

That was filled with connection.

This is not.

I ache for Tyler. The Tyler who felt like the other half of my soul, but this man isn't him. This man is broken by events that he can't share with me, and the fierceness of his need is shattering me too.

But I can't stop.

I can't break the spell.

His desperation is what I want. The harshness of his touch is easier to bear than softness and sympathy. Like this, we're two different people than we were. Two people so changed by our past that we no longer fit together.

Except, when he hauls me onto the couch, rolling until he's over me, it feels like it used to. The thickness of his cock grinds against my pussy, and my body reacts in just the same way. His hands are up under my cami, squeezing as he kisses me deeply. Muscular thighs push my softer ones apart, and all that is between us is a tiny pair of satin shorts and his cotton underwear.

Everything feels like a dream; the darkness around us a comforter that fogs my mind so I can push aside all the reasons that this is a terrible idea, and I can forget that we're in a communal part of his shared house, and anyone could stumble upon us.

There was a rhythm to the way we were together that beats so deep in my soul that fighting it is impossible. My fingers dig into the firmness of Tyler's ass, and his hips shift until the blunt head of his cock notches at my entrance. The barriers are still there between us, but the intention is plain.

And I want him. I want him so badly that tears leak from my eyes and trail into the hair at my temples. My chest hitches with a sob that builds so fast I can't hold it in. But Tyler doesn't notice. In a second, his cock is free, and the slip of fabric between my legs is shoved aside. I brace for the stretch that I know is coming, and when he pushes deep inside me in one thrust, I don't even care about the sharpness of the friction or the way my cervix aches because this is meant to be.

I'm sure of it.

My car has always been reliable.

I've never driven out this way before.

Something bigger than both of us put us in the same place at the same time, of that I'm certain.

Tyler's face is buried in my neck as he fucks me so deep and hard that I'm whimpering and grasping at his back. There's a new precision in the movement of his hips that tells me he's had other women in the past four years. But none of that matters because this is us.

Sandy and Tyler.

We were always meant to be together, like the moon and stars or like ice cream and chocolate sauce. My heart knows his heart, and when they're pressed together, they synchronize as though they become one.

His teeth nip at my neck, then his kisses soothe, and I stroke over his broad, strong back, needing to ground myself against him because while this is happening, we are both okay. But when it's done – when he's torn us both open – we won't ever be the same.

There's a tidal wave coming that is so tall it's going to knock us both off our feet and send us spinning into the churning waters.

A tidal wave of our own making.

Between my legs, the ache turns into a well of pleasure that's ready to overflow. His rough hands palm my breasts and pluck at my nipples, and I'm lost in the sound of his desperate breathing by my ear. When I come it is a slow slither into darkness, interspersed by a flash of bright light, and the waves of contractions must trigger something in Tyler too because he shouts, swelling inside me, curling into my body so that there isn't a part of us that isn't touching.

My neck feels wet where Tyler's face is buried, and I'm just about to turn to touch his cheek when feet thud at the bottom of the stairs. There's no time to disentangle ourselves. No time for Tyler to come around and realize what we've done.

It was all a dream of a time in the past when things were so easy.
But when Greg appears around the door and his eyes meet mine in the darkness, everything becomes difficult.

7

GREG

It takes a couple of seconds for the sight of Tyler on top of Sandy to come into focus. Her legs are wrapped around him, and his face is buried in her neck.

Shit.

I knew this was going to happen. From the moment he brought Sandy's car into the repair shop, and I realized who she was, I knew.

Life has taught me enough to know that some people are drawn to each other like moths to a flame. It's impossible to keep them apart.

I've had to work hard in my own life to stop getting dragged back down by my family and my neighborhood friends. Distance has been the only thing that has kept the old part of my life, the part where I ended up back in jail every few months, from taking over. My brothers at Deep Repairs have kept me on the straight and narrow. They've given me a chance to build something that is worth fighting for. They didn't give up on me, even when my choices were bad enough for them to leave me behind.

But Tyler is getting dragged down.

I know Sandy doesn't mean to do it. She might have an idea of what has happened to Tyler since they parted company, but she doesn't know. She'll never be able to imagine the full extent, even if he tried to explain. You had to be there to see it.

Her being here is a bad idea.

I told Andrew, and he agreed, but what could we do? There was no way that Tyler was going to push Sandy away. Not when everything in him remembers how good things were between them.

Sandy shifts, sliding her fingers into Tyler's hair. "Tyler."

I turn my back, but I don't leave.

"Tyler," she says again.

"What's going on?" From his bedroom door, Andrew's line of sight catches me standing in the kitchen, but he can't see Tyler and Sandy yet.

"NOTHING," Tyler barks. "Get out of here. For fuck's sake."

I stride into the hallway, shaking my head as Andrew puts his hands out, palms to the ceiling, searching for an explanation. "They fucked," I mutter.

Andrew mumbles an expletive under his breath and rubs his face in a way that screams frustration.

Rustling sounds emanate from the kitchen, but I have no idea what's going on.

Have Tyler and Sandy made up? I doubt it very much. Tyler can't talk about what happened to Jake, even to the people in his life who know and would never judge him. There is no way he'd open up that way with Sandy.

"Fuck." It's Tyler's voice, laced with frustration and distress, and the urge to go back into that room and yank my friend out of the situation that is only going to cause him to hurt is so strong that I have to grip my hands into fists to control it.

Tyler was the one who brought me back from the brink. He visited me in jail as often as they would allow, and he was there, the last time, to collect me. He was the one who told me I was never going back.

"It's okay," Sandy says, her voice soft and soothing. At least she's not freaking out at him, because that would make everything so much worse.

"Shit." Andrew paces in front of me, his face constantly turning back to the kitchen door. He's having the same trouble staying out here that I am.

"I could say that it'll be okay, but I'd be fucking lying." There's a deadness to my tone that I don't like. There was a time when that was the only kind of tone I used, but since we opened Deep Repairs and I've had a chance to see what normal life can be like, that side of me was put to bed. Now it's back.

"I'm coming in," I say, losing a grip on my control. I'd rather Tyler was pissed at me, and I had a handle on the situation.

"Stay the fuck out there," Tyler growls, and I stop abruptly in the doorway. It's Sandy who rounds the corner, her face twisted, her pajamas still disheveled.

"He's gone blank," she says. "He won't look at me. He won't let me touch him."

"Shit." Andrew puts his arm around Sandy, and she slips into his embrace so comfortably that I'm left with my mouth hanging open. When did he cultivate this level of familiarity? She's hardly spent time with any of us.

"I'll go," I say. "You take Sandy back to Tyler's room."

Andrew nods once, and then I'm rounding the kitchen door, searching for Tyler in the darkness. "Hey, T." I approach him slowly like I would a dangerous animal. It's not that I'm worried that he might attack me physically. I have him by at least twenty pounds of muscle and ten years of violent experience. I'm the eldest in the group by a long way, the unofficial pop or big brother. It's more that he's going to be emotionally volatile, and I don't want to antagonize him.

"Don't 'hey' me, man," he says. It's muffled because he's sitting with his face in his hands, curved over like someone with a ton of brick on his shoulders.

"How'd it happen?" I ask, leaning against the counter. Getting closer will just piss him off.

"I had a nightmare, and she was there, and I don't know…it was like muscle memory. It was like it took nothing at all to slip back into what we were."

"So you didn't talk."

Tyler shakes his head. "I'm done talking, G. I just want the ghosts in my head to shut the fuck up."

"But Sandy isn't a ghost. She's a real person, and you're probably going to need to have a conversation with her."

Tyler clears his throat, glancing up at me through eyes that are pinched at the corners. "There's nothing that I can say that will fix things."

"Better leave them broken then," I tell him. It's not that I believe my words, more that I know Tyler isn't capable of fixing anything if he doesn't have the strength to tell me I'm wrong.

"If it was just me…" he trails off, eyes flicking back and forth as though he's searching for something in the dark.

"If it was just you, what?"

"Then I'd leave it…but this is Sandy. I fucked up once. I can't fuck up again, for her sake."

"Can I give you some advice?" Tyler nods, his face open and his expression desperate. "Don't do this tonight. Discussions never go well at night. Our minds can't take the complex shit when we're tired. Leave it until tomorrow."

"But she's upset," Tyler says.

"I don't think so. She was more worried about you. Andrew's taken her back to your room."

I'm expecting Tyler to be pissed about that. Sandy was his girl, after all, so it'd be understandable if he was territorial about her, but that isn't what I see. Instead, he seems relieved.

"Andrew will look after her." Tyler lets out a long breath and stands, pacing a little before he heads to the sink to fix himself a drink. "Andrew always knows what to do."

He's right. If I'm the big brother of the group with the wisdom that comes with experience, then Andrew is the conciliator. He always knows what to say when things are getting heated. Whenever we got into trouble as kids, he'd know just how to smooth things over. I avoided more than one bloody nose because of his negotiation skills. Most importantly, he can make all of us see a different viewpoint, and with that strategy, there are rarely arguments that can't be solved.

"Maybe he'll help her understand," I say.

"Maybe he'll fuck her too," Tyler mutters. At least, that's what I think I hear.

"What?"

Tyler shrugs, placing the empty glass on the counter and then turning to look at me. "What do you think of Sandy?"

I take a step back in surprise. No good ever comes from a man asking another man what he thinks of his woman. There are boundaries between men for a reason. Boundaries that you cross knowing no good will come.

"She seems like a great girl," I say. That's the line. No further.

"Pretty?"

"Sure. A real peach," I say. "You were a lucky man." Definitely no further.

He nods, a small and strange smile ghosting at his lips.

"I was."

Nodding just once, I fold my arms across my chest. It's a defensive move, but I can't help myself. There is something about this conversation, about this whole situation, that doesn't strike me as right. There's a natural order to life, and when it's broken…

"Thanks," he says when I don't reply. "I must have been making some racket for you and Andrew to come sprinting down here.

"We're always here for you," I tell him.

"And for Sandy?"

"Sure," I say as he pauses in front of me. "Your friends and family are my friends and family," I say. "Ride or die. You know that."

"Good," Tyler says. He flops back onto the sofa. "Night, G."

"Night, man." It doesn't feel right to leave him when everything is telling me that he's messed up and needs me. Everything is telling me except my eyes. My eyes detect something completely different.

Tyler is planning something.

I have no idea what it is, but whatever it is…I'm going to make sure he's okay.

At the top of the stairs, the door to Sandy's room is closed, and so is the door to Andrew's. If I knew this girl better, I'd knock to check she's okay, but apart from the stories that Tyler had told us all when he was drunk, I don't really know her at all. I'm just about to close my own door when a latch clicks behind me. Andrew emerges from

Sandy's room, our eyes meeting across the hallway in the darkness. "Everything okay?"

Andrew shrugs then nods and purses his lips as though neither of those gestures really communicates what he thinks.

He closes the door then makes his way closer, his hand coming to rest on the handle to his own room. "She seems okay. Better than I thought."

"So does Tyler," I say, cocking my head. None of this really makes sense. "But he said something funny."

"Funny ha-ha?"

I lean against the door, thinking back to the odd moment in the kitchen. "I think he said that maybe you were going to fuck Sandy."

Andrew's eyebrows shoot up. "Fuck her?"

"Yeah, and he…he seemed okay about it."

"He was okay with the idea of me fucking his ex-girlfriend?" Andrew says, his voice higher than usual.

"If my ears weren't deceiving me…he looked strangely calm about the idea."

Andrew snorts. "The man's going soft. Earlier, he was telling me about the wedding he went to today. The bride married four grooms. Apparently, it's a thing."

"Polyamory," I nod. It's something that happened in my old circles, although it was usually one man and two women.

"I guess." We both shrug at the same time as though neither of us really knows how to deal with any of this.

When I'm within the confines of my own room, I slump back into bed. The memory of Sandy's messy hair and kiss-swollen slips into my mind, too overpowering to push away. My hand slides to my cock, thinking about how she looked in the darkness, pinned underneath Tyler, spread wide open.

A frantic fuck in the dark…just the kind of fuck that I like best.

Across the hall, Sandy lies with the feeling of Tyler between her legs. Would she enjoy the feeling of Andrew and me there too?

Who the fuck knows?

But imagining her moaning my name into my ear while I pound hard into her pussy is what makes me come harder than I have in a long time.

8

SANDY

I should feel secure and content tucked under the covers of Tyler's bed, but I don't. When Andrew was here, I pretended that everything is fine. I told him I was okay. I told him that what happened in the kitchen wasn't a big deal.

I lied through my teeth in a way that makes me feel dark and icky inside.

As I curl my legs up, more of Tyler's cum leaks out of my pussy into the already soaked gusset of my satin shorts, and I whimper into the pillow. In this room, I'm surrounded by the man who pushed inside me, who tried to reclaim me. I don't hate him for what happened. I wanted it as much as he obviously did.

Or needed it?

Want and need are brothers but not twins.

I whimper because I miss the feel of his body over mine, the smell of him, the press of his fingers and lips on my skin. I whimper because there was no time for us to come to terms with what happened before we were parted. I whimper because even though I wanted it, I know deep in my heart it was a mistake.

Pressing my fingers to my lips, I flush as I think of the frantic kisses. Heat slides over my body as I recall how big Tyler was looming over me; how powerful too.

I whimper again as I remember the dampness on my neck that could only have come from his tears.

Tyler doesn't cry. At least, it's not something I ever witnessed. He had his fair share of troubles in his life, but he was strong. He had backbone and fists that could crush a skull. My Tyler was my rock, and without him, I was pulled under life's choppy waters.

But he's not a rock anymore.

What am I going to do? Before we fucked, things were okay. I could have stayed here for as long as it took to fix my car and driven off into the sunset without looking back.

Now everything is more complicated. We're entangled, and chopping away the roots and tendrils that have fixed around each other again is going to hurt.

But I have to do it. I have to push aside all the simmering feelings that are making my insides ache and be strong for us both.

I have to, otherwise who knows what will happen and how long it will take for me to recover all over again. And Tyler? I truly don't know how he feels, and that's enough not to risk this for either of us. A plan to leave tomorrow begins to form, just as the handle to the door begins to move.

I tense, waiting to see who it is. There are six men in this house. Six men I barely know.

But it's Tyler who appears in the opened doorway. He doesn't ask my permission to enter. He doesn't say a thing as he closes the door behind him, plunging the room back into total darkness. Words remain trapped in my mouth that I should be brave enough to say as I watch him round the bed to the empty side. His eyes meet mine in the darkness, tortured and pained. They make my heart skitter. As he slides between the sheets, my breath freezes in my lungs.

Face to face on the pillows, he reaches out to touch my cheek, tucking a lock of hair behind my ear. His gentleness stings more than his frantic, clawing touch did. His gaze drifts over my features, lazy but uncertain. "I'm sorry," he whispers.

Sorry for what? I want to ask him so badly, but he closes his eyes, ending the conversation before it begins. Maybe it's better this way.

It should be hard to fall asleep by the side of the man who hurt me so badly I thought I would never recover, but it isn't. He drifts off first, but I stay awake, etching his relaxed features into my memory, and it feels good. Like a broken part of me that needed answers finally settles just a little.

I don't know everything, but maybe I don't need to.

Maybe just having a few days with Tyler will be enough for me to let the past go.

9

TYLER

I wake with a start as my leg drops off the edge of the wrong side of the bed. My mind scrambles over where I am. I never sleep this side. Except that last night, Sandy was in my bed.

I roll slowly, finding her facing me, a sleeping angel with her wavy hair spread over the pillow. Her sweet, pouty lips are parted, revealing just a hint of her straight white teeth.

I kissed those lips last night. I slid my tongue over those teeth, deep and then deeper.

My breath leaves my chest in a rush.

Last night feels like a dream. In fact, the past twenty-four hours is a long blur of disrupted emotion and overwhelming feeling. A fucking mess of desperation and pain and grabbing, grasping need.

We fucked.

My dick kicks at the memory, already hard as a rock between my legs.

How the hell did it happen?

One minute I'm flailing in the recuring dream that never seems to leave me alone. The next, Sandy is there with soothing words and fingers that feel like a warm balm on my skin. I shouldn't have reached for her. I should have told her to leave me alone, but I couldn't. In that moment, with my heart beating like I'd been sprinting and everything in me terrified, I needed her.

My girl.

There was a time when I wouldn't have thought anything about waking up next to this woman. It was just a part of my life, like eating and breathing and showering—a routine.

Now it feels like the greatest gift I've ever been given.

She stayed.

After I barked at Andrew and Greg to leave me the fuck alone, I waited with my head in my hands. I contemplated staying on my makeshift bed, but I couldn't just leave things with Sandy in a mess. I had to make sure she was okay. When she didn't tell me to leave, I took a chance. There were no words I could find to tell her how I feel, and she didn't ask for any explanation.

She gave me peace in the way she always used to.

And what have I given her?

My face flushes with shame. I used her body knowing that she's conflicted, knowing she's wounded, and knowing there is too much unsaid between us to go that far. But she wanted it. My shoulders still hurt from the way her nails dug into me. She kissed me hard and deeply, in a way that matched me completely.

But what do I do now?

If I lie here and she wakes, there will be so much awkwardness between us. We will need to have conversations about what happened, now and in our past, but I'm not ready yet. We both need some time and space.

DEEP 6

It takes a lot of control to slide myself out of the bed without waking her. I pad to the door as quietly as possible. My jeans are downstairs, and I'm sure I'll have some underwear and a fresh shirt in the drier. If not, I'll borrow someone else's. We're not precious about our belongings in this house. If it fits, we wear it. Sharing has become second nature to me.

Sharing.

The wedding yesterday has planted a seed in my mind that feels fucking alien but also strangely right. Sandy's friends are all freaky as shit, marrying multiple men like they're buying multipacks of candy. I don't know if Sandy was telling the truth about getting introduced to the cowboy cousins or whether she was saying it to rile me up, but the fact that polyamory is something ordinary to her has gotten me thinking things that would have seemed crazy to me yesterday.

Greg is already in the kitchen. When he sees me, he nods, still chewing a mouthful of cereal. "You're playing a dangerous game, my friend," he says, lowering his spoon. Without a shirt on, his prison tats are dark and distracting. Greg is the kind of guy who looks like a murderer but would never hurt a soul unless they threatened someone he loves. Then, well, I wouldn't want to be the man in his path.

"Nothing happened after…I just…I couldn't leave it."

"You should have left it. That poor girl up there. I don't think she knows if she's coming or going."

"Neither do I."

Grabbing my jeans from the end of the couch, I tug them on. I need a shower, but it can wait, and I'm not about to have a deep-and-meaningful with Greg in my spunk-encrusted boxers.

"And that, my friend, is the problem."

"What do you think of Sandy?"

Greg lifts another monster spoonful of cereal into his mouth and chews. The crunching hurts my frazzled brain, but I flop onto the chair across from him, holding down my frustration at his stalling tactics. I get why he's thinking about how to answer. Commenting on another man's woman can be a dangerous path to tread. He doesn't know what I want to hear, and if he gets it wrong, he could offend me or piss me off. I know he wants to do neither. "She seems like a great girl," he says.

"She is." I fiddle with a pen that someone left on the table. Probably Andrew. He's always filling out forms or paying bills. Taking care of us the way he always has.

"Why do you care what I think?" It's a good question. Of all of us, Greg is the most astute at reading other people. I guess when you're banged up with a load of violent assholes, you learn to take your time and be observant.

"You guys are my brothers." He nods, knowing full well the weight of what I've just said. "It matters what you think."

"But she's just passing through, isn't she?"

Leaning back on the chair, I place my hands behind my neck, trying to release the tension that has my whole body knotted. "Maybe."

Greg's eyebrows respond, but the rest of his face remains impassive. "You got something on your mind, T? If you do, just spit it out."

A deep breath settles the buzzing in my temples, but my gut is still twisted. It hasn't been this bad for at least six months, and I know it won't get better unless I do something. Something that's gonna seem crazy to the rock of a man sitting in front of me.

"I want her to stay."

Greg's jaw goes tight, but I don't miss the flicker of interest that passes through his hell-dark eyes. "Stay?"

"Yeah." I slump forward, taking the pen into my jittery hands again. "Four years ago, I didn't…I couldn't…but I can't let Sandy go again."

"Can't or don't want to? Those are two very different things." Greg rubs the corner of his mouth, looking as thoughtful as he ever does.

"Both," I admit.

"But she has a life, T. She has a home. And so do you. You might have fit together easily in the past, but it won't be so easy now. You're both older, and a lot has happened to change you."

I click the pen over and over as Greg remains watchful and quiet. "You ever loved a woman deep in your bones? Like, you can feel them there. Like when you're inside their body, there's nothing between you…no separation. You ever fucked a woman and shed a tear when you came?"

Greg's eyelids lower slowly, his hands dropping to his thighs beneath the table. He exhales, long and slow. "No, T. I haven't ever felt like that about a woman."

"But if you did. If you found that other part of you…would you fight for it?"

I'm expecting him to shrug because we don't do serious and heartfelt conversations in this house. We talk shop and football, and about girls we fuck but have no feelings for. Sometimes, when we're drunk, we talk deeper.

That's how the boys know how I feel about Sandy. It's how I know how devastated Damien is that his brother enlisted, and when I've heard Greg confess terrible things he saw in the slammer. Drunken-night conversations are where Arden admitted that he can't read, and where Able spoke about finding their momma after she took an overdose. They're where Andrew cried about finding a fucking child molester standing over him in the night, and the beating he took when he resisted.

None of those things ever gets mentioned again when we're sober.

The sound of the refrigerator whirs in the background as Greg juts his chin forward. I've forced his hand. Put him in a spot where he can't answer a question with a question easily. His hands brace around the edge of the table, and he leans closer, his eyes searching mine. "I'd kill for it," he says in a voice so low and menacing that I believe every word.

"So you understand."

He nods firmly once, and I allow a flicker of relief to tip the corners of my mouth. I've gotten him onto a path now, but I need to push on. This next question will reveal to my friend the alien seed that has now grown into a fully grown tree in my mind. It's dangerous, and if there's one thing I don't want to do, it's piss him off. The rest of the men in this house could laugh about something like this, but not Greg. For an ex-con, Greg is as straight down the line as any man I've ever met. No nonsense. Hard as a rock.

I inhale deeply and let it out slowly, bracing myself for his response to my next question. "Do you think you could feel that way about Sandy?"

Greg's neck flexes with a swallow that must have felt like a gulp, and his knuckles whiten as his grip on the table intensifies. "You're playing with fire, Tyler," he says, and I know he means business because he's switched to using my full name. "Don't you think that girl has been through enough? You want to confuse the shit out of her too? Confuse and insult her?"

"You don't understand. Her friends share men. It's not a big deal to her."

"Some of my friends are banged up for killing a man, chopping him into pieces, and dumping his parts in dumpsters around town. Doesn't mean I want to live the same life."

"Yeah, but she went into a long spiel about all the pros. She was supposed to get introduced to these rancher cousins of her friend's husbands. When she told me that, she didn't sound angry at the idea."

"Maybe she was just telling you this stuff to shock you or to make you jealous. Maybe the part about the cousins was made up just to hurt you."

"Sandy's not like that." Or at least she wasn't. I'm not the same man I was before either, so should I be expecting Sandy to be? Greg spoons another mouthful of cereal while I sweat over the viability of my own idea. Then I realize that he never answered my question.

"Maybe she has changed. Maybe she made the whole thing up. I guess I won't know until I have this conversation with her. What I need to know is would you want to share her with me?"

His nostrils flair like an annoyed bull. "What the fuck are you asking me, Tyler? Would I fuck your woman? Would you want that? Man to man, Tyler. This is your girl. Not just any girl either. And you think you could share her with me?" His arms raise at his sides, aiming to show off the full extent of the man he is. His huge, inked biceps bulge, and the broadness of his chest is enhanced.

He's a massive man.

A massive man who I'm inviting to put his hands on my girl. I get what he is trying to do, but it's not going to work. He thinks the idea of Sandy touching him, kissing him, fucking him should be something that fills me with bitter jealousy, but it's not like that. Knowing she'd be in good hands, hands more reliable than mine, would only be a relief.

Eye to eye, something deep and fucking heartfelt passes between us. I blink, deciding my next words carefully, knowing I have this one chance to convince him of what I already know deep in my marrow. "You're my brother in every way but blood. I'd give my life for you. I'd share the love of my life with you. And if anything happens to me…"

Greg's hand shoots up to halt me before I finish. "What the fuck is going to happen to you, T? Is there something you're not telling me?"

"No. There's nothing I'm not telling you. I broke this girl once, G. I won't bring her back into my life without knowing she'd be in good hands if something happened to me. I know enough to know how fickle life can be. There's no certainty, or at least, I can't pretend that I believe there is."

The cereal bowl is shunted across the table by Greg's huge, tattooed hand. The word HATE is emblazoned across his knuckles, the word LOVE missing from the other fist. He told me once that when he got it inked onto his skin, he didn't believe there was anything other than HATE that would ever touch him. I'd like to think he's changed his mind since we all ended up together as a makeshift family, but deep down, I know he needs to feel the love of a woman to make him truly believe.

Sandy's touch did that for me.

"Fuck," he mutters, his palms shaping into fists big enough to kill with a single punch. "You think these are good hands, T?"

It's not the first time that I realize that most of Greg's fierce exterior has been crafted to cover something softer and a whole lot more vulnerable.

"Of course. There's no one I'd trust more." And it's true. Even though Greg is the only one of my boys who's seen the inside of the pen, he's the one I know would fight to his last breath to keep Sandy safe. The rest are good strong men with big hearts, but Greg is ride or die. He's been to the brink and come back again. I need him on

Sandy's team.

Greg's neck swallows around nothing again, or maybe it's around something this time. I'd like to think it's a lump of positive emotions because that's what I've got wedged in my throat right now too. He shakes his head as though he can't believe the conversation we're having, or his own thoughts.

"I'd share your girl with you, T. If she'd have me, that is."

I grin at my friend, who looks more like a thug or a criminal than a man you'd entrust the love of your life to. "The universe sent her back to me, G. On the day of her friend's wedding. If this is fate at play *'if'* won't come into it."

10

SANDY

The bed is empty when I awake to the heavy thump of vehicle doors closing. Tyler's curtains are awesome at keeping out the sun, and from the groggy feeling in my head, I'm pretty sure that I've slept for longer than I usually do.

Sex used to do that to me, or at least the mind-blowing, soul-shattering orgasms that only Tyler could ever yank from my body. And sleeping next to him too. There used to be so much comfort in having his body next to mine, and surprisingly, it was still the same after so many years and so much pain.

I run my hands over my face as my mind flitters over what's going to happen today. Tyler will probably want to talk. Or maybe not. Maybe he came to sleep next to me without touching me to let me know that cares, but not enough to be more with each other again.

Maybe he just needed time to think about what he wants to say.

Maybe it's all a huge mistake to him.

A huge mistake to both of us.

Ugh. I need to use the bathroom and take a shower. There's no way I'm padding around a house filled with men with semen-encrusted satin shorts and a cami that's been torn in a frenzy. It's not the only thing that feels a little torn. Between my legs there's an unfamiliar feeling, the ghost of a cock that penetrated too fast and felt too good.

A bubble of emotion rises in my chest, but I suck in a quick breath and push it back down. It's something I've become an expert in. Inside me, there are so many feelings I have to keep closed away. Feelings, and secrets that need to be kept.

One of Tyler's shirts rests over the back of a chair, and I tug it over my arms, breathing in the scent of him that makes me lightheaded and heavy-boned all at the same time.

When I'm clean and presentable, I pad down the stairs and into the kitchen, wondering if I'm alone. It's 10 am, so well after the time – I'm assuming – Tyler and his friends need to be at work. Except, just as I'm about to fix myself some coffee, awkward as hell about making myself at home here, footsteps sound in the hallway. The thud of my heart, expecting Tyler behind me, is deep and anxious. When I turn, I find that it's Greg instead.

I'm anxious for a different reason.

Of all the men in this house, Greg has the most intense air about him. There's power in his body and a forcefulness to his presence that concentrates into an imposing air that sends a shiver up my spine.

"Sandy." He nods once, the sparsest greeting that anyone has ever given me.

"Oh, hey Greg. I was gonna make myself a coffee." I

show him the mug I managed to find in the many cupboards.

"I'll do that for you," he says. There's no way I'd disagree with such a forceful statement. "Would you like toast or cereal? We have fruit, eggs, or I can rustle up some pancakes."

Pancakes. This man who looks as though he could rip my head right off my body is capable of cooking sweet treats? It just goes to show you can't judge a book by its cover. As much as I'd love to see this man whipping batter and flipping pancakes, I don't want to put him to any trouble. I'm not an invited guest as such, even for Tyler. For Greg, I'm just an inconvenience.

"Just cereal would be great."

"It's in the pantry. Go choose, and I'll grab the milk."

I shuffle over to the large door in the corner and find a well-stocked cupboard with at least ten different boxes of cereal to choose from. I pick the ridiculous multi-colored option that I used to eat when I was a kid, which elicits an amused snort from Greg. He hands me the mug filled with steaming black coffee held by a hand with the word HATE emblazoned across the knuckles.

Shit.

Maybe he notices me looking because as soon as the mug is safely in my grip, he drops his hand, rubbing across the tattoo as though he'd like to be able to erase it.

"Cream or sugar?" he asks with a slight dip of his head.

"Neither," I say.

"Sweet enough," he mumbles, retreating to the fridge for the milk and returning with a bowl and spoon too.

I perch on a stool at the counter, and Greg passes me everything I need to assemble my breakfast, then leans his hip against the counter on the other side, watching.

Making breakfast has never been a process so fraught

with nerves.

"Did the others already go to work?" I ask.

Greg nods solemnly. "Tyler had business he has to deal with today. He asked me to take care of you."

Take care of me, I think with a huff. I'm a grown woman used to fending for myself. I don't need an overgrown doorman to watch over me like a princess trapped in a castle. "I'm okay," I say, spooning in my first mouthful and chewing. If I was sweet before, I'm going to be positively saccharine by the time I've finished this. "I can entertain myself. Tyler shouldn't have forced you into becoming a babysitter."

"You're not a baby."

"No. I'm a grown woman. Unless Tyler is worried that I'll steal stuff from your house."

Greg's shoulders bunch, reacting to the confrontation. "That is not what's on Tyler's mind."

"So what is, then? If he thinks I'm too fragile to cope with a few hours by myself, he's mistaken."

"That isn't what he thinks."

"So what is it then?"

Greg's dark eyes flash with something that looks like a challenge, and although it's impossible to tell, something that tickles like arousal too. I get the feeling that this big brute of a man likes a woman who's a handful.

A hot pulse of heat pools between my legs at the thought of being in Greg's hands. It's a startling-enough response that forces a little squeak to leave my lips, causing his eyebrow to raise. I've never been attracted to a man like Greg before. He's so broad he could block a doorway, and his muscles are so thick that I suspect he must live on steak and protein shakes and dedicate hours each week to their maintenance. Tyler is muscular but in a lean, cut way that is more about sharp edges and angular plains. Greg is all brawn and potency and more mature in years too.

"You being here has done something to Tyler," he says.

"I didn't mean for us to run into each other," I blurt, but he holds his hand up to stop me.

"I'm not saying this to allocate blame, Sandy. I'm telling you this because he's my friend, and I don't want things to go down the way I'm foreseeing."

"What do you mean?"

Tension rolls off Greg, making me lower my spoon and rest it in the milky bowl. "The Tyler now isn't the Tyler you knew. He's different, and that's what's making him do crazy things and come out with crazy shit."

"You mean what happened last night?"

"He should have been thinking clearly. He shouldn't have let his heart drive his actions."

In my chest, the ache I've been suppressing begins to bloom like a blood-red rose, splitting me inside. "I wanted it too, in the moment."

"So you realize that it was a mistake."

"I realize that having this conversation with you seems odd. This is for me and Tyler to discuss."

Greg rests his skull-crushing hands on the counter, HATE barking at me from his skin. There's no LOVE on Greg's other hand to counter it, telling me that this man is hard on the inside as well as the outside.

"He's gone and got some ideas in his head. Ideas that have come from your friends."

"What ideas?"

"I'm going to share this with you for Tyler's good. In normal circumstances, I would take the conversation that I had with him this morning to the grave, but there is too much at risk here."

"What conversation?"

Greg's knuckles whiten, and his face hardens with the effort it's taking to break his friend's trust. It tells me that he's a man of honor, despite outward appearances to the contrary. "He asked me if I'd be willing to share you, like your friend's husbands share her."

"Share me?" I huff out a small stream of breath in shock. There is so much buried in that statement for me to process. What happened between Tyler and me last night wasn't just a one-off for him. He wants more. So much more, in fact.

"He loves you, Sandy. I know that might sound strange to you because of what happened four years ago. Your feelings towards him must be complicated. They say a broken heart is never fully mended."

"He loves me so much he's contemplating pimping me out to his friends." Who the hell does Tyler think he is?

"That's not what this is about, woman," Greg hisses.

"Woman?"

"Will you just listen to me? He loves you, and he doesn't trust himself to be what you need. He doesn't believe that you would be able to rely on just him."

"Why not? I don't understand."

"Because of what happened four years ago."

Tyler's reaction when I mentioned Jake and Luna flashes back through my mind, and Andrew's words last night. Maybe Greg will finally tell me what happened. "Did Jake die?" It's a horrible guess to make, but I have to find out one way or another.

The way Greg drops his hands from the counter to his sides tells me all I need to know. My hand flies to my mouth, holding in the sob that wants to break free. I only met Tyler's little brother once. He was a cute kid. Well, more like a gangly sixteen-year-old who still needed to grow into his face and body. He had the same eyes as Tyler and a wicked grin and sparkle in his eyes that told me he was going to be a heart breaker.

"The date on Tyler's arm?"

"The date he passed away," Greg says, shaking his head.

Three months after Tyler disappeared from my life. "What happened to him?"

Greg rubs his chin, shifting his weight on his feet in a way that reminds me of a boxer trying to dodge a punch. "Road accident. He was in a coma."

"For three months?" Greg nods. "Fuck." A wave of nausea knocks me back in the chair, the sight of the cereal floating in the bowl now repulsive. All those nights, I cried, imagining Tyler in bed with another woman, imagining him moving on happily and forgetting me like I was nothing. All the days, I held my phone waiting for him to return my call, believing he didn't want to. Cursing him for leaving with no warning. Cursing him for shattering my life and leaving me to struggle through the process of putting everything back together. All that time, he was dealing with the trauma of losing his brother.

"I hated him," I whisper. "I hated him so much."

Greg shoulders bunch, but I can't look at him anymore. I let my eyelids fall, and I breathe slowly and deeply through my nose, feeling like I'm fracturing all over again.

After the darkest days, I came to a point where I could see the truth. Tyler wasn't the man I thought he was. I'd been duped into falling in love with a liar and a manipulator. I told myself he pretended to love me to take my virginity, and when he'd had his fun, he moved on to another unsuspecting girl. In my mind, I made him a villain of our story.

But it was never that simple.

"You didn't know." Greg's voice is low and smooth, but it doesn't iron out the self-loathing and pain I'm feeling. Knowing I couldn't have done more doesn't make me feel better either. I fold my arms across my body like they have the capacity to keep me together, but a sob still rattles my shoulders, and before I know it, I'm folding in on myself, and there's no way to prevent it.

Tyler needed me, and I wasn't there. He chose to deal with the most terrible time in his life without me. I could have supported him. I would have done anything he needed me to do to make things easier, but maybe that's the point. Nothing would have made it easier.

Pain is a personal and private thing. Even when it's shared, it's still something we experience alone. Was that why Tyler disappeared? He couldn't see a way of sharing his grief with me. His loss was too great, too overwhelming. I couldn't imagine what it would be like to lose my sister. She's always been my greatest supporter, and from the age of nine, she's taken over the role in my life that my parents abandoned for my father's job overseas.

I'm too wrapped up in my own scrambling thoughts to notice that Greg has moved closer. When he rests a tentative yet heavy hand on my shoulder, I feel the weight of it through skin and flesh and bone to my aching heart. I turn, finding him crouched on the floor next to my chair, his dark eyes as black as night but drawn wider with concern. There's such a steadying presence to him, and just like that, I realize why Tyler would ask this man to share me.

It's not to do with sex. It's not some weird kink that he's acquired since we parted.

This is about sharing the burden.

It's about providing more for me than Tyler believes he's able to provide alone.

Stability. Continuity. Steadiness. Permanency.

Greg is unmovable. An anchor in the roughest of seas. An impenetrable tank of a man.

And I'm weak enough to need what Tyler wants to give me.

My life is a mess. No job. No home. I'm about to take ten steps backward, and I don't want that. But wants and reality are often unaligned.

It should feel unnatural to turn into Greg's arms like a child seeking solace. It should feel like a betrayal to Tyler and me. I vowed to hold my emotions tightly bound with bitterness and hopelessness and to never trust again.

But the vows we make to ourselves are the most easily broken.

And when I turn my face to kiss Greg, I don't only break my vow.

I shatter it into a million pieces.

11

GREG

When Sandy's lips touch mine, the world stops. Her face is wet with tears for my friend, but her mouth is hot for me.

This is not where I expected this talk to go.

Tyler is mad to think he can share this girl with all of us. I thought she'd never accept it.

I thought wrong.

Instinct drives me to pull her closer. My hand slides into her pretty curls and grips harder than I intend. The feeling of a loss of control rushes through my veins, setting my heart off like a jackhammer, but as her knees hit the floor between my crouching legs, I have her in my power.

The taste of her mouth is as sweet as the sugary cereal she was eating, the tentative slide of her tongue against mine like a licked stripe against my balls. The muscles on my shoulders and back bunch like my body is ready for war, not affection. Every instinct running through me is scrambled.

This is wrong. This is Tyler's girl, but I want her, and he wants to give her to me. Her hands pressed to my face are tender, telling me she wants to give me something too, and instead of drawing back, instead of telling her she needs to talk to Tyler and fix what needs fixing, I'm pulling her against me.

Fuck, she's tiny. Tiny against my huge, hulking body.

Soft in all the places that I'm hard.

When I use my grip on her hair to angle her face, going deeper with my kiss, she whimpers. When I use my other hand to slide down her back, relishing the curve of her waist and the roundness of her ass, she shivers.

We are black and white, bad and good, wickedness and purity, mistakes and virtue.

There are a million reasons why this can't happen, but I'm bullheaded enough to ignore every one of them.

It takes nothing to haul her up until I'm on my feet and her legs are wrapped around me. For a moment, we draw apart, and her eyes meet mine.

The deep thudding in my chest echoes in my ears as I really focus on this girl who's been like a ghost in our lives. Wavy hair that's glossy and soft tickles my arms, hazel eyes that could look a thousand different colors depending on the light blink with arousal and confusion. A smattering of freckles kiss her cheeks, flushed from crying and her reaction to this thing between us.

This confusing thing.

This thing that makes me want to burst out of my skin and be a new man.

There are tattoos on my body that I despise. Tattoos that reflect a different man from a different time. Tattoos that are on show for Sandy to see and judge. But she isn't judging. She's waiting.

Waiting for me to get a grip on myself.

"This is what Tyler wants," I growl. "But is it what you want?"

She presses her hand to my face, running her thumb over the soft skin above my cheekbone and my eyes drift closed. "What about what you want?" she asks. "Does that just get forgotten?"

Forgotten.

How did this girl get so perceptive that she can see right to the heart of me when I've told her nothing at all? Has there ever been a time when anyone cared about what I wanted and then gave it to me? I can't think of one. I've always had to take. Plunder. Tear what I want from the world. And here is Sandy, thinking about me.

Tyler's right. She's perfect.

"If you could see what I want from you right now, you'd run and never look back."

She strokes my face again, but this time I don't shutter myself to her. This time, I allow her feline eyes to search the deep blackness of my soul. "You think I'm a fragile flower," she says. "You think because I look this way and talk this way that the hardest thing that I've ever dealt with in my life is breaking up with Tyler."

"You've never been with a man like me before," I tell her.

"How do you know?" Her hand drifts to my collarbone, playing with the neck of my shirt.

"Because a man like me would never have let you go."

The long exhale of breath she makes sends blood pooling to my cock. If she was naked and I had my eyes on her pussy, I know she would have squeezed tight at my words. If I was buried inside her, I would have felt it like a vice around my dick.

"I've never been with anyone except Tyler," she says,

lowering her gaze. Is she embarrassed or ashamed about that? She shouldn't be. She should be fucking proud that she's kept the wolves from breaking down her door. Until me, that is. Now she's got the biggest baddest wolf of all with his cock pressed against her cunt.

And man, does he want to get inside.

It'll be warm in there. And comfortable. I know before I even get my fingers inside Sandy that I would lose myself in her body.

Fucking this pristine woman would be like washing myself clean. All the mistakes I've made, the wrong decisions, the other women I've used for release, all gone.

She'll cleanse me of every wicked thing that life has extracted from me and make me better.

Tyler thinks his idea is good for Sandy, but it's better for me.

I told her it wasn't a good idea for her own good, not mine.

And now I've tasted her, I'm weak. My resolve to put her interests in front of mine is gone.

"I could change that," I say, pulling her tighter against the iron bar of my cock. Her eyelids droop with arousal, and I've got her. I know I have. Right where I shouldn't want her, but I do.

So much that I want to throw my head back, bare my teeth and growl like a bear.

My bed is thirty paces away. Thirty paces to get Sandy where I want her. Naked. Spread open for me. Begging me to soothe the ache I know is building between her legs. Thirty paces, and I'll give Tyler what he wants.

But can I take them?

12

DAMIEN

There's something going on with Tyler. He's wired and jittery, like he's high on meds or strung out and stressed. I can't put my finger on what it is, but as I work on the engine of Mr. Doncaster's old truck, I'm half focusing on the oily mess and half on Tyler.

"How come you left Sandy with Greg?" Andrew asks, and I'm glad someone is trying to get to the bottom of what's going on. We're not busy today, and Tyler's spent most of the morning with his feet up, reading something on his phone.

He could have stayed home with Sandy. He could have been trying to fix things between them if that's what he wants. We all know he fucked her last night. Andrew made sure to share that with us on the ride to work.

I told Tyler he's a lucky bastard. Sandy's a real peach. I expected him to warn me off even looking at his girl. Men can be territorial like that, but he didn't. Instead, he grinned at me like he just hit a hundred on a scratch-off.

None of it stacks up.

Or maybe it does. Maybe Tyler's lost the sense in that pretty head of his. Perhaps he's gotten used to the single life, and he doesn't want Sandy the way he used to.

I've heard him shout her name in the night many times before she showed up out of thin air. I didn't think that four years have dampened down his feelings for her.

But maybe I know shit about what's between them.

"They're bonding," Tyler replies, and I go from hunched over the engine to back straight as an arrow. Bonding. What the fuck?

"Why the hell is Greg bonding with Sandy?" Andrew says.

Arden chuckles behind me. The guy has got a permanent grin on his face and finds just about everything in life amusing—especially my occasional inability to cover up what I'm really thinking. As soon as I open my mouth, I'm an open book. It's why I've learned to keep it shut, watch, and listen.

Except when I hear crap like what just came out of Tyler's mouth.

"I want her to like you guys," Tyler says.

"Like us? Why the fuck would you care if she likes us or not?" Able asks, wiping his hands on a rag, his eerie ice-blue eyes scanning over everything. I swear that guy has another level of perception – matrix-level shit.

Andrew mutters something under his breath, and Able raises an eyebrow. "You got something to say?"

"This is Tyler's bullshit," Andrew says. "I'm not wading into it."

Tyler shifts on the stool, dropping the phone onto the messy counter where we keep everything we can't be bothered to pack away: receipts, free calendars featuring half-naked big-breasted women, empty bottles of soda and half-finished packets of chips. This place is a mess.

"What, T? What's Andrew talking about?" Able tosses the rag, and it lands on the counter next to Tyler, who focuses on it more than he should. What's he avoiding here?

"You ever heard of poly relationships?" he asks.

"Poly what?" Able takes a step closer, his hand rubbing over the tattoos on his arm.

"For fuck's sake," Andrew mutters. "You're seriously going to do this?"

Tyler tries to ignore him, but the way he scratches at the skin around his thumb tells me that Andrew's comments have knocked some of the certainty out from under him. "Poly relationships basically involve more than two people."

"You mean like one dude and two chicks?" Arden asks. "I didn't think that was about a relationship. I thought that was porn."

"It can be one man and two women, or one woman and more than one man."

Andrew picks up a tire that he needs to fix an old Toyota out front and shakes his head. "Dude goes to one wedding, and he thinks he's an expert on alternative lifestyles."

"The wedding was for one woman and two guys?" I ask.

"Four."

"Four guys?" Arden whistles high and then low.

"But what the fuck does that have to do with Greg bonding with Sandy?" Able says, and I see the moment the penny drops for him without needing a response from Tyler. "Wait. You want to share Sandy with Greg?"

"Fuck." Arden shakes his head, his whistle at the craziness hitting an even higher note.

"Just Greg?" Andrew asks, dropping the tire. It hits the ground with a thwack, much like the sound of my jaw doing the same at this conversation.

"Not just Greg," Tyler says. For once, Deep Repairs is stunned into total silence. I guess Tyler wasn't expecting the completely shocked response because he holds his hands up, palms facing out. "You're all looking at me like I'm crazy, but I'm not."

"You lost your last grain of sense," Able says. "There is no way that sweet girl is going to go for an idea like that."

"You didn't hear her yesterday. She's seen her friends do it. She's seen them happy."

"Do you even know if she's single?" Able has a point.

"I think last night is evidence that she is," Tyler says.

"Just because a girl is single doesn't mean she's going to be up for Dickfest 2021." Arden rubs his hand over his thick beard as though he's already imagining Dickfest for himself. I'll admit that some images have passed through my mind with Sandy at the center. Images that no decent man should ever think about his friend's girl.

"This isn't about dick," Tyler says, and for the first time, I see a cloak of exhaustion curling his shoulders. He looks worn out, tired to the bone. Hunched with the weight of whatever is fueling this train of thought.

I take a step forward. "Chill out, guys. Let him talk," I say quietly. Although I'm a big guy, the biggest among us all, I know that strength doesn't come from size or volume. Shouting switches off ears. I learned that growing up, trying to block out my abusive fuck of a father.

Tyler nods at me gratefully, his green eyes staring deep into mine. He fiddles with the leather strap he has around his wrist. "I never meant to leave Sandy behind. I...you know shit happened. Now she's back, I want her, but I can't be what she needs alone."

Arden's jaw twitches, and his eyes widen slightly as

though he's holding back, saying something about Tyler not being man enough. It would be a joke, and those are his MO, but for the first time in a long time, he keeps his mouth shut.

"Anything could happen to me," he says. "Anything could happen to any one of us. What I learned from Jake is that life is short, and we shouldn't count on there being a tomorrow."

"You can't live thinking that way, T. Fear of dying makes life not worth living," Able says. He's right about that, but I put my hand out to stop anyone else from interrupting Tyler. The dude needs to get it all off his chest, and he doesn't need any of us making it harder.

"I know I made Sandy suffer. She already lost me once. It was there in the way she was with me last night. I just…you guys are as close to me as brothers. I'd trust you with my life. I'd trust you with my girl. I'd trust you to be what she needs if I'm not around."

"You're speaking like you know something bad is coming," I say.

"I don't have a crystal ball. I just have enough humility to know I'm nothing special. If the universe could take Jake, it can take me."

"So you're saying that sharing Sandy would be all about her protection," Andrew says.

"Yeah. And for us too. This business…the house…nothing would be the same if we all meet different women. They'll want to have their own space. Maybe they'll want us to start up something on our own. Everything will change, and I don't want that."

"So you're talking about keeping us together?" I ask. For the first time since Tyler began explaining, I see sense in his thinking. I still think he's crazy, but maybe that's just because this isn't the way normal people live, and I always imagined the wife and kids and house for myself sometime in the future. Was I doing that because it's what I want or because I just have this deep need to do better than my own parents did?

"She's never going to go for it," Able says. "I mean, look at us. Six fucking giant men with grease under their fingernails and mouths stuffed with curses. She's a nice girl. She could do a whole lot better finding a nice white-collar guy, maybe a doctor or an attorney or some shit, and settling down with him."

"She loved me once," Tyler says. "Last night, it felt like she still does. I don't know for sure...I don't really know anything for sure, but I need to know what y'all think before I even think about broaching the subject with Sandy."

"You're asking us if we want to bring Sandy into our lives as our girl. One girl and six guys?" Arden says. His expression is strangely serious in a way that confuses my eyes. It's like looking for your reflection in a funfair mirror. What you see is only half what you expect.

"One girl. Six guys." Tyler nods.

"Fuck," I mutter, flexing my hands.

"You got something to get off your chest, D?" Tyler asks me.

For a moment, I contemplate retreating into my reserved shell and holding everything back like I usually do.

When Dad's fists were raining down on my mom, and I was too little to help her, I'd sit in silence with my brother. Silence was a safe place.

It would make this simpler to stay quiet. I could just follow the crowd. There are four other guys getting invited into this situation. I don't need to be at the forefront of the response. Except I can see what this is costing Tyler to say.

For whatever reason, he's opening up this vulnerable

part of himself. He's telling us his biggest fears, his greatest weaknesses. If he can do that, then I should be willing to step forward too.

"I get you, T. I get where you're coming from. You guys are my brothers. I never want anything to come between us. The family shit we've all been through…well, it's enough to tell me that what should work sometimes doesn't. This might all sound crazy, but maybe you're right. Maybe we could be something good for Sandy, and she could be something good for us."

Tyler nods at me, and a flicker of a smile tweaks the left side of his mouth.

"You'll get jealous," Andrew says. "Fuck, if I was you and I had Sandy, I'd go fucking crazy if another guy tried to lay their hands on my girl."

"She's not a steak, Andrew. She's not something you can consume and there will be nothing left for me. She's a person with so much love in her heart, and she'll have enough for us all. I'm sure of it."

"Look at us," Arden says, the grin firmly back in place. "A girl who crushes on Tyler isn't going to crush on Damien. And one who likes Greg isn't going to look at my blond-haired, blue-eyed brothers and me and want to jump our bones. We're all too different to appeal to one woman."

"Maybe," Tyler says. "Maybe Sandy will think I'm crazy and leave, and I'll be back to where I was yesterday before she blew back into my life. Maybe I'm just a fucking coward for not trying to get her to forgive me and keep her to myself. But I don't think I am. For the first time in a long time, I feel like I've got it all figured out."

"This is going to end in tears," Andrew says, hefting the tire back off the floor.

"But you're in?" Tyler asks of his retreating form.

"I'm in," Andrew shouts, not bothering to turn around.

The smile that lights up Tyler's face is like pure satisfaction. "If he's in, we're in," Able and Arden say at the same time. If it was going to be easy for any of us to share, it would be them. More than one woman has staggered out of our house after getting in the middle of that triplet sandwich.

"What about you, D?"

I shove my hands into the pockets of my bright blue overalls. When we started this repair shop together, we couldn't land on a name. Nothing seemed to fit. It was me who came up with Deep, and it was because, for the first time in my life, I had my people around me. I wasn't on my own anymore. Together we were rolling deep.

No man is an island. We need people around us to be content. Six deep, and I was happy. Adding another, well, that could make us the lucky seven.

"I'm in, T," I say.

"Good man." Tyler picks up his phone. "Good man."

The next hour passes like I'm walking through quicksand. Tyler is on fire, laughing and joking like he threw off that cloak of exhaustion and let it float away on the wind. The rest of the guys seem their usual selves but occasionally, our eyes meet, and something passes between us.

Anticipation.

Nerves.

A feeling that things are never going to be the same again.

Can I be the kind of man that Sandy needs?

I don't know. I never loved a woman the way you see in the movies, but it's what I want.

As I shut the hood of Mr. Doncaster's truck, knowing I fixed the unfixable, I think maybe I have it in me to do anything I put my mind to.

And if Sandy agrees, I'm putting my mind to her, deep and then deeper.

All the way.

13

SANDY

When Greg hesitates, all of my working organs seem to freeze in anticipation.

I can change that, he'd said, telling me he could be the man who'd wipe out Tyler's status as the only man I've ever let between my legs. Instantly I became a woman possessed with a demon exactly like the one emblazoned on his bicep. I was willing to beg Greg to make it so. Beg him to take away the lasso that Tyler still has on my heart and body. Wipe away some of the pain.

I know he would.

The man currently holding me as though I weigh nothing more than a feather would have no trouble erasing things. The hands that are gripping into the soft flesh of my ass could pulverize all of my problems. He could pound me until I forget how much my heart hurts for Tyler and how much my heart hurts for me. He can show me that there is life out there that doesn't involve pain. At least not in a bad way.

Am I a fool?

Yes.

Am I reckless?

I want to be.

Until two months ago, I was a chaste schoolteacher, with nothing on my mind except imparting wisdom to my students. Then a man stole that from me, and now I don't even recognize myself.

Greg's chest is heaving, his heart pounding like a bass drum against my palm. His eyes are like obsidian, but within all that darkness lies a raging inferno that threatens to consume me.

And I want to be consumed.

"I'm yours," I tell him, and he actually growls, sending an animalistic shiver up my spine and slickness between my legs. He doesn't even have to touch me, and I'm primed for him like a bitch in heat. His lips find mine again, and then he's walking with all the purpose of the Terminator until my back hits the wall.

"I want to take you to my bed," he says as he mouths a hot path up my neck, tugging my earlobe into his mouth. "I want to fuck you against this wall, so you're clawing at my shoulders, begging me to stop."

"I'll never beg for that," I say.

"Oh, you will, girl." His teeth graze my jaw, and he bites down hard enough to make me yelp. "I'm going to get you so you don't know what you're begging me for."

"Do it." My fingers dig into his shoulders, and light sparks in his eyes.

"Tell me again."

"Do it. Take me upstairs and fuck me until I don't know which way is up and which is down."

"You won't know your name by the time I'm finished with you."

Those are the last words he speaks before he carries me up the stairs, not even breaking a sweat.

Greg's room is nothing like I expect it to be. It's entirely white, with luminescent cotton sheets, a white wooden bed frame, and white walls. It's as sparse and minimalist as a modern art museum, with absolutely nothing out of place. The contrast between the room and the man is mind-blowing.

When my back hits the bed, I don't have a chance to think before Greg's hands are unbuttoning my jeans and yanking them off my legs. My panties end up halfway down my thighs, but he takes no time to savor their removal, simply tossing them onto the pristinely clean wooden floor like you'd discard an old rag or a piece of litter. "Take off your top," he growls, "And then show yourself to me."

Show myself. What does he mean?

When I fumble to pull off my shirt and deal with my bra fastening, he watches with cool anticipation.

"Show yourself," he says again.

"How?" Hot blood seeps into my cheeks as he puts his hand on the inside of my pressed-together thighs and eases them open.

"Show me your pretty pussy, Sandy. Use your hands to hold yourself open."

Oh God. Understanding what he means just makes me blush even harder, but I do what he says because everything about his voice and demeanor commands it.

But I don't do it fast. I leave my legs to flop open slowly, running my palms down the soft skin of the inside of my thighs, eyes fixed to Greg's that never leave my center. When my fingers find my labia, I almost slide them over my clit, but something tells me that Greg wouldn't like that. Pleasure is something he wants to give me. Letting me take it would involve surrendering his control.

Instead, I use my thumbs to part my labia, displaying my most private place to his hungry eyes.

"Good girl," he says, low voice rumbling like vibrations against my core. "Now stay like that."

Greg walks around the bed, slowly picking up my discarded clothes, shaking them, and hanging them over a chair. Only when the room is tidy does he begin to strip. That first tug of his tight gray shirt over his head by one brawny arm makes my pussy contract, but he doesn't see because he's inside the shirt. The sound of him pulling his belt from the loops of his jeans causes the same response, and this time a flicker of a grin forms at the corner of his mouth. Nothing about his expression speaks of amusement. It's wickeder than that. It's as though he thought he knew something about me and has now had it confirmed.

"You're ready for me, aren't you," he says, resting the belt over the chair and then returning. His finger slides up the inside of my thigh and ghosts over the spread hole of my entrance. He rubs his fingers together, savoring my wetness, and my pussy squeezes again.

I'm ready. Readier than I ever would have thought possible for a man I barely know. Readier than I could have imagined if you'd told me how this would have been. I didn't know I'd get turned on by a man's orders or his cold appraisal. These things are new and strange to discover about myself.

The unsnap of Greg's buttons down the front of his jeans seems to take forever. Beneath, I get a glimpse of tight gray underwear that does nothing to conceal his cock, which is hard and straining within the fabric. It's not concealed for long.

Greg removes everything in one rough flourish, and when his clothes hang tidily, he crawls up the bed between my legs like a bear on the prowl. The wait for him has gotten me antsy. Every nerve under my skin primes for his touch, and I guess that was the whole point.

Mind games are sexy as fuck, and a man who knows how much sex is in a woman's mind will be a master of her body.

His arms come down either side of me, and he braces himself above me, his bottom lips drawing in for a long moment and reappearing moist. I don't know where to look. His eyes are like shadows that can see into my soul. His broad shoulders and chest scream power and a past bleaker than anything I can imagine. Lower, his abs are like a ladder to the underworld of his cock. Hades hangs there, between his legs, the dark god waiting to drag me under. A shiver runs through my whole body, peaking my nipple and flooding my skin with prickling goose flesh.

"Don't be scared," he whispers. "Even when it hurts, it feels good."

His lips find mine, but he doesn't close his eyes. He watches my reaction, the jittery blink of my eyes, the widening of my pupils as his formidable beauty comes close enough to touch me.

If the devil had a human form, he would choose Greg's. Of that, I'm certain.

Then he licks a long stripe along my jaw, and for a moment, I slip beneath the surface of reality. "I can see why Tyler hasn't been able to forget you," Greg whispers close to my ear. "I can see why he can't let you go."

I whimper as his lips close around my nipple and then his teeth, biting hard enough for tears to spring to my eyes. "I can see why he'd do anything to keep you, including giving you to me. But he didn't really, did he, Sandy? He just gave me permission. You handed yourself over for this. You gave me this body to play with, this heart to know." The flat of his broad palm rests over where my heart is pounding with a mixture of trepidation and arousal.

I nod because he's right. Tyler may have given the green light, but I was the one with my foot on the accelerator. I didn't just drive; I floored it into Greg's arms like a woman on the run from the cops and into the arms of a gangster.

"Tell me what you want," he says, his mouth hovering over the curve of my belly, so close to where I need him.

"Your mouth," I say.

"Where?"

"Everywhere." It's not until the words have left my lips and I see an even darker glint in Greg's eyes that I realize my mistake. In a flash, he has me rolled onto my front, grabbing my hands and holding them over my head. His whole body rests against mine; 220lb of caged animal, and I'm powerless.

"Keep your hands there," he says.

"What are you going to do?"

"You'll have to wait and see." One hand releases and begins a long, languid stroke from my fingertips, down the soft underside of my arm, along my ribs, and across my waist, then lower. His hips buck just once, pressing the huge bar of his cock against the seam of my ass. Then he's pushing himself up and grabbing a pillow.

The loss of his weight and warmth leaves me adrift until he hoists my hips upward and plants the pillow beneath me like I weigh nothing more than a rag doll. But whatever he's trying to do, it isn't enough for him. Another pillow is added, leaving my ass in the air.

Everywhere.

The word echoes in the recesses of my mind as his rough palm, crafted from years of hard work, strokes the soft cheek of my ass. I hold my breath, bracing for what comes next, not knowing what it might even be.

Is he going to spank me? I don't know if I'd like that, but nothing can surprise me about any of this. I'm so far out of my comfort zone.

Instead, his thumbs stroke down either side of the seam of my ass so slowly that I have to wriggle.

"Still," he says, as they stroke back up, this time a little deeper. Holding back my reactions is like torture, but I do it because one word from Greg and I want to obey. Then his thumbs part me, and I have to close my eyes from the shame.

And when his tongue touches my taint, I can't breathe. I told him *everywhere*, so this is where he's gone – the naughtiest, most forbidden part of me. Greg is a man of extremes.

The part of me, the buttoned-up part that thinks I have to stay my daddy's good girl for the rest of my life, dies a little inside. The other part of me, the one that wants to be explored, wants to be owned, wants to be claimed and possessed and wrecked, wants to beg him to give me *everything*.

But Greg is in charge, and when his tongue circles my taint and I whimper, I can feel the smile creeping over his face. I can tell that he loves not only the act of sex but the process of breaking me down into pieces whose shape I don't recognize. My hips push back of their own accord, and my voice whispers, "Please." I'm so empty, and I want this man to fill me. I want him to break off the parts of me that have wrapped around my hurt and leave me open, heart pounding, mind splintered, everything yearning and desperate and ready to live again.

And he can.

I know he can.

Maybe better than anyone else.

Maybe that's why Tyler chose him. Maybe it's because he has the utmost confidence in a man who looks like he's spent his life pulverizing the rules.

Greg's tongue drifts lower, licking into my entrance

and then back up, circling, circling, circling, never stopping even when I'm trembling so much it must be hard for him to focus. Even when I jerk away because it feels too good, and he has to grip his hands into the soft flesh of my hips and hold me where he wants me. Even when I'm making sounds that don't sound human, his tongue keeps its unholy rhythm, and a realization hits me.

He's going to make me come without even touching my clit. Without putting a single finger or his cock inside me. Just the sheer forbidden feelings and his manhandling are enough to tip me over the edge.

It's like being set free.

My legs snap closed, and everything draws up and inward, my pussy and ass fluttering over and over and over and over until I actually start to worry it might never stop. Has he broken me so that I'll remain in a state of perpetual orgasm for the rest of my life?

My mind is as black as the ink that covers him until I hear him chuckle, and I'm suddenly back in the room.

14

ARDEN

"I need to go and see a man about a dog," I tell my brother. He's under a car, so really, I'm only speaking to his feet and bent legs.

"What kind of dog?" Able asks.

"It's a phrase," I say. "Don't get your panties in a bunch. I'll see you later."

I'm out the door before anyone can question me, jumping in the truck that we all took to work this morning. An easy way to make sure none of them can easily follow me.

I mean, there's no reason they should.

We often leave the repair shop in the middle of the day to run errands or get lunch.

My belly rumbles, but it's not lunch I'm after.

Tyler said that Greg is bonding with Sandy, and I want to see what it means for myself.

Yes, I'm a nosy fucker, and yes, Tyler's plan to let us

share his girl has my dick harder than the wrench on the floor of this truck.

The fact that Greg got a heads-up has me antsy. I love that dude like my blood brothers, but he's seen and done things that could blacken a wedding dress at forty paces. His hands on sweet, angelic Sandy…well, what I'm saying is I'm worried that if he goes first, she'll change her mind.

I feel stupid for even doing this. If Greg has tried to make a move, he probably has a Sandy-sized handprint on his cheek. She'd wither him with a hazel-eyed stare and a scowl twisting her pretty lips. I'll probably arrive at the house to find him downstairs and her upstairs.

I change the radio station from Andrew's favorite to something with a whole lot more bass. The rhythm of the guitar and the beat of the drum is loud enough to vibrate through my jittery mind. My brain isn't like my brothers'. Even when I'm exhausted, it never seems to rest.

It doesn't take long to reach the house. We bought it for that very reason. The other trucks are still in the driveway, so I'm certain that Greg hasn't gone anywhere. Inside, the house is quiet.

There's no one downstairs.

The den is like it was left last night, and, in the kitchen, a single half-filled bowl of cereal, with milk sloshed over the side, remains on the counter. That's how I know something's going on. Greg would never leave a mess like this unless he's distracted by something big. The brute looks like he should live without a care, but he's the neatest freak I've ever met.

I toe off my shoes in the hallway, wanting to maintain as much stealth as I can as I make my way up the stairs. Greg's room is the one before mine, so I have a legitimate reason to pass it without it looking as though I'm purposefully snooping.

A whimper vibrates the air in the hallway. It's a

desperate keening sound that fondles my balls and stiffens my cock.

A sound that tells me Greg's got Sandy on her back.

I knew it wouldn't take him long.

He's a devil with the ladies, and it's always the pretty, uptight, librarian types that spread their legs for him the fastest. But I have to admit that I'm surprised. Greg has strict codes and expectations around behavior. Of all of us, he's the one I thought would have the most concerns about Tyler's suggestion to share Sandy.

But it would seem that I was wrong about him and Sandy. I guess there is more to this whole thing than meets the eye.

I wait, my left ear tilted up to catch more sounds. Another whimper from Sandy, and my cock is rock hard. I adjust it with my hand, giving it a squeeze for good measure, then Greg makes a low growling sound that reminds me of a lion at the zoo, and the headboard begins thwacking rhythmically against the wall.

Fuck.

He's giving it to her slow and hard, just my tempo. I like to push in deep in one thrust and then roll my hips, keeping an even rhythm that makes a woman's toes curl.

I take another step forward until I'm close enough to see through the crack in the door to the bed beyond.

Greg is on top of Sandy, his hand around her throat, his eyes open and fixed on hers. Her legs are spread wide, angled on a pillow that tips her hips up, setting her up for deeper penetration. And I know it'll be deep. Greg has a huge cock. No wonder the poor girl is whimpering. He's pinned her hands above her head with his other hand, so she's completely in his control, but I don't miss the roll of her hips beneath him. She's moving against him, loving every minute.

I squeeze my cock again, imagining what it will be like

to get inside Sandy myself. Maybe she'll be up for being with me and my brothers, all at the same time. Girls love triplets. It's like a triad of pleasure. Three holes to fill and three dicks to do it.

But after the sex, what will Sandy want? Does she know about what happened with Tyler? Has Greg told her Tyler's idea, and she's into it or has he just seduced her, keeping everything a secret?

Maybe Sandy's changed from the girl she used to be. Tyler built her up to be an angel rather than a real woman. Soft, kind, perfect. Almost untouchable.

But that's not the girl I see beneath Greg. This girl is begging him. "Fuck me harder," she moans, but Greg doesn't listen. He's playing games with her, slowing down until it's an unhurried drag out and an even slower push back in. A sob leaves Sandy's throat, and I can't take any more.

If I didn't think Greg would cut me in two, I'd be barging into that room and joining in. But what's normal for me and my blood brothers hasn't spread to the rest of the men who live in this house. Only time will tell if they'll want to take sharing to that other level.

I pad back downstairs, making sure to close the front door without making a sound.

I've found out what I wanted to know.

Now it's back to work.

My time will come to feel the tight, warm heat of Sandy's cunt. And after, I guess I'll find out if she's as sweet and good as Tyler's always told us.

Sex is one thing, but I'm looking for something more permanent than that for all of us in this household.

Maybe Sandy could be the girl who warms all our cold, ragged hearts.

15

GREG

My body is hers.

Everything I have, I want to give to her.

Sandy moans beneath me, her eyes glazed and her lip trembling with each inhale. I feel her swallow against my palm, and I almost come from that feeling. There will come a day when I'll slide my cock into her throat and feel that swallow reflex from a different angle, but not today. Today it's all about Sandy.

She's already come on my cock once, clenching her little pussy so hard that I grunted with pleasure. The noises she makes are like a tickle on my balls.

The way she moves is driving me fucking crazy.

Best of all, she loves me being in control. Most women do. They give it about wanting to be independent, but in the bedroom, most want to be dominated. Maybe it's a primal thing—something from our reptilian brain that keeps the order of things.

It's what I need.

"Fuck me harder," she hisses through gritted teeth, her hips shifting.

Even though she's already had an orgasm, her pussy is still a hungry little thing. I can give her more. Harder, faster, deeper, but I love the slow build. I'm relishing this perfect little princess, marking my territory. If Tyler wants to share her with the rest of the Deep six, I want to make sure she has me imprinted on her first.

Well, not quite first. Tyler will always have that status.

Things between us are different, and that's okay. She's never fucked a man who's almost a stranger. There has to be something illicit about that. Something forbidden that's setting her on fire.

"Please," she gasps. "I'm so close."

Her begging sounds pitiful in the best possible way. My dick is going to break her down until she can't take anymore, and then it'll set her free.

Maybe it's time to give her what she needs. Hooking my arm beneath her knee, I hitch one leg over my shoulder, driving so deep that her eyes roll. My ass clenches, my thighs power me forward over and over and over, my cock slipping in the perfect mess of her arousal. With each devastating thrust, she cries out, fingers now free to grip into my flesh, driving me forward.

"Fuck," she hisses. "Fuck, fuck, fuck…"

Then like a lasso around my cock, her pussy tightens over and over.

This is what it's meant to be like between a man and a woman. Slickness and sweat, darkness exploding into light, power, and release.

I'm so close that all it will take is…

…her nails on my back, her moans of pleasure.

My balls draw tight between my legs as deep, dark, sinful heat pulses through my cock, buried so deep inside her that I'd be writing my name if I hadn't wrapped my cock in latex.

Sandy insisted, and I'd complied, but not before realizing that she hadn't insisted on the same from Tyler. I saw him cleaning up their mess from the sofa.

The trust that exists between them is complicated. For the first time ever, I want to build that kind of trust with a woman.

It takes her longer to come back to reality. My eyes watch as her lids flutter, then open, gazing guilelessly into mine. She's an open book that I just scribbled my signature on, like a little kid spray painting his gang tag on a white wall. Her lips part, but whatever words she had to say die before they reach her tongue.

I release her leg, lowering it slowly to allow her tendons to relax without twinging. I'm aware of how overwhelming the power in my body can be.

Then I bring my hand to her face.

Aftercare isn't something I generally think about. Rolling onto my back and falling asleep, or even more often, grabbing my clothes to make a hasty retreat, tends to be my pattern, but not with Sandy. Her soft peachy skin tickles my calloused fingers. Her sweet breath ghosts my lips as I lean down to kiss her. "Are you okay?"

"Yes," she says softly. She blinks, and something passes across her face, but I can't put my finger on what it is.

"What about here?" I let my thick, now semi-hard cock draw out of her slowly, and when it flops out of her heat onto the mattress beneath, she winces. There's a caveman part of me that loves seeing that little bite of discomfort, knowing I've left my mark.

"I'm okay," she says softly.

"This was..." I trail off, not really knowing what to say.

"Unexpected." A tight smile pulls at her lips, but I want more. I want her straight white teeth to flash me with a smile filled with appreciation and contentment.

"Unexpected."

Her hand trails over my shoulder and the ink demarcating the mouth of hell, lower over my side where an angel cowers under the devil's trident. "These marks must have hurt."

"I was at a point in my life when just feeling something was a relief." My words are true, but I'm surprised that I spilled them to Sandy.

Sandy's head nods gently as her fingers trace more of the lines on my skin. On the other side of my chest, a dark wolf cowers beneath the looming face of a white wolf. "Good and evil," Sandy whispers.

"What?"

"The tattoos. They're all different, but through them all, there's the thread that links them; the battle between darkness and light."

I look down at myself, noticing for the first time that what's she's said is true. On my other bicep is a swirl of birds in flight, some black and some white. The white ones have the black cowed. On my back is a man dressed like a biker, with one huge white wing and one huge black looming over him. He's turned in the direction of the black wing.

Yin and yang. The duality of the world and what's inside us.

Sandy is perceptive enough to see something that I didn't even realize about me, and in just that one observation, she's stripped me down to my barest parts.

"Just pictures I liked from the book at the tattoo shop," I dismiss, but her jaw twitches as though she doesn't believe me. She'd be right. Each of the tattoos on my body comes from a design I created. Someone else did the work, but they were always based on my inspiration.

"Chosen by you," she says softly. "So, which are you,

Greg. The dark or the light?"

"We're all made up of both, Sandy."

"We are." She draws her lip under her upper teeth as though she's thinking and holding something back at the same time.

"Our mistakes are the black. The times when we've done things that have hurt us or made decisions that have hurt someone else." Sandy's eyes drift closed, and after a while, when she opens them again, they're glassy with tears. "Hey," I say, holding her by the chin. "What are you thinking about?"

"Some mistakes can never be undone."

I nod. "There's plenty in my past that I'd erase if I could."

"But then you wouldn't be you." She touches my eyebrow and trails lower over the scruff on my cheek. "You wouldn't be able to see the world the way you do. You wouldn't touch people the way you do."

"You like the way I touch?"

She nods. "You touch me like you know everything inside me...all the good and the bad, and none of it matters—just the heat between us. Just our skin touching, our bodies joining. The sweat and the slickness."

It's been a long time since I had a lump in my throat. Maybe two decades since the last time my dad beat me, and I was too small to retaliate. Sandy's words burn in my neck because she's put her finger on exactly how it was to be with her.

For the time it took us to fuck, her touch sank deeper than I could ever have predicted. She's the angel, and I'm the devil. We fit together just right; two sides of a coin that I want to polish and slide into my back pocket for safekeeping.

"You're mine now, Sandy girl. I'll share you with my boys, but you're mine, and I'm yours. I'll never let anyone hurt you ever again."

Her eyes flutter closed and then open slowly like she's savoring the taste of my words on the tip of her tongue and relishing the flavor. "I believe you," she says eventually, hand trailing over the white wolf, but what if it's one of your boys that does the hurting?"

My breath gets trapped in my lungs at what she's insinuating.

Everything—all of Tyler's ideas and the success of it—rests on unity. We take care of Sandy, and Sandy takes care of us. But if that unity isn't there, then more than just our relationship will fall apart. Friendships could be shattered.

"None of my brothers will hurt you," I say, with as much certainty as I can find.

Sandy smiles sadly. "It's happened before. It'll happen again."

My instinct is to draw her into my arms and hold her tightly, so I do it, rolling so I'm on my back and she's resting in the crook of my arm. "Baby, don't look for the bad before the good. Life can make us that way, but we gotta fight it. It's the only way to get through it all in one piece."

Sandy hides her face against my chest, and although her whole body is rigid and still, I know that she's crying.

I hold her until whatever she needed to get out of her system has passed. When she falls asleep in my arms, I wait until I know she's settled. Then I disentangle from her, tucking the comforter around her shoulders.

There's an angel in my bed—an angel with broken wings.

And although I should know better, I make a vow to her that I'll help her heal them. Whatever it takes.

16

TYLER

Greg's message lights up my phone just after lunch.

It's done.

Although it's what I want, my gut clenches at the images that flood my mind, Greg stripping Sandy, her whimpering, letting him take out all of his tightly coiled rage on her body. I didn't think it would happen so fast, but I'm an idiot because whatever Greg puts his mind to, he ends up achieving, good or bad.

When I look up from my phone, Able's watching me closely.

"Everything alright, T?" he asks. He places the carton of oil on the floor, tightening the cap.

"Everything's good." The smile I force would probably be enough for Damien or Andrew or Arden but not for Able. He's the guy who can read emotions like words on a billboard.

A little while later, I spot Able and Arden whispering out front. Whatever they're talking about has Able's eyes widening and Arden's hands gesticulating. When he cups his own throat between his broad fingers, those images of Sandy and Greg come back to me.

I love these men, but that doesn't mean this is going to be easy.

Sandy is gentle and kind, and these men are rough and flippant about most things. I know they'll treat her with respect out of their love for me, but it still makes my hands curl into fists.

Maybe it'll get easier when we're all together. The feelings of unity that I have with my brothers will be magnified with Sandy at the center. If I can just hold it together through this stage, it will all be worth it. When I know Sandy is safe and well cared for, whatever happens, I'll be able to rest. When I know she'll stay, and I won't have to lose her again, I'll be at peace.

I find the keys to Sandy's car and decide to distract myself by looking it over inch by inch to make sure it's safe. There's no way I'm letting her out on the road in something with a fault, no matter how small. On the first inspection, one of the tires is a little worn on the inside. Maybe it wasn't balanced correctly when it was fitted, or maybe she damaged it in a pothole, and it's caused an uneven pattern of wear. Underneath, her brake pads are almost down to the discs—another thing to add to the list. I don't get to the engine because I know it's been inspected and the parts ordered. We just have to wait for them and then fit them. That gives us a timeline to work to. Not enough time for one woman to get to know six men, although at the pace Greg has managed to get between her legs, maybe it won't be so hard for the rest.

That doesn't make me think badly of her. I'm not some raging misogynist who thinks women need to stay virgins until marriage. It's just about me learning who this Sandy is. She's not the girl I fell in love with but a woman now—a woman with needs that I want to satisfy and wants that I need to provide for.

I can prove to her that I'm reliable and trustworthy. I can prove that what happened between us four years ago to end our relationship isn't a pattern.

I'm about to order a new tire to replace the worn one when the sound of an engine rumbling from outside draws my attention. It's Greg's truck, and he's sliding out and throwing the door closed roughly. The sound of his boots on the concrete echo around the shop. Andrew, Able, and Arden look up like meerkats scouting for predators. Damien is somewhere under a car and probably oblivious to what's been going on today.

When Greg nears the desk, he looks at the chair as though he isn't sure whether he should be stand or sit. His black eyes meet mine, and I nod to the chair. Better to have us both at the same level. Greg is enormous.

"What-up, T?"

"Just ordering," I say. "You good?"

"I'm good." He raises his right eyebrow, scanning every part of me that he can see for a hint of my mood. He's a master at reading body language, probably honed from his time in the can when it could be a life-or-death situation.

"Sandy good?"

"I left her at the house. She was sleeping."

"Okay."

"I know what you said, T," he says, rubbing his hand over his closely cropped hair. "I know what you told me you wanted."

"It's okay," I said. "I'm fine."

Greg shakes his head, flopping his big arm back to his side. "I told Sandy about your idea. I told her that you were crazy. I told her about Jake."

Jake.

Just the mention of his name takes me back to the

hospital room on the night I got the phone call. The doctor came out to talk to me before I could see Jake in the ICU. He told me my little brother was in a critical condition and that he was fighting for his life.

I went so cold inside as though all my blood turned to ice in just one tick of the clock.

"But…your message…you made it sound like everything was good…" I stutter, trying to drag myself back to the present.

"I know what I said." Greg turns in his chair, resting both palms flat on the desk in front of him. We're eye to eye, man to man. "She was upset. She told me she wanted me. She…" He pauses, inhaling so deeply that his nostrils flare. "She begged me to explain, and at the time, I could feel what she needed, and I wanted to give it to her. I couldn't see her cry and refuse what she was asking me for to make her feel better."

"That tells me I was right in suggesting this," I say. "You put her needs before your own concerns. That's what I want you to do."

"But now I think she might regret what we did."

"Did you get the feeling that she did…after?"

"No. She was fine. We talked. We…we…cuddled, but after…" he pauses again, looking around the repair shop as though he wants to know where each of the boys is before he tells me. "She told me she's worried about getting hurt. I told her none of us would hurt her, but she said, 'It's happened before, and it'll happen again.' She was crying, T. You gotta do something…you gotta talk to her. This thing you want for all of us, it's not going to work based on broken foundations. Your relationship with Sandy is the bedrock for everything that comes after, and I really like her. I don't want anything to fuck it up."

Slumping back in my chair, it's my turn to run my hands over my hair, frustration, and anxiety burning under my clavicle. Talking is what comes the hardest to me. Not the everyday kind of talking but the conversation that tears out your heart and leaves it bloody and bleeding on the counter for someone else to prod at. Talking to Sandy will mean opening up about Jake. I've never told anyone new about what happened. My boys were there through it all. They know everything from my drunken rambles and grief-stricken breakdowns, but I've never told them directly and consciously how I feel. I don't know if I can.

Instead of Greg simplifying things for me, he's now making this more complicated. But maybe I don't have to open up to Sandy. Maybe, if we can keep her busy with other things, the past will become less relevant.

I drop my hands as relief sweeps through me like a plow through fresh snow. "I can make it good with Sandy. You'll see." Greg doesn't need to know everything about my interactions with Sandy. I can show her how much she means to me without spilling my guts all over the sidewalk. There's a way around this where I can keep my shame buttoned up.

"You better," Greg says. There's a warning in his voice that is low and possessive.

"Yo, Greg," Arden says, strolling past us like he has a joke bubbling on his tongue.

"Yo, yourself." Greg shakes his head, frowning at Arden's retreating form. They get on great, but they're at opposite ends of the spectrum when it comes to character. When he's out of earshot, Greg turns to me. "That guy…did he leave here at any point today?"

"Yeah. To run errands."

Greg nods, and he doesn't say anything else, but I know what he's thinking. Arden went snooping. That's what the whispering and throat holding was about.

I glance down at Greg's huge hand that is still resting on the damaged wood of the desk. HATE is there, winking at me. Was that the hand he held around Sandy's throat when he was fucking her. Will he have left marks?

I guess there's only one way to find out, but I'm not going home without the rest of these boys for distraction. Tonight, I'm going to make chili for dinner, and then we can hang out and show Sandy just how awesome it will be for her to live with us.

If she says anything to me about Jake, I'll have a practiced smile to paint onto my face. I'll tell her everything's okay now, that I'm over what happened. Maybe she'll believe me. Maybe she won't ever find out that under everything, I still blame myself.

DEEP 6

17

ABLE

There's some crazy shit going on at Deep Repairs. Shit so crazy that even in my most warped moments, I haven't ever fantasized about something like this.

Sandy breezes in with a broken-down car, and suddenly Tyler has lost his mind.

But I know enough about our group of six that Tyler's crazy is just the kind of madness that we'll follow him into.

I say his plan is crazy, but the idea behind it actually makes a whole load of sense. The last time any of us had a girl who we wanted to stick around for more than one night, she caused a ruck between Andrew and Arden that it took weeks of a careful diplomatic effort to repair. I hate seeing my brothers fighting, but to be honest, it just made things difficult in the house.

Maybe T is right. Maybe sharing one girl will build on the harmony we already have.

Deep Repairs is important to me. My five brothers are important to me. Having something better than what I grew up with is my main goal in life, and that isn't just about living in a better place or having money to eat stuff other than hotdogs and ramen. It's about harmony and love too.

I'd never admit that to the rest of them.

They already think I'm soft for being the one who rescues stray cats from the neighborhood. When I nursed a bird that had a broken wing until it healed, they thought I was crazy. Greg suggested breaking its neck as a kindness, but I fought against him. In the end, that bird flew away to live its life. Who knows where it is or what it's seen since? All I know is that, when I released it from my bedroom window, a weight from inside me flew away too.

Second chances in life can be hard to accept when the first chance you have is terrible. But I have accepted the good life I have now, and I want to protect it. Whether it involves Sandy or not remains to be seen, but I'll only be ready to participate so long as we all stay united. At the first sight of back-biting, I'll withdraw my support.

Tyler has been brooding ever since Greg came to the shop, and when we all heap into two trucks, I choose to travel with him, watching the jitter of his leg and the way he's picked the skin around his fingernails until it's raw. I'm going to need to stay close to Tyler for sure.

Back at home, I'm the first through the front door, and as soon as I step into the hall, the smell of something delicious hits me square in the face.

"Fuck," Andrew mutters behind me. "That smells good."

We all troop into the kitchen, finding Sandy stirring something in a large pot. On the counter, cooling on a rack, are twelve huge blueberry muffins—my favorite.

If I'm not mistaken, the food in the pot looks like beef chili. It's usually Tyler that cooks it, but Sandy's definitely smells better. There's something richer about it that tickles my tastebuds without having to touch my tongue.

Not only that but Sandy's also dressed in the cutest outfit—a pretty yellow summer dress that's short enough to get a look at the milky skin of her curvy thighs. It's sheer enough that I can see the outline of her panties through the fabric—her very small panties.

Fuck.

"Hey," she says, turning and smiling, shrugging her shoulder as though she's shy about her efforts. I glance at the rest of the boys, finding them all with the same expressions, mouth open and eyes slightly wider than usual.

They never look at me that way when I cook!

"It's nearly ready, so you can go wash up." Sandy looks pointedly at our hands. We've all gone through the motions of cleaning up at the Deep Repairs workshop, but that's the thing about being a mechanic: the grease stains around my nails never seem to go completely, even if I scrub them almost raw.

No one says anything. They're gawking as though someone removed their brains. "Come on, guys," I say to jolt them out of their frozen states, and we all troop out of the kitchen to use the bathroom.

"Did you see that?" Damien says with a whistle.

"What part?" Arden asks.

"All of it," Damien says, his voice light and impressed. Tyler chuckles, squirting soap into his palm.

"You ain't seen nothing yet!" he says proudly.

Is it weird that he's so cool about us ogling his girl this way? I guess if you follow society's expectations, then of course it is. Pride in your girl is one thing, but Damien's comments went beyond just normal appreciation. They were packed with unsatisfied lust.

"She always cook like this?" Greg asks.

"Yep," Tyler says. "Sandy's the whole package. I told you. Smart, funny, cute, sexy, good cook…" He trails off as though anything else would be a step too far, but I know what was on the tip of his tongue. Knock-out in bed.

From what Arden told me, Greg gave her the fuck of her life, and she was taking it like a trooper. She'll have to be a trooper to take us all, that's for sure.

I'm the last to wash up, taking my time to get my hands as clean as they can possibly be. I even wash my face, patting it dry with a towel, and then straighten my hair. After all Sandy's work, looking presentable is the least I can do.

In the kitchen, Tyler is helping Sandy find plates and silverware. Greg is hunting out enough cold beers to go round, and Damien is even laying out napkins. The table is almost laid, and I smile at the effort the guys are making. We usually serve ourselves with whatever someone has been decent enough to cook and then slump onto the couch to watch whatever sport is on the TV.

Sandy loads up huge plates of chili, which she serves with homemade cornbread.

We all take our seats, and I'm amazed that everyone waits for Sandy to sit before tucking in. It's like having a woman around has resurrected all the manners that were lying dormant behind the testosterone in this house.

"Dig in," she says, smiling.

I am not exaggerating when I say it's heaven in a bowl.

"It's better than yours, T," Damien says carelessly.

"It always was," Tyler says, grinning in the lopsided way that makes him look younger than he is. It's his smile that reminds me of Jake the most, and that always makes me sad.

"Amazing," Andrew says, tearing off a chunk of bread and heaping it with rich meat and beans.

"It really is, Sandy." For once, Arden doesn't have a joke, and I catch a hint of redness on his cheeks when he looks at her.

At least he still has some shame. Dickhead shouldn't have come snooping. If you're going to watch people having sex, they should at least know you're doing it. Anything else makes a peeping tom in my book.

I wonder if Greg realized Arden was there. If not, and he finds out, Greg's massive shovel of a hand might end up wrapped around Arden's throat! As much as I love my triplet, I would probably enjoy seeing that.

Sometimes he needs to be taken down a peg.

As soon as I think it, I regret my feelings. Arden has always had it harder than me and Andrew. He struggled a lot in school and developed his cocky joker persona to cover up his issues. Even now, I think he was drawn to come home today to work out where he's going to stand in this whole arrangement. He'd hate it to be last to get with Sandy. He'd hate it if he felt like she didn't want him.

Everything comes back to his insecurities.

I hope Sandy will be careful with him if it gets that far.

"So, how was work today?" Sandy asks. She's so sweet, trying to make polite conversation while we're all tucking into dinner like pigs at a trough.

"Good," Tyler says. "We ordered you a new tire and some brake pads too. Yours were worn."

Sandy stops chewing. "I..." She pauses, rubbing her mouth with her napkin. "Is that going to cost me a lot?"

Tyler shakes his head, his eyes flicking between Sandy and his food as though he's worried that he'll turn into a pumpkin if he looks at her too long. "We've got it, okay? You don't need to worry about it."

Sandy's hand comes out, palm facing Tyler. "I can't do that. You're not responsible for my car."

Greg clears his throat, and we all focus on him immediately, including Tyler. There's a second where I think all of us are expecting Greg to bulldoze in and tell Sandy that paying to fix her car is nothing. Would she listen to Greg more than Tyler? These are complex dynamics that I'm not sure about. In the end, Greg surprises me. "Listen to Tyler, Sandy. Honestly, it's not a big deal for us. The parts come at cost price, and the labor is ours to give."

Sandy seems to slump down a little in her chair. I guess it must be weird for her to accept gifts from us, so I understand her response.

All of this Is very new.

She seemed very worried about the money. Tyler told me she's a literature teacher. Surely that pays well enough to cover a few minor repairs. Something in her response doesn't feel quite right.

"We still going to The Passage tonight?"

"Shit, I forgot about that," Tyler says. He glances at Sandy, pausing as he tries to decide.

We usually race at least one night a week. The day changes to keep the cops on their toes, and the location varies too. Tonight's race is in an almost deserted part of town where the old factories used to be. The road there is wide enough to take delivery trucks, so it's perfect for racing. There are no residential homes either, so the risk of getting spotted is minimal.

Usually, it would be a no-brainer. The cars are in the double garage next to the house. We take it in turns to compete against the other racers. Sometimes they're local, but sometimes they come from further afield. With social media, there's an increased awareness of what we're doing, which brings amateur race enthusiasts from long distances.

It's always the most interesting when there is someone

completely new to race. Everything is unknown.; the car and the spec under the hood, the driver and their skill and attitude toward risk. Add all that to variable road conditions and weather, and you have a nail-biting situation.

The adrenaline is a buzz that's hard to recreate.

"What's The Passage?" Sandy asks when Tyler takes too long to answer.

Again, there are glances between us. Is this something we're going to share with an outsider or something we're going to keep to ourselves?

"It's a road downtown," Greg says. There's a look between him and Tyler and a nod.

"We road race," Tyler says.

"Race…like with cars?" Sandy asks.

"Yeah. Big shiny cars," Arden says. "You should see them and hear them. Fucking sexiest things ever."

Greg huffs as he breaks off another chunk of cornbread. Arden's overenthusiastic blurting isn't his style.

"Can I come to watch?" Sandy asks, her sweet voice all high and hopeful.

"It's not strictly legal," Tyler says.

"Not legal at all," Greg snorts.

"We'll keep her safe," Andrew says. "Whoever isn't racing needs to watch over Sandy like a hawk."

"Maybe it's best if she stays here," Greg says. "One of us could stay."

"I want to go." Sandy's tone leaves no wiggle room. Where Greg would probably put his foot down under usual circumstances, he's reluctant to here.

We're all treading on eggshells, trying to make a good impression, trying not to scare away the prettiest girl who ever walked through our front door and not piss off our friend whose heart has been like a raw piece of meat for too long.

"It's dangerous," Tyler says.

"Life is dangerous, Tyler," Sandy says. She doesn't know how right she is, or maybe she does. I'm expecting Tyler's face to go red the way it looks when he's thinking about Jake, but instead, he exhales, his shoulders slumping.

"Who's racing?" Tyler asks.

"It's supposed to be you and Greg tonight," I remind him.

He nods once. "So, you boys will look out for Sandy."

"Sure, T," Damien says. He's the biggest of all of us. Maybe not the toughest—Greg has that title—but his hands could crack a man's skull. If I was going to leave my girl in someone's hands, it would be his.

"Okay then. We need to eat up, then check the cars over. I want to get there early. Make sure we have time to check out the competition."

I guess that life goes on the way it did before Sandy arrives. That's a good thing, I think.

But racing comes with risks. I just hope that nothing bad happens tonight with Sandy as a witness.

18

SANDY

When the boys head outside to take a look at the cars, I follow them. I want to see what the big fuss is all about. The way they were all looking at each other like they were discussing a terminal illness has me intrigued.

Are their insinuations about the danger involved just male bluster?

Whoa. The cars are something else.

One is low, red, and sleek, with black and white stripes painted down the side. The other is fluorescent green, slightly higher and wider with bigger wheels. I'm not a car person outside of loving my old Lexus. Even if I had money, it wouldn't be the place that I would spend it. But I can tell how much the boys love this. They trail their fingers over the sleek paintwork as Tyler jumps into one and Greg into the other. Hoods are popped, and engines started. The purr of both cars in a confined space is as loud as jet engines at the airport. The floor seems to rumble with the power.

Greg leans over the engine, his right ear tilted closer. He's listening intently, but for what, I'm not sure. Is it possible for him to be able to determine a fault with the mechanics just by the sound? That would be some kind of super skill.

They both make checks, Tyler leaning into the car and fiddling with something. It's too dark for me to see what.

"What do you think?" Arden asks me, rubbing his beard thoughtfully. He has a quirky smile on his face like he has seen something funny but hasn't shared it with anyone yet.

"They sure are noisy," I say. "And impressive."

"The power under your foot…it's like ejaculating."

"TMI," Andrew says, his nostrils flaring.

"Well, how would you describe it?" Arden asks indignantly.

"Not like that," Andrew scoffs. "I mean, are you hoping that Sandy knows what ejaculating feels like?"

"I'm sure she's had an orgasm before," Arden says. His eyes unconsciously drift to Greg, and it hits me that they all know what happened here today. Blood seeps to the surface of my skin, heating my cheeks. It's not unexpected but still embarrassing. Sex isn't something I do easily, and trust is a big part of it. Still, Greg isn't exactly breaking my trust by kissing and telling. Tyler's looking for a relationship similar to Connie's, or at least I think he is.

Relationships involve sex.

We're all on this planet because someone ejaculated.

Does Tyler realize how Connie and Natalie are with their men? Does he get that they all fuck as a group?

Carmella told me that juicy fact. Apparently, Connie has the best sex this side of the Atlantic, and I can believe it. Just one of her husbands would be enough to blow a woman's mind, let alone four of them.

But OMG…just Greg on his own almost put me in a coma today. And Tyler didn't even have to try yesterday, and I was exploding like Fourth of July fireworks.

What would it be like to be with six?

Crazy. Stupid. Dangerous.

My mind hasn't stopped racing since I woke up naked in Greg's bed and realized that I was alone.

It's why I made dinner and dessert. I had to do something to keep my mind off what's going on here because although I know it's the most ridiculous idea that Tyler ever had, I haven't felt as safe as I did in Greg's arms for a very long time.

His words and his touch wrapped around me like a bulletproof blanket. Next to him, all the shitty things that have happened in my life just melted away.

It was only temporary, but feelings like that can be addictive.

I catch Damien looking at me, but when I smile back, he blushes and turns away quickly. He's such a big guy. That body is broad as a tree trunk, and his hands are like snow shovels. How can a man so tough on the outside seem so sensitive on the inside?

Tyler is done with his car first, closely followed by Greg. They have a conversation, their heads drawing close together and voices too low for me to hear. There's lots of nodding, then Greg slaps Tyler on the shoulder.

"We're good to go," Andrew says.

"I need a jacket," I tell him. "It's a little cold already, and it'll only get worse later."

"Sure. Go get it. We'll wait."

I dash into the house and up the stairs, finding Tyler's room. My suitcase is unzipped and open on his bed, and on top, my denim jacket is draped. Taking a quick look in the mirror, I find my cheeks flushed and my eyes sparkling. I look different than I did yesterday morning. The last couple of months have been particularly hard on me. Deciding not to go ahead with the tribunal was a relief but also a big disappointment. I'm a fighter; at least, I thought I was. Turns out, what I actually am is a quitter who's scared of starting something I can't finish.

Deep inside, I knew that the stress would push me back into the dark place that I've worked hard to claw my way out of.

For the first time since that asshole touched me without permission in the teacher's lounge, I feel uninhibited. With these men, I feel protected. No one would dare come near me with six men surrounding me, let alone these six men.

And I love it.

After feeling exposed and alone for so long, it's a welcome change, but I don't want to start making it into more than it is. Me and Tyler proved that one amazing relationship could go to shit. Forget trying to keep six relationships healthy and happy.

Connie and Natalie are managing, but their men are brothers. All they've done is find working family units and become absorbed into them. These men are all so different. Yes, they're friends, but it's not the same as being real blood brothers. I always say that Carmella is like a sister to me, but Suzanne would always come first in a life-or-death situation. That's just how it is.

"You ready, Sandy?" someone shouts from downstairs. I dash out of Tyler's room, making sure to grab the handrail, so I don't fall down the unfamiliar staircase. Outside, Tyler is in the driving seat of the red car, and Greg is in the driving seat of the green. Arden is a passenger for Tyler and Able for Greg. That just leaves me, Andrew, and Damien to ride separately.

As I slide into the back seat of the truck in which Tyler drove us to the wedding, I'm hit with a wave of nerves. I'm alone with these guys I don't know very well, and the two guys who I do know—Tyler and Greg—are about to race two scarily fast cars.

I'm not a risk-taker. I never have been. The only risk I ever took was dating a boy from the wrong side of the tracks. Suzanne warned me about Tyler. She told me we just weren't on the same page for something serious. She suggested that I date the captain of the football team, whose father owned the local country club. "You'll never want for anything," she told me. "You have to think practically rather than with your heart. I mean, look at me and Vernon. I made a pragmatic decision, but we couldn't be happier."

When I asked her about what she meant, she told me she'd dated a bad boy before she met her husband and had to decide between the two. She didn't regret her choice one bit.

But I'm not like Suzanne. I never have been. My heart decides, and the rest of me follows. Being pragmatic about love is like trying to hold water in your hands, at least for me.

From the moment I met Tyler, I knew he was my missing piece. Yes, we were different, but it never mattered to me. We matched where it counted. He was all I wanted.

Now here I am, and Tyler has a business and is a homeowner. He's settled into himself a lot in the past four years, but he's still taking risks that I don't like. The image of him sitting on his shiny black motorcycle with a cocky grin on his face flashes through my mind. I hated him riding it. I told him it was a death trap and that he should sell it, but he wouldn't listen.

Now he's traded the motorcycle for a shiny red car.

Maybe I should tell him I don't approve. Maybe he'll listen to me this time and let one of the others take his place, but somehow, I doubt it. Anyway, I've only been back in his life for five seconds, so I don't have the right to dictate how he lives, however much I might want to.

It doesn't take long for us to arrive at The Passage. It's an odd, eerie place surrounded by deserted industrial buildings with windows like broken, blackened eyes, and graffiti that tells the story of the deprivation in this area. The road itself is wide enough, and there is already a long line of vehicles parked up and a swarming crowd of people. "We'll park up here," Andrew says, glancing over his shoulder at me. He finds space behind a flashy purple truck, and I leave the vehicle tentatively.

Tyler told his boys to watch over me. I'm sure he wouldn't have bothered with that if there wasn't the real chance of danger.

I place myself between the towering walls of Andrew and Damien as we weave our way forward to where Tyler and Greg have parked up nearer the front. I guess there is space left for the racers.

"Cory is here," Andrew says.

"And Greeno," Damien adds.

"The boys will have their work cut out to beat those guys." Andrew glances down at me. "You sure you're alright here, Sandy? We can take you back if you want."

"I'm fine," I say, even though we just passed a guy who had a very obvious gun stuck down the back of his low-rise jeans. "Who's racing first?"

"There are two cars further ahead in the line-up. Then it'll be Greg first and then Tyler."

"Right, and are there prizes, or is all of this just to make men feel like they have bigger cocks?"

Damien snorts, and even though it's dark, I'm sure I can see the hint of a flush across the tender skin beneath his eyes.

"None of us have anything to worry about in the cock department," Andrew says, his mouth quirking at the side into the cutest smile, revealing one very endearing dimple.

"So, then there must be prizes?" I raise my eyebrows, then lose concentration as we pass a girl wearing a pink bikini who's draping herself over Greg's car, blowing kisses in his direction. "Seriously?" I say to Andrew. "I guess this is what you guys come down here for."

"Not tonight," he says.

"Hey, Tina. Get off my car," Greg yells out the window.

"What?" she says, pouting in his direction. I can see the outline of her pussy through the thin fabric, and a tattoo that says SPANK ME comes into view across her lower back as she stands by his window.

"You're clashing with my paintwork," Greg says.

"Never bothered you before." Tina switches her hip, resting her hand in the dip at her waist.

"That was before. This is now."

"And what's so different about now?"

Andrew clears his throat, and Tina turns, her other hand going to her sunbed-bronzed hip. Her eyes rake over Andrew, then Damien, before stopping on me.

"Well, who's this little princess?" she says.

Greg gets out of the car, drawing himself up to his full slight slowly and for maximum impact. He looms over Tina, but he's not interested in her. Instead, he walks around her and ducks to press a soft kiss on my cheek. "You ready to cheer for me?" he asks as my heart flutters like a butterfly pinned to a board.

"I don't think you need my cheers," I say softly, stumbling into the lulling effect his dark eyes have on me. This close, I can smell his scent. This close, I'm overwhelmed by the memory of his body over mine.

"Oh, I need them, Sandy," he says. For just a second, his hand finds mine, sliding down the edge of my pinkie and then letting go. It's a fleeting touch that buzzes my nerves in crazy ways.

"I'll cheer for you then," I say softly.

"And what about me?" Tyler steps in front of me as Greg moves aside.

"Do you need my cheers too?"

Tyler blinks, his pretty green eyes obliterated by the flash of his long black lashes for just a second. "I need them." He takes my hand, holding it tenderly, then brings it to his lips, pressing a featherlight kiss to my knuckles.

"Who the fuck is this?" Tina shouts. "All of a sudden, there's a new girl in town, and you're all fawning over her."

"Leave it, Tina," Tyler says, mouthing "Sorry" to me.

"Yo, Tina," a big guy shouts from the other side of the road. In a flash, she's gone, tottering across the road on her killer heels, switching her hips like she's on a fashion runway, not a run-down deserted road in the ass-end of the town.

"That girl is going to get herself into trouble," Andrew mutters.

"That's why she always comes around us," Greg says. "She knows there's not going to be any trouble for her here. The same can't be said for those guys." He nods his head over to where Tina is currently sandwiched between two huge guys. One has his tongue down her throat and the other his hand in the back of her bikini bottoms. I don't get the feeling that she asked for the attention either.

"Poor girl." I shake my head, pulling down the cuffs of my sweater so they cover my hands. The night chill has set in, and even in a jacket, I'm feeling a little cold.

The car behind Greg's cranks up the tunes. It's something from the vaults of old-school hip-hop, and some of the people in the crowd start to dance. It's a race meet, but it's also a social event. I feel like a fish out of water amongst these people. I wonder what my students would think of me attending one of these events. They'd probably freak out.

But as much as I feel uncomfortable, I'm also happy to see another part of Tyler's life, even if it is a dangerous one. He's been lost to me for so long. Each hour we spend together is like reading another chapter of his story.

The cars that are participating in the first race take their positions. Even though it's an illegal race, someone has taped a yellow marker across the road, and there a man dressed in black on the start line with a pistol. The first race has a blue car with lightning down the side pitted against a darker blue vehicle with a white stripe. Both have two huge round silver exhausts, which rumble as they rev the engines. It's all for effect. Even I know that much. The noisier the engine, the more their opponent is going to worry the engine is more powerful.

"My money's on lightning," Damien says.

"You think?" Andrew shoves his hands in his pockets, cocking his head to one side. Of all of the Deep six, he's the one who's the most reserved.

"Yeah. That guy has a death wish. It's always the ones who love treading the line between life and death who win because they're not scared to take the necessary risks."

Andrew faces back out to the cars that are getting ready for the start. Brake lights flash, and engines rev until it's hard to hear any kind of conversation, but I'm close enough to Andrew not to miss what he says next. "Is that why Tyler always wins?"

Damien doesn't hear, so there is no discussion about Andrew's theory, but a swelling feeling of anxiety wells inside me. Does Tyler have a death wish? He always loved riding his motorcycle, but he was careful and responsible. I never worried that he'd have an accident that was his fault. If something bad happened, it was going to be the other driver that caused it.

What's changed?

Is it Jake's death? Is that why he's living life like it's disposable? Is that why he wants to share me with these men?

I don't really understand anything that's happening in my life right now. I feel like the wheels of the vehicles as they speed away, leaving behind a belch of fumes and a sound so loud my eardrums hurt. All the things I'd achieved after Tyler have gone, and I'm back in the same place I was, without roots to hold me in place.

Connie wasn't so different from me. She had a job she hated and an apartment that was so small you could barely swing a cat. She needed something different in her life and found it with the Banburys. Is it weak of me to want to find the same thing?

But these men aren't the Banburys. They're rougher around the edges. They're not brothers by blood but by choice. Life experiences brought them together. Could I build something with them that could be as good as what Connie has?

Should I even try?

I'm not coming into this with a life that's fulfilling and stable. In a couple of weeks, my bank account will be dry. I'll be a burden. Maybe they'll think that I'm just with them so they can pick up the bills. That's not the kind of woman I want to be.

I glance back to the race.

Lightning wins.

It was as Damien predicted.

If winners need to be the ones who aren't afraid to walk the line between life and death, I think I'm always going to be a loser.

19

ANDREW

Just standing next to Sandy is driving me crazy. She's wearing this soft blue sweater with a sequined heart on it that skims over all her curves in a way that's modest but tantalizing. A minute ago, Tina was practically draping herself naked in front of me, but my mind was on Sandy and all the things that I know she's got going on under her sweet preppy clothes.

She's not all sugarplums, though. Underneath, she's a girl with a strong backbone and enough sass to keep us all on our toes.

We don't need a pushover.

We need a girl who has the gumption to keep six men inspired and tethered. That isn't an easy job. In fact, I'm doubtful that it's possible, but that's just me.

Out of all of us, I'm the one thinking with his head, not his dick or his lonely heart. I'm the one who's pondering over all of the things that can go wrong rather than imagining how it's gonna feel so right.

And it will.

Taming this girl has my dick twitching in my jeans in a way that hasn't happened for a while.

I just don't trust that Tyler knows what he's doing.

It's not that I don't love him, far from it. I'd take a bullet for the guy, but he's never been one to think things through. He acts on impulse. He lives life close to the edge. It's almost as though he likes to tempt fate or death, or whatever power there is out there who gets to decide how long we have on this crazy planet.

So, here I am watching Tyler get ready to race. I don't know if Sandy's conscious that she's moved closer to me and Damien the nearer it gets to Tyler racing. Her arms are wrapped around herself as though she's braced against the cold, but to me, it looks more like she's trying to hold herself together.

Leaning in closer to her, I breathe in her sweet floral scent. "He'll be okay, you know."

"Will he?" Her pretty eyes stare into mine, searching for how I really feel. She doesn't buy the platitudes. She wants the truth.

"I'm hoping that you being here will make him think before he acts," I tell her.

"You're hoping that I'll be an incentive for him not to risk killing himself in a race that doesn't matter?" There's anger in her voice, and something scathing and sharp that I realize comes from fear.

"Yes. He needs you. Always has."

Sandy shakes her head, and I get an urge to stride over to Tyler's car, yank him out by the scruff of his shirt and tell him to sort his shit out.

Somehow, he's managed to sleep with Sandy without telling her what's kept him away for four years and managed to encourage Greg into sleeping with her too. This web is already tangled, and it's only going to get worse because I know Tyler. He doesn't talk about what's in his heart. He buries everything, then acts out because of it.

But is telling Sandy how much Tyler needs her the right thing to do?

Who the fuck knows? It's not like I'm in charted territory here.

The race begins, and Tyler is the fastest over the start line. Arden and Able have moved to the finish, but I've kept Sandy here just in case. If there's any kind of accident, we'll be too far away to witness it in detail.

"He's not going to win," Damien says, shaking his head.

"How can you tell?" Sandy asks.

"I just can." Damien glances at me, and when our eyes meet, I see what he's trying to convey. Somethings different now Sandy's here. Tyler's different.

For the first time since Sandy walked through the door of Deep Repairs and I found out who she was, I wonder if Tyler could be right. Maybe she is what we need—the glue to fix our individual wounds that can also solidify our bonds as a group.

Sandy shivers noticeably, and it's an instinct that drives me to put my arm around her shoulder and pull her closer. She doesn't resist but gazes up at me, her eyes filled with something I can't define. It's not fear or wonder or awe or anticipation but some strange mix of all of that. It's what I feel in my gut too, a sense that I'm standing on the precipice of something, about to tumble forward so fast that I won't ever find a way back.

There's an explosion of cheers for the other rider as he hits the finish first. I see Greg swear under his breath, his competitive spirit caring more for the short-term win than the longer-term gain.

"Just Greg to go," Sandy says.

"Greg will win," Damien says. My gentle giant of a friend smiles down at where Sandy's nestled against me, keeping warm. There's no jealousy there. He's just happy when we're happy.

"Why?"

"Because he wants to impress you," Damien says.

"And Tyler didn't?" Sandy asks. It's a valid question.

"Tyler needs you to stick around more than he needs to impress you."

I feel Sandy nod just slightly in response. I'm not sure of Damien's logic or what it means about the current connection between her and my two friends.

The race is nail-biting. For a second, Greg's opponent veers to the side, almost clipping the tail of Greg's car. Whether it was purposeful, or the result of a pothole is hard to tell from the angle we're at, but the way Sandy flinches tells me a lot.

When Greg wins, I hear my brothers cheering and the sounding of the horn we have as a code for a win. The Deep Six live to face another race.

Damien and I don't hang around when the racing is done. Sandy's hands are icy, and we don't want to risk getting picked up when the cops eventually make it. On the ride home, she's quiet, staring out the window, even though it's hard to make much out in the darkness.

Back at the house, she stands awkwardly in the kitchen as Damien tosses the keys into the bowl by the front door. She's holding back from saying something, that much is evident, but I don't feel like it's my place to pry. Maybe whatever she has to say is for someone else.

But then Sandy turns, facing both of us. "Before the others get back, I want to talk to you about something."

"Sure," I say.

Damien is staring at the floor but nods too. The guy

can never stand to look into the eyes of a beautiful woman. They're like his kryptonite.

Sandy focuses on me. "You know what Tyler wants," she says.

Fuck. So she's really going there. "Yes."

"And what do you think about it?" She clasps her hands together in front of her, twisting her fingers as though she's nervous.

"Are you asking what we think about the idea of sharing you?"

She nods, twisting her fingers again, her face too blank for me to read. Damien doesn't say anything, just shifts uncomfortably on his huge feet.

"If you'd asked us about the idea last week, we'd have said you were a fruit loop," I answer.

"And now?" Her voice tips up at the end sweetly.

"Now, I have reservations, but I'm up for trying," I say, wanting to keep things matter of fact.

Sandy nods as though she appreciates my candidness. "And you, Damien?"

My mountain of a friend blushes scarlet above his beard, only managing to look at the bright light that is Sandy for a second before his eyes focus on the window. Headlight beams shine in the driveway as one of the cars pulls in. "I think you're the prettiest girl I've ever seen," he says eventually, and it's Sandy's turn to blush. I guess that answers her question, but with a lot more romance than I managed.

Maybe I'm going to need to up my game.

"And your brothers?" Sandy asks me.

"I can't speak for them in detail," I say. "But I know they're in agreement to try if you are."

Sandy nods again, her chest rising with a long inhale as though she's letting the information settle inside her before deciding how to respond. "Can I sleep in your bed tonight?" she asks me, and for the first time in forever, I'm lost for words.

"Uh…"

"He means yes," Damien says, grinning at me. It's so funny how he can joke so easily and poke fun at me, but when Sandy asks him about how he feels, he's like a blushing schoolgirl.

"Will Tyler mind?" I ask Sandy, even though I know she has no idea. I guess I feel like I need to at least acknowledge that it's a possibility.

"It's his idea, isn't it?" she says. "Can you take me now?"

"Uh…sure," I say. As I make my way toward the hallway with Sandy trailing closely, I hear Greg and Able stomping inside. We're on the stairs as Damien begins relaying what just happened in a hushed tone that's still audible because of his ridiculously deep voice.

"Thanks for this," Sandy says. As we pass Tyler's room, she ducks inside and grabs her small case. My room is at the end of the hall, opposite Arden's. When I throw open the door, I'm glad to see it's mostly tidy with just a few pairs of jeans and sweaters tossed over my chair and a messy pile of paperwork on my desk. Sandy glances around, taking everything in.

"You like cityscapes?"

The pictures on my wall tell a story of my fascination with architecture and engineering that I would have pursued if I'd had a family who supported education and had the money to help. Instead, I ended up needing work that could pay bills as soon as I was a teen.

"Sure," I say. "Some cities are all about the modern, like Dubai, but then you have cities like London where old and new coexist. The challenges are different." She stands in front of the black and white image of London that I ordered from a photographer in England.

"Charles Dickens loves to mention St. Paul's Cathedral." Her finger traces the outline of the domed building at the center of the photograph. "In David Copperfield, they go to the top of the cathedral to look at views over London. I'd love to do the same one day."

"Me too," I say. "And maybe go to the top of The Shard. It's the tallest building in London."

"Is it this one?" She points at the building that looks like a glass stalagmite, spearing its way from the ground into the sky.

"Yeah. There's a viewing platform on the seventy-second floor."

"Sounds high," she says.

I lean against the door jamb, folding my arms, watching as she turns to place her case on the end of the bed. "Are you afraid of heights?"

Sandy shakes her head, her pretty curls bouncing a little with the movement. "I don't think so. I've just never been that high."

"Me either," I admit.

"So, I can sleep on the couch downstairs," I say.

"You think I've asked to steal your bed for the night," she smiles.

"It's safer not to assume."

"I figure it's probably a good idea for us to get to know each other. You guys are working, so the evenings are going to be the only time."

"Talking in the dark can be fun," I say.

"Whispering secrets like we're at camp." She bites her bottom lip like she's remembering something naughty from her past and fuck me if my cock doesn't come to life at that one tiny gesture.

"I don't have many secrets," I say, venturing into the

room and closing the door behind me. Sandy's eyes follow all of my actions.

Below, I hear the slam of the front door and the rumble of voices in the kitchen and den. Eventually, someone flicks on the TV, and my unease settles. If Tyler wasn't happy with Sandy being with me, he'd have made it known by now. As for Greg, I can't imagine that he's pleased she's chosen me. After their little rendezvous today, he was probably expecting her to want to sleep in his bed tonight.

"You wanna use the bathroom?" I ask. "It's through there."

"Yeah, that would be good," she says. There's an awkward moment where our eyes meet, and a buzz of nervous electricity zaps between us. Sharing a room and a bed is a step into intimacy before we've done more than hug in public. It's natural for it to feel awkward.

Sandy begins to riffle through her suitcase, reaching for the nightwear she was dressed in yesterday before freezing. "Do you have a shirt I can sleep in?" she asks.

"Sure." The top drawer of my dresser is filled with shirts, and I find her my favorite soft gray one that's been through the washer a thousand times. It's big on me, so it'll be big on her. When I pass it to her, and our eyes meet again, there's another jolt of feeling between us.

Sandy takes her washbag and towel into the bathroom and closes the door. I don't hear the click of the lock, but I don't imagine that constitutes an invitation. The pipes squeal to life as she twists the squeaky shower handle, and my mind drifts into a fantasy of Sandy's naked body stepping into the water, rivulets running between her breasts and down the seam of her peachy ass.

Fuck. If I was in that room right now, she'd be getting dirtier, not cleaner.

I tug my shirt over my head, loosen my belt and let my

jeans drop to the floor. I usually sleep naked but tonight, I pull on a pair of loose gray shorts for Sandy's sake. I don't want to scare the living daylights out of her.

While she washes, I take some time to put my room to rights, and by the time she emerges, pink and pretty from the shower, I'm stacking paperwork at the desk. Her eyes roam my naked torso, landing eventually on my bare feet, and mine scan her like I'm a starving man at an all-you-can-eat buffet. In my shirt, the outline of her breasts is evident enough for me to work out that she's not wearing a bra, and man, does this girl have a rack on her. Little pointy nipples jut through the soft fabric, just begging to be touched. At least, I wish they were begging because I'd happily get my fingers and mouth on them.

"Everything okay?" I ask to break the sizzling silence.

"Sure," she says, dropping her clothes onto the bed and beginning to fold them. The hair around her face is damp, and her curls have the cutest little frizz. Without makeup, her face has some freckles, which I love. I drift to the nightstand, switch on the side lamp, and then turn off the main light, ready to settle in. I feel Sandy's eyes on me, taking everything in. We stand on either side of the bed and smile awkwardly at each other. "Is that your preferred side?" she asks.

"I don't have one," I say.

She's the first to pull back the comforter and slide in, sitting with her back against the black headboard. I do the same, shaking my head at how weird it is to be getting into bed with someone this way. I guess married people do it all the time. When I'm hooking up for sex, it usually involves a lot of frantic kissing and clothes removal standing up before tumbling together onto the bed.

When I slide into bed next to her, there's an awareness across my skin that she's near. Just a few inches, and I'd be touching her. As I'm getting comfortable sitting, Sandy slides further down until her head is resting on the pillow, so I do the same. We smile at each other like newlyweds who've been waiting for the honeymoon to pop their cherries.

"It's funny," she whispers, "but I can already tell you apart from your brothers."

"Well, Arden always has a beard, so he's obvious."

"Even without that," she says. "It's in the eyes," she says. "They're supposed to be the window to the soul."

"And what do you see through my windows?" I ask.

"Someone who doesn't like taking risks," she says. "Someone who measures out life in increments, so you don't make a mistake."

"There wasn't much measuring done tonight," I say.

"Which is why your shoulders are bunched. You're not relaxed." Her hand reaches out to touch my shoulder, and she's right. I am tense, but that tension slips away as soon as her fingers trail over my skin.

"What is this for you, Sandy?" I ask. "I just want to understand what you're thinking. I mean, one minute you're driving down a road to a wedding, and the next, you're here and in this situation. It seems like everything's moving fast."

"It is," she says.

"And that's okay with you?"

Sandy blinks slowly, pursing her lips slightly as she thinks carefully about how to respond. "Have you ever had a time in your life when you feel like everything is out of control? You've done your best to get your life in order, but nothing stays that way."

"Yes," I say. "It's frustrating."

"So, when you're in that situation, do you fight it, or do you go with the flow?"

"That would depend," I say, playing with the edge of the pillow that Sandy's head is resting on. "I think it's in my nature to fight."

"I'm tired of fighting," Sandy says. "I'm tired of battling to keep my head barely above water. It doesn't seem to matter how hard I try; life sends me challenges, and then I'm drowning."

"You don't seem like you're drowning to me."

Sandy shrugs, her teeth digging into her bottom lip. "I don't have the fight in me anymore," she says eventually.

"But that isn't good for us. I don't want you here with us because you're too broken down to do what you actually want."

"It isn't about what I want or don't want. It never has been. It's about how I think things should be. What's expected of me. What I should be doing versus what I shouldn't, and I don't even know anymore whether it's me I'm trying to please, or my parents, or my sister, or the world in general. But in the end, I don't seem to be pleasing anyone."

I know I'm not imagining the glassiness to her pretty eyes. "All I need to know is that you want to be here with me. In this moment. Just tell me what you need, and I'll give it to you."

Her eyelids drop and stay closed for long enough for her to compose herself. "I need to let go," she says. "I need to not fight anymore and let life happen around me."

"And what do you want to happen?" I whisper.

"I want to make new memories…to wipe away some of the old ones."

Sandy's fingers touch my face, running softly down my jaw, grazing over my lips, down my neck, and over my chest. Her eyes follow the path, mapping out my face and body as though she wants to commit it to memory.

This doesn't feel simple. It feels so complicated that I don't know what's best for any of us—Sandy's right about me. I need to measure risk, and I don't like making mistakes. But I also hear what she's saying about life. Sometimes we battle it, but the fight just feels overwhelming, like an old man waving his walking stick at a tumultuous sea. There is something tempting about what she needs. Maybe letting the waves of life lap over your feet is better than resisting. Maybe succumbing to Sandy's charms and indulging Tyler's fanciful ideas is what I need to do.

Maybe taking risks is part of the path to love.

Tyler loved Sandy once. The way he talked about it was like a fairy tale, and I can see why. She's strength and vulnerability, beauty, temptation, and coiled pain. In her eyes, I can see weakness and fortitude. She's unmeasurable, and it's scary.

When she shifts closer, bring her lips an inch from mine, my whole body comes alive. "Will you let go with me?" she whispers.

I don't answer with words but with the softest ghost of a kiss that sends tingles down my spine, pooling heat and power into my cock.

Sandy doesn't want to fight this, and neither do I.

But as I pull her against my body and slide deeper into our kiss, I wonder how my friend Tyler has managed to get us all into this freefall of a situation.

20

SANDY

Like Alice, I'm tumbling down the rabbit hole with no idea how I'm ever going to get back out. When Andrew's tongue slides against mine and his arms wrap around me, I feel as though I'm drinking a magic potion, but instead of getting taller or shorter, I'm filling up like a balloon.

I can still feel Greg's fingers inside me. I can still taste Tyler on my tongue. And now Andrew is giving me what I need; the chance to journey with him under the covers, filling my empty chest with warmth and helping me forget everything that's going on back home.

Andrew is so different from his friends. Where Greg is darkness, Andrew is light. His blond hair is like a slick of gold, and his eyes burn like blue flames. His touch isn't as possessive as Greg's, either. There's a smoothness to him that's all about the push and pull between us. He's leading, but he wants to feel me following, and that's good for me.

I don't know how far I want to go with him. Just being in this bed feels good. Being in his arms feels better. His lips kissing a trail down my neck is awesome, and his hand sliding up the inside of the shirt he loaned me is shiver-inducing. I'm naked beneath, my nipples already drawn into tight little points, just waiting for his mouth to make them ache.

I run my fingers through his hair, and he moans deep in his throat as his palm finds the soft curve of the underside of my breast.

There's no rush in his touch, just a liquid flow of his body against my body. I close my eyes, allowing myself to tumble further, arching my back into his touch, parting my lips when his palm grazes the very tip of my little nipple.

"You're like a drug," he whispers. "An intoxication."

"I'm just a woman." I exhale long and low as his hot mouth sucks the peak of my breast, tugging rhythmically in a way I can feel between my thighs.

He's half lying on top of me now, his thigh pushing higher until it's resting against my pussy.

Just a scrap of white cotton fabric between us, the barrier to my final descent into a new world.

Not quite final. There are three other men in this house who want to be part of Tyler's group. Three other men whose mouths want to taste me, whose cocks want to fuck me. Three other men who can transport me further into this land of dreams.

I hear Suzanne's voice in my head; *just come live with me...it'll be great.*

Except it won't be. It'll just be a huge reminder of what I lost and what I don't have.

At least here, I'm walking forward.

The path might be winding, and with Tyler on it, my heart is likely to be shattered, but a small part of my heart is hoping that I'll be as lucky as Connie and Natalie. Could this be my place in the world? Could I find a way to patch up my wounds here?

Andrew's hand trails over my waist and then slowly lower, mapping the curve of my hip and drifting over the roundness of my ass. The urge to press up against Andrew's thigh is too much to resist, and when I grind against him, he groans against my skin.

"You're hotter than fire," he murmurs, fingers playing with the edge of my panties. Now would be the time to tell him we shouldn't go so fast, but that would be the old Sandy talking. The new Sandy wants to tell him to lick me until I come and then fuck me until I come again.

I want to drown in his fresh scent and get lost in the movements of our bodies that are as old as time.

He hooks his finger into the side of my panties, and his eyes find mine in the low light. "Is this what you want?" he asks.

A small dip of my head is all it takes, and then he's easing my damp panties away from my aching pussy, gazing down at my belly and thighs as though my body reveals the secrets of the universe.

People talk about the power between a woman's thighs. The power to stimulate pleasure. The power to create life. I've never felt it until now.

As Andrew's fingers slide into my soft curls, gently parting my labia and finding my clit for the first time, I feel like a goddess with the strength to topple an empire.

Maybe topple is the wrong word. I feel like a goddess with the strength to build an empire.

That's what we would be. This group of men and me. The establishers of an empire. This body of mine, flesh and bones and blood, can unite them and create another generation. Their seed could fill my empty body with life. It could take me back four years to before my heart was broken, and maybe I could be that girl again. Filled with hopes and dreams. Imagining that life can be overflowing with joy, not wondering when the next heap of shit is going to fall from the sky.

The first touch of his warm, rough tongue between my legs feels like a rebirth of sorts. I don't have to be something broken. I can be something put back together again.

I can open my legs and not remember sadness but crave the building of pleasure that I surrender to.

Andrew is a master of reading me. Every twitch and quiver has him changing tempo until I'm begging him not to stop, and he doesn't. He does what I asked him for and gives me what I need, and when I come, I hold his blond head against my pussy, owning every moan and every pulse of pleasure he's elicited from me.

He kisses my belly and the soft, tender inside of my thighs. When I'm relaxed, he licks long and slow from my entrance, almost to my swollen clit like he wants to taste my orgasm for himself. I understand that urge because I have it too. For the first time in a long time, I want it too.

Andrew's wearing soft shorts with an elasticated waistband that I explore, trailing my finger over the V of muscle at his side and the undulation of his perfect six-pack. Even though his hair is blond, the happy trail running down from his navel is a little darker. I want to follow that trail to the prize beneath—the prize that has tented his shorts to extreme proportions.

He doesn't resist when I get on my knees to push his shorts down. He has to lift his ass, and when he does, his abs clench in a way that makes me whimper. Damn. This man has a body built to arouse women. It's a sacrilege that he's a mechanic, hiding all this good stuff under greasy t-shirts and worn overalls. He should be a model or a stripper or something that would involve fewer clothes.

When his cock snaps back, tapping his belly, my mouth fills with saliva and my body with power.

His eyes are on me, watching with a mix of

bemusement and fascination. He's wondering what I'm going to do. Does he want my mouth or my pussy more? Or maybe my virgin ass. The memory of Greg's tongue there has me shivering all over again.

Whatever he wants, he gets me slowly bending forward, nuzzling against the light brown patch of soft hair surrounding his cock. His arm drifts across his eyes as though watching me and feeling me is too much of a sensory overload. My lips buzz as they trail up the bar of his cock, and the first taste of him that I get sends me lightheaded. I swear that giving oral sex can be as pleasurable as receiving it if you're with the right man and in the right frame of mind.

And this feels like both.

He's big, but that never stopped me with Tyler. All it takes is a little more effort to relax my jaw and a conscious effort to open the back of my throat. When I swallow him deeply, the groaning he makes sounds like it's driven by pleasure and pain.

"Fuck," he hisses, his hips jerking forward enough that my eyes water, but I don't care. I'm powerful and capable. I can make him feel better than he's ever felt before. I use all my best techniques, running my tongue around his wide head, rolling his tight balls in my palm, and taking him so deep that my nose presses into his belly. When I look up into his eyes, he's staring at me with disbelief, and I have to pull back to smile.

He's seen me in my preppy sweater and my pastels and imagined that I'm one thing, and now he's discovered I'm something else entirely. Being a surprise is awesome, but I don't pause for long. My mission is to make this man explode in my mouth. I want to taste him on my tongue and swallow him down. I want to devour him the way he devoured me.

And I do.

Andrew can't keep still, even though I rest my hand on

his stomach. His whole body flexes beneath my palm as I bob my head, breathing in the growing scent of his arousal. His muscular thighs want to work. His ass tightens against my palm, and my mind is filled with images of what he would look like, fucking into me, everything so tight and fierce. He'd have me whimpering again, of that I'm certain, but Greg's left me too sore to go that far tonight.

His hand hovers over the back of my head as though he wants to control my motion but doesn't feel it's appropriate. When he can't hold off, his touch isn't domineering. He doesn't force me down, although I wouldn't mind. Instead, he throws his head back, clenches his eyes closed, and *feels*.

And I love it when his cock kicks in my mouth, his arousal salt-sweet and warm as his heart. I love it when his fingers tangle in my curls as he jerks and twitches through his release. I love how he gazes up at me like I'm Aphrodite in the flesh.

And when he laughs like I'm the biggest birthday surprise he ever received, I laugh too.

We don't sleep right away. He wraps himself around me, like a big spoon to my small spoon, and I ask him how he met Tyler. When I find out they met in a group home, the ache in my chest is too much. I know Tyler's history wasn't as peachy as my own but finding out that some of his darker moments were with Andrew and his brothers makes it worse and better all at the same time. They've been together through thick and thin, and suddenly I see why Tyler's idea has been adopted by these men with so few questions.

They bonded in hardship, and bonds like that are the most difficult to break.

21

DAMIEN

When Andrew comes down for breakfast, the rest of us are already chomping through cereal at the table. The conversation has been sparse, more delivered to break the silence than to share anything in particular.

He appears in the doorway, freshly showered, his blond hair still wet. There's a sparkle in his ridiculously blue eyes that wasn't there last night. I swear it's like a weight has been lifted from his shoulders.

Man, if that's what sex with Sandy can do to a man, I want to be next.

"Morning," he says, heading to the coffee pot to pour himself some black wake-up juice.

"Morning," Arden says, the smirk on his face even more pronounced than usual.

"Everything okay?" Tyler asks. He's holding a spoonful of Cheerios in the air, waiting for Andrew's reply.

"Everything's fine," Andrew says. Then after he takes a sip of his coffee, he adds, "Sandy's fine."

Tyler puts the cereal in his mouth and chews, staring at

the table in front of him. I catch eyes with Greg, which is always like falling into the black abyss but today is somehow less terrifying. If fucking Sandy can take the darkness out of Greg, it must be like experiencing real magic.

"Damien," Tyler says. "You can stay and look after Sandy today."

Everyone turns to me, and I feel my cheeks heating like a fucking volcano. It's the thing I hate about myself; my inability to hide my embarrassment.

Although why I should feel embarrassed, I have no idea. I'm not a virgin by any stretch. I know my way around a woman's body better than I know the route to Deep Repairs, and I can drive that in my sleep.

"Maybe you can take her shopping?"

"She needs pajamas," Andrew says.

"She wouldn't need them in my bed." Arden snorts, stuffing a huge spoonful of his ludicrous multicolored cereal into his mouth.

"Well, she isn't in your bed, is she," Tyler says. He pulls out a wad of notes from his back pocket. "Use this. Get her whatever she needs."

"I've got money, T," I say, but he shakes his head.

"Let me do this."

I guess if he really wants me to spend his money on Sandy, I will.

I wouldn't mind spending my own. Seeing her dressed up pretty in something I bought her would feel awesome.

Everyone finishes their breakfast in awkward silence, and I'm glad that I'm missing out on the ride to work this morning. I'm sure that Arden will loosen them all up within the hour. He has a way about him that no one can resist for long. I guess every group of friends needs a joker to lighten the mood.

When they leave, I clear up the mess, and I'm elbow-deep in dishwater when I hear footsteps on the stairs.

Sandy appears in the doorway, dressed in one of Andrew's shirts and what looks like a pair of his shorts. Her hair is mussed from sleep, and maybe whatever they got up to last night. "So you get to chaperone me today." She rolls her eyes but smiles at the same time.

"At your service," I say, with a mock bow. "Tyler's instructed me to take you shopping. He's left me with a bundle of cash that is at your disposal."

"Shopping. What does he want me to buy?"

"Pajamas...well, Andrew suggested that." My gaze drops down over her current attire, and Sandy snorts.

"Maybe he's got a point. Maybe some underwear too," she muses. "I wasn't expecting this kind of vacation."

I turn to face the window, my cheeks hotter than the surface of the sun. "Whatever you need," I say with as much of a carefree tone as I can muster.

"Okay, I'll go and get dressed."

"What about breakfast?" I ask her.

"Do you have one of those travel cups?" she asks. I search for one in the cupboard and present it like it's a silver goblet.

"Perfect. I'll take some coffee in that and one of the blueberry muffins I made."

"There's only one left," I laugh. "The rest disappeared with the boys."

Sandy smiles broadly. "I won't take too long."

She's actually a lot quicker than I thought she'd be, appearing in the same outfit she wore last night. The sweater really brings out the pretty color of her hazel eyes and hugs curves that I shouldn't be noticing if I want a chance in hell of keeping a normal complexion. I hand her the filled coffee cup and the muffin in a paper bag.

"Breakfast to go," she smiles. "Thanks."

Damn. There go my cheeks.

"Let's go." I duck my head and grab the keys from the counter, trying not to let her see me blush. Outside, the truck is parked at a funny angle, and it takes me little back and forth to get us on the road. All the while, Sandy is breaking off bits of delicious muffin and popping them through her pretty lips, and I can barely focus enough to drive.

The mall is on the other side of town, so I know we're gonna need to make conversation, but my mind is blank. In the end, Sandy asks me questions, and I start feeling a whole lot more relaxed.

"I've known Tyler since middle school," I tell her. "He was one of the cool kids, but he wasn't an asshole. If he saw me hanging by myself, he'd always drag me into whatever he was doing. I got involved in football because of him, and then things were easier. My size became a positive thing."

I see Sandy smile out of the corner of my eye, but I'm not sure at what part of my story. Is it that Tyler was a good guy, even back then, or that he helped me find my way? Or maybe both.

"And you guys hung out ever since?" she asks.

"Mostly," I say. "When he hooked up with you, he kind of disappeared for a while."

"Yeah." Sandy takes a sip of her coffee. "We were kind of intense. I always asked him about his friends, but it's like he wanted to keep his worlds separate for a while. I'm still not sure why?"

"You ever buy something so pretty that you didn't want to take it out of the packaging?" I ask her, and she nods in agreement. "Well, maybe that's how Tyler felt about you. Maybe he was trying to keep everything perfect for as long as he could?"

"Perfect? But why wouldn't things have been perfect with you guys involved too?"

"Greg was already locked up. I was with a girl who was causing a load of trouble between us all. The triplets were getting involved in shit they should have been staying clear of. We were all pumped with testosterone and making a mess of our lives."

Sandy blinks slowly and shakes he head. "He was trying to protect me," she says softly.

"Of course." We are waiting at a stop sign, so I get a chance to face her. "And himself."

"And when Jake died?" she asks. "He just disappeared, and I had no way of contacting him except his phone. He never answered."

"He was trying to protect you then too."

"I'm not a fragile flower." Sandy's voice matches her screwed-up features. "I can deal with life, you know. I've had to deal with a lot…" she trails off, blinking a few times and then staring out of the window. I want to ask her what she's talking about, but it's not my place to pry. If she wanted to share the details, she would.

"We always try to do what we think is best for the people we love, Sandy. You might have wanted Tyler to do something different, but he did what he thought was best. He did what he could deal with."

"Well, he should have done better. He left me behind, and he had no idea what was going on with me. I needed him."

"I'm sorry," I say. "But none of us can go back as much as we wish we could. We blame ourselves, and we blame each other for things that can't be changed. That bitterness doesn't help anyone."

"I know," she says, rubbing her leg. "I wish I could let it go."

"You can," I tell her. "I've had to let go of a lot of my past because dwelling on it was only hurting me more. The now is what we can influence, and the future. We have to focus on that."

"I want to ask Tyler about what happened," she says.

"Don't." The word flies out of my mouth too quickly, and she flinches. "I just mean, if he wants to, he'll talk to you, but don't ask him. Don't risk opening an old wound."

"There you go, trying to protect someone you love," she says eventually. "But what happens when protecting Tyler hurts me?"

"Then we're all in a fucked-up situation," I say.

"Maybe we are." She sips her coffee again. "Can we listen to the radio?"

"Sure. Anything in particular?"

"Nah. Just put what you like."

The station I choose plays country music, but I make sure it's upbeat. Neither of us needs some old-timer singing about his woes.

Thinking over what she said, I know I need to challenge her black-and-white view. Spending time with Sandy today must help her see the potential in this relationship. I don't want to be the one to fracture the fragile progress.

It's not often that I feel I have life lessons to share, but right now, I do and as hard as it might be for me to open up, I have to try. "You know, Sandy. Sometimes the people we love hurt us, and sometimes we have to accept that they decided to do what was best for them at the time, like my brother. I practically raised that kid. I did everything I could to keep him safe. I fought for us to stay together, and I helped him to do well enough at school that he could have gone to college, but he chose to join the army, and now he's overseas, risking his life. I was mad as hell at his decision. He's the only blood family I have, and he made a decision that could end his life. But I can't hate him for it. I can't take that decision and turn it on myself. I have to see that it's something he needs. In the end, we are all our own people. We can think about our impact on others, but we can't always sacrifice what we need even if it's going to hurt someone else."

"I guess," she says, staring out of the window. I don't know if she believes what I've said or if she's just avoiding getting too deep into the subject.

By the time we get to the mall, Sandy has finished her breakfast, and we've both had a chance to decompress from the serious conversation.

"You ready to hold some bags?" Sandy asks me, smiling in a way that feels like an apology. Not that she has anything to apologize for.

"Yes, ma'am." I give her a mock salute that makes her laugh. God, I'd do anything to hear that again.

Sandy's right. This is a fucked-up situation, but I'm going to try my best to make things right for everyone. The time has come to make Tyler realizes that if he really wants this beautiful girl, he's going to need to tell her everything.

22

SANDY

Damien is a gentle giant. A man filled with more wisdom than I ever would have guessed—wisdom that is hard to hear, but I appreciate anyway.

As we make our way into the first store, I can tell he's uncomfortable being in the women's underwear section, and it makes me want to laugh and punch his shoulder for being so ridiculously cute. Instead, he's inspired my naughty side.

"What do you think of these?" I ask him, holding up a barely-there, sheer red thong with a row of diamantes at the back. They're tacky as hell, but probably most men's wet dream.

"Uh..." Damien's cheeks end up almost matching the underwear.

"Or this," I say, grabbing a black bralette and pantie set of delicate lace.

"Whatever you like," he stammers.

"How about you tell me what you like?" I say.

Damien shifts on his feet, his eyes darting, panicked around the racks like I've asked him to search for a single diamond in the Grand Canyon. I expect him to dodge my suggestion as he shoves his hands into his dark jeans, pulling the fabric across his tree-thick legs. I never asked him what position he played, but it must have been something in defense. With a body like that, he'd have been like facing a brick wall on the field.

I'm about to tell him I'm only joking when he notices something and makes his way across the store. I follow, fascinated when he picks up a cream satin bra and pantie set with just a simple bow to decorate them. It's plain but classy, something I would have chosen for myself. "This one," he says. "If you like it, that is."

"I love it," I say, smiling. I take the one he's holding and put it back on the rack, finding my size. "Anything else?"

Damien rubs his beard, his warm brown eyes searching again. The flush has gone from his cheeks, and there's determination in the set of his jaw. He likes being given a task. This shopping trip is telling me a lot about him that I might never have found out in other circumstances.

"This one," he says, picking up an emerald-green lace bralette. The panties are like shorts that cut high on the ass. It's pretty as hell.

"You have an eye, Damien," I smile, searching out my size again.

"What about pajamas?" he asks.

"Yes. I need some of those."

He strides across the shop, looking more like a lumberjack than a personal shopper. His shoulders are so broad. I reckon he could pull a tree out of the ground and tear it apart with his bare hands. Somehow, his brown curls don't fit with the rest of him. They're too soft. Too innocent looking. Too tempting for me to run my fingers through.

"These," he says when I eventually catch up to him. He's holding a pink satin cami and shorts, and a black satin button top with long pants.

"Those will be perfect." He's even managed to search out the correct size for me. "You know, maybe you're wasted at Deep Repairs," I smile. "Maybe you need to become a personal shopper."

"Now you're teasing me, Sandy," he says, but his chocolate eyes are sparkling.

"No, seriously. You've got taste, Damien. Most guys would have picked the scarlet whore underwear."

"Most guys wouldn't have been imagining what would look good on you, though."

There is a flicker of electricity between us as Damien manages to look me in the eye and pay me a compliment without blushing. I guess he's getting more comfortable in my presence.

"What do I look like in your imagination, Damien?" I ask, gazing up at him.

"Like an angel," he says, and my heart skitters, making my head swim. This guy doesn't just have shopping moves. He's seducing me in public without even touching my hand.

A shiver of awareness passes over my skin as I imagine him. I know the outline of his body but not what it'll look like without the sweater. Is he smooth across his wall of a chest, or does he have a dusting of hair that would fit with his mountain-man look? Is his cock in proportion to the rest of him? I'm actually scared to find out.

"Maybe we should pay for these and hit another store," I say breathlessly.

"Sure," he says, taking everything from my hands and heading purposefully to the register. Everything is wrapped beautifully in dark blue tissue paper and placed into a thick paper bag that ties at the top with a ribbon. Damien pulls a huge stack of cash from his pocket and counts off more bills than I would ever have spent on myself.

A pang of guilt runs through me, but I push it down. This wasn't my idea. I would have been happy to wash my clothes and wait for them to dry. My car will be ready soon, and I can go home where I have plenty of clothes to manage.

This shopping trip is about Tyler keeping me here and showing me that he can give me what I need. What he doesn't realize is the thing that I really need—a discussion about what happened between us—is the one thing that seems forbidden or that he isn't willing to give.

"Where next?" Damien asks when we're in the echoey, high-ceilinged central part of the mall.

"How about here?" I point to a small boutique that I'm not familiar with. The clothes in the window look like they're good quality, and I can see at least one sweater that I like displayed on a mannequin.

I browse the rails, pulling out clothes and hanging them back up. Damien follows patiently behind me, carrying my underwear bag in his huge hand. "You see anything you like?" I ask him, fascinated to find out if his shopping skills are confined to undergarments and sleepwear.

Without responding, he begins to search out jeans, sweaters, t-shirts, and even a cute dress. He hands me a bundle of hangers. "What do you think of these?"

"I think I'll try them on," I say, smiling.

The store worker watches us with a bemused expression on her face, probably as surprised as I am that Damien has excellent taste. There's a dark wood and crimson velvet chair in the center of the dressing rooms, and when Damien takes a seat, he looks like the giant from Jack in the Beanstalk perched on Prince Charming's throne. "Show me," he says before I disappear behind the black velvet curtain.

As I begin to remove my clothes, my body is hyperaware that Damien is just a thin sheet of fabric away from seeing me in just my underwear. The jeans and shirt look great, and I prance out, giving Damien a twirl. "You're definitely getting that outfit," he says, nodding appreciatively. Next, I try a pair of black jeans with a soft gray sweater, and Damien nods with approval.

The last item is the dress. It's white cotton with dainty white embroidered flowers, in a floaty but short style. It's pretty rather than sexy, but in it, I feel amazing.

Damien called me an angel, and this dress makes me look like one, but underneath it, I feel like a devil.

The dressing room is quiet. It's just us here, cut off from the rest of the store. When I'm in front of Damien, his eyes rake over me, lingering on the swell of my breasts and the point on my mid-thigh where the dress finishes. I move closer until I'm standing between his spread legs, watching his brown eyes darken as his pupils dilate. "What do you think about this?" I whisper. "The fabric is so soft."

"You're definitely getting it," he murmurs huskily.

"Getting what?" I ask, looking pointedly down at his cock.

The flush on his cheeks is evident, but the tick in his jaw tells me everything I need to know about his pent-up frustration.

"Want to feel the fabric?" I say, touching the hem of the dress.

His hand drifts to the point I just touched, and he rubs the material between his thumb and forefinger. "Soft," he says. Then his palm presses against the outside of my leg, and I almost crumble with arousal. "But this is softer."

Damien's eyes stay glued to mine as his palm slides up the outside of my leg, disappearing under the skirt until his fingers reach the underside of my ass. My whole body twitches with a shiver as he strokes so gently around the back of my leg toward the inside of my thigh. "Are you wet?" he asks me, and I want to drop to my knees with weakness. Wet? Wet would be an understatement, but I nod anyway.

"If we were somewhere private, I'd pull you onto my lap and settle you onto my cock. I'd let you ride me wearing this pretty dress until we were both sweaty and sticky and messy." His finger finds the dampness of my panties, and his eyelids drop closed. When he opens them, his hand falls away. "Don't take off the dress. Just break off the label and fold up your clothes. I want you to wear this now."

"Okay," I say, my chest hitching as I breathe fast enough to compose myself. In the changing room, I glance at myself, finding my cheeks flushed and my eyes sparkling. I used to look this way when I first started dating Tyler, as though my fluttering heart lit me up from the inside. When I emerge through the curtain, Damien is waiting for me. He gathers the purchases and the loose ticket from the dress, leaving me with my folded jeans and sweater.

"I'll get a bag for those," he says.

The store clerk's eyes bulge as I follow Damien. "She's wearing the dress," Damien says. "Can you ring up the ticket and the rest of these?"

"Sure," she says. The bill isn't extortionate, and when Damien is handed the bag, he opens it so I can surrender my clothes. As we leave the store, he takes my small hand in his huge work-roughened palm and leads me back to the parking lot.

"You didn't need anything?" I ask as we emerge into the sunshine, and I shade my eyes with my hand.

"What I need is under that dress," he says. "But I've got to get you home for that."

DEEP 6

"Maybe," I say.

The look in Damien's eyes is a mix of fierceness and surrender. I think he'd agree to anything if it meant getting under my skirt.

"It's broad daylight," he says huskily.

"And the truck has tinted windows."

"Fuck," he mutters, picking up the pace. When we get to the truck, he opens the door for me and then tosses the bags into the trunk. He turns the ignition, shoving it into gear and reversing way too fast.

"Where are you going?"

"To the emptiest corner of the lot," he says.

It doesn't take long to find a place that has a tree on one side and a wall in front. There are no other cars parked nearby. As soon as he's switched off the engine, he flicks off of my seatbelt and hauls me into his lap as though I weigh nothing. All the breath leaves my lungs as he tugs me so my legs are on either side of him, and my pussy is mashed against his cock.

His big hands cradle my face, warm eyes searching mine. "You know how I know Tyler loves me like a brother?" he says. "Because he wants me to share what he loves most in the world, and you know how I know he loves you?" he continues. "Because he's not selfishly trying to keep you to himself."

Tears burn in my throat, but Damien kisses them away. For such a big man, he knows how to kiss with finesse. His hands are so gentle, mapping the line of my jaw, my neck, the curve of my shoulder. His lips drift to the top my breasts that are revealed by the dress he chose for me, and he inhales against my skin. Between my legs, his cock is a rigid bar against my damp panties.

"Have you got a condom?" I ask. Flicking open the glove box, he pulls out a strip and tears one off. I shift back, and my fingers search out his belt, unfastening it first and then moving to the button fly of his jeans. "Let me," I say, as my fingers trail the impressive outline of his cock through his underwear, making him jerk with sensation. Damien tears open the foil package with his teeth and passes me the ring of slippery latex. He adjusts his position so he can push his jeans a little lower and pull his cock out. And what a cock it is.

My mouth goes dry at the sight of the thick, long bar in his palm. My hand finds the hem of his shirt so I can pull it up and see more of him. His stomach is tight, and higher up, he does have a dusting of soft hair on his chest that I want to bury my face into. I place the condom on the rounded head of his dick and begin to roll it down. My fingers fumble and tremble, and his hands cup them on either side.

"Relax," he whispers, helping me to ease it into place.

Between my legs, I'm an aching mess. So much that I'm embarrassed when he slides up the hem of my dress and gets a look at everything there. His fingers trail a line down the front of my panties, his eyes fixed there too. "You're soaking," he says in awe.

Now it's my turn to blush. "Give me what I need," I say. "I'm ready."

"What do you need, baby?" he asks.

"What you promised me in the store."

His thick finger slides under the edge of my panties, testing my entrance and dipping just inside. There's no resistance, just slickness and building need, and he must sense it because before I can ask again, he's raising me up and angling his cock where his finger was and gripping my hips to help ease me down.

And oh God, I need help.

Rocking my hips, I take thick inch by thick inch, stretching so wide that it burns before it feels good. Damien's eyes are tightly closed, his nostrils flaring as I ease myself down and down, realizing that I'm never going to be able to take all of him. There's just too much.

"That's it," he says, his hand on my lower back, pressing me against him. His breath gusts over my cleavage as my clit rubs against his body with each thrust. I'm so wet that the sound of me moving is slick, just as he promised.

The skirt of my pretty white dress covers everything, the innocence of it such a contrast with what's happening beneath.

My legs begin to tremble as my pleasure builds. "My angel," Damien whispers against my ear, drawing my earlobe between his lips. "You know, from the moment I saw you, I wanted you. When I found out who you were, I thought it would never happen, but it has."

"Oh God," I groan as his hips begin thrusting upward, making the penetration even deeper.

"You like this big cock?" he hisses through gritted teeth as his cock seems to swell to even huger proportions inside me.

"I love it," I gasp.

"Yeah, you do," he says, anchoring me closer and grinding me into his body. My clit feels swollen, and my pussy stretched to its limits, and I know I'm going to come before I do.

"Don't stop," I whisper against Damien's neck. He smells of lemons and mint and sheer masculinity. And he doesn't stop. Instead, his thrusts get faster and shallower, pushing against the bundle of nerves inside me exactly the way I need.

This moment is everything I need. The rush of fucking in public like two college students such a change from the serious teacher role. I throw my head back, my eyes clenched shut and let go of everything. All the worries and hurt. All the feelings of not being enough, because Damien makes me feel like I'm all that he wants and all that he'll ever need.

And then I'm coming and coming and coming, deep clenching waves of pleasure pulsing through me.

"Fuck," Damien grunts, still moving through it all. My palm is slick where it rests against the bare skin of his chest, and when he comes inside me, I get to feel the frantic racing of his heart and the swelling of his mammoth cock.

I get to feel the surrender of a man who could crush me with just one hand but who never would.

Damien. My gentle giant.

A gift from Tyler, or am I a gift to Damien? Who knows, and who cares?

As I come down from the stratosphere, I rest my face on the soft hair in the middle of his muscular chest and listen to the pounding of his heart, wondering how long I can let this version of life wash over me before I need to return to Suzanne's basement and the fragments of my life from before.

23

TYLER

"Sandy's car is finished," Greg says, just as we're packing up to leave for the day. I was hoping it was going to take at least another day, but Greg's a fast worker. He obviously isn't as worried as I am that this could end things with Sandy before they've even started.

"Leave it here," I say. "I'll tell her tomorrow."

"Tomorrow?" Greg rubs his grease-covered hands on a cloth.

"Yeah, tomorrow. Let's have one more night before she can even think about leaving."

"You're worried she's going to leave?"

I nod, tossing my empty bottle of water in the trashcan by the wall.

"But we're all doing what you wanted. She's with Damien today. Then it's just Arden and Able to go."

"We don't know what's happened with Damien," I say. "We don't know she's receptive."

"She wouldn't have fucked me and sucked off Andrew if she wasn't receptive."

I close my eyes and rub my throbbing forehead at images that I should feel rage over but actually fill me with relief.

"But maybe you should talk to her about it," Greg continues. "It seems to me that she did her best to avoid you last night."

"She was tired," I say, not believing my own words. From what Andrew disclosed, they stayed up late talking and whatever. Sandy was definitely using Andrew as a way of keeping her distance from me. I don't know why. Is she angry at my idea but going through with it anyway? Or is she just fucking all of my friends as revenge for me wanting to share her? The thought of Sandy hating me that way fills me with slick black fear.

Maybe I'm using my friends in a way too. While Sandy's with them, I don't have to deal with what is resting unsaid between us. They'll be an anchor for her too. If she cares for them, there's less chance that she'll get into her Lexus and leave us all behind.

I don't think I can deal with losing her again.

"Leave the keys here. If she asks, we'll tell her we need to take it out for a test drive before we can release it."

"Okay."

I can tell Greg doesn't like it, but he'll do it because I asked.

On the journey home, I message Damien with a question mark. He replies with, **It's done**, and I know that Sandy's two-thirds through the Deep Six and still here. I trust that my boys have made her feel good and will have put her needs before their own. There's not a man in our group who's a selfish asshole when it comes to fucking. I've heard enough screaming orgasms in the middle of the night to be confident of that.

DEEP 6

At home, Sandy is wearing a pretty white dress that looks new. She's barefoot with her shiny chestnut hair tied in a messy bun. Damien is next to her at the counter, chopping tomatoes. It's the picture of domesticity.

"Hey," I say. "Something smells awesome."

"Fried chicken," Damien says with a grin. "All homemade."

"Fucking hell." Arden leans over Sandy's shoulder to take a look. There's a platter fit for a banquet, loaded with crispy fried chicken and a bowl of potato salad with scallions.

There's even a giant chocolate cake drizzled with a shiny chocolate topping.

It's like I've stumbled into heaven.

"Go wash up," Sandy says. She passes Damien, gently touching his shoulder as she looks for the silverware in the drawer. It's such a small touch, but it tells me so much.

She wouldn't touch him that way if this was about revenge. I don't know how I could have thought that about Sandy. The mind can play funny tricks on us, forcing us to imagine the worst when the worst has already happened to us in some capacity.

As I wash my hands, I say a silent prayer that what is happening today will still be happening next year. I want to come home to this woman and find her happy and content. I want her to kiss me and touch me gently like she used to and see her the same way with my buddies.

I want the kind of home life that I never experienced before, and I want kids that will grow up surrounded by security, not exposed to hardships that would challenge even an adult.

I'll never be the man I was four years ago. Sometimes our experiences change us for good. But maybe what I am now will be enough.

DEEP 6

The food is awesome, and Sandy makes us laugh with tales of Damien blushing at panties in the store. Arden shares some funny high school stories where he and his brothers would all date the same girl, but she thought she was only dating one of them. Sandy's shocked and swats Andrew on the arm, telling him she's disappointed in him. He blames everything on Arden, which is probably true. Out of all of them, Arden's the one who loves looking for trouble.

I tell Sandy to relax in the den while we deal with the clearing up. It's the least we can do after the best meal we've had in a very long time. When Sandy's out of the room, I grab Arden and Able by the arms and gently shove them toward the door. "Get in there. We've only got tonight. You guys need to make your move."

"Both at the same time?" Able whispers. "Is Sandy into that?"

"I don't know…just work it out."

Able looks worried, but Arden's got the confidence of a hundred men. "No problem, T."

He rubs his shaggy light brown beard, his crooked grin out in full force. "And don't worry about Able. He's never had a problem sharing in the past."

"Sharing bar coochie is one thing. Working on a good girl like Sandy is something else."

"Well, her car is ready. You need to show her what you've got. The icing on the cake, yeah!" I say.

"Okay, okay." Able shrugs as he makes his way to the den. Arden follows him with way more swagger. Do I think they can do it? I reckon Arden will make it happen. Fingers crossed.

"After this, we need to make ourselves scarce," I say to Andrew, Damien, and Greg. They share glances but nod. I get that they must be wanting Sandy for themselves. It's how I feel too. My cock has been throbbing like a fucking alarm for days. My heart misses her kisses and the feeling of her arms around me. But the sacrifice will be worth it in the long run. I just hope these boys can see it.

It doesn't take long to put the kitchen to rights, and then we head out to the local bar for a few drinks and to watch some sports. Connor's Bar is a place that I've always felt at home, but tonight I'm restless. I tell Greg to shoot some pool with me to try and keep distracted, but panic's hand is clutched tight around my guts.

Will all of this be enough for Sandy to look past what happened before? Can she love me, even though I'm not the same as I was? Can she forgive me for leaving her and never going back?

Can a broken person get close to another without cutting them open too?

I just don't know, but I hope with all my heart that they can.

24

ARDEN

I'm sitting on one side of Sandy, and Able is on the other, and we're watching a ridiculous show that Sandy chose, where women try on wedding dresses, and their moms are bitches. This is not what I call entertainment, but whatever makes her happy.

The thing is, I don't think Sandy's really watching the show. I keep catching her glancing at me out of the corner of her eye, and she's fiddling with the hem of her gorgeous white dress so much that I can't take my eyes off her thighs. She shifts in her seat every so often, like she's thinking about sex. I know I am. My cock is stirring, and I have to keep running through the process of draining oil from an engine to take my mind out of the gutter. No woman wants to sit next to a man with a tent in his shorts they haven't consciously put there.

Able is restless too, but probably because he feels awkward. We might look alike, but we always have been chalk and cheese.

I'm not a teenager anymore. The prospect of sitting here, sliding my arm tentatively around Sandy's shoulders and waiting to see if she's going to lean into me or push me away does not appeal. We're all adults. This doesn't have to be about playing games.

It could just be about three people having a whole truckload of fun.

Or a truckload of fucks. The latter sounds better to me.

I snort at my inner dialogue, and Sandy glances at me again. There was nothing funny on the show. In fact, the bride-to-be is currently in tears.

"That momma doesn't deserve kids," Able says, practically growling with anger. He always gets fierce when we watch shit that has abusive parents in it.

"Some parents don't," Sandy says.

"Do you have good parents?" Able asks.

"My parents always prioritized other things above my sister and me," she says. "It's not that they're bad people as such. They didn't beat us or make us feel bad about ourselves. They would just leave us with babysitters and go away for weekends. Then, when I was thirteen, they decided to move away. They left me and my sister the house, and she's nine years older than me, so she could take care of what needed to be done, but I wasn't done needing them. My dad got a good job overseas, and that was it."

"Shit, Sandy. That sounds rough," Able says softly.

"It was," she says with a shrug. "Some people are violent, and some people are emotionally hurtful. My parents just didn't care enough."

"But your sister was around?" Able asks. "I know I always relied on my brothers."

"Yeah. Suzanne's been amazing. More of a mom than our mom ever was."

"Well, that's good." Able reaches for Sandy's hand and gives it a squeeze, then doesn't let it go. And I thought it was me that was going to touch her first. I guess I need to give Able credit for his subtle, thoughtful moves.

"Yeah, Able is like the father I never had," I say.

"Funny," Able replies, shooting me a disapproving look out of the corner of his eye. I guess humor isn't what's required right now. But what is?

"Did you have a good time with Damien today?" I ask Sandy.

"Yeah. It was awesome. I'm still reeling at how good he is at picking clothes out for me. Like, everything looked amazing and fit perfectly."

"That part's because he's been imagining your body nonstop since you arrived. I reckon we could all draw our version of you naked with our eyes closed right now."

Sandy gawks at me, her mouth open and her eyes wide.

"Dude," Able says disapprovingly.

"What? I'm just being honest."

I hold my hands out, palms up, protesting my innocence, even though I know in my heart that I am deliberately trying to get a rise out of Sandy. It's my way of covering up how I really feel because I never want anyone to know that I want or need them more than they want or need me.

I guess having a shitty start in life leaves its mark.

And for the first time in my life, I can't see a way to making Sandy want me. Why the hell would she? She's a fucking literature teacher, and I can't even read.

"Excuse my brother. Sometimes he doesn't know when to keep his mouth shut," Able says.

I know when I'm not wanted. I grab the edge of the couch to pull myself up, and I'm halfway there when Sandy's hand covers mine. "You know, Arden, you don't have to act that way with me."

"Act what way?" I say, pretending I have no idea what she's talking about.

"Act as though nothing can touch you," she says. "I know what it's like to put on a front. I had two years, after…" she pauses for a moment, her eyes drifting closed, then regroups, "…I had two years of trying to pretend that nothing touched me. I joked my way through awkward situations, and I acted like I was Teflon coated, but no one is, Arden. We're all just muddling through."

"Wow," Able says. "Sandy just got you."

"Nobody gets me," I say. "Teflon is sticky compared to me."

"Really?" Sandy releases Able's hand and turns to face me. "Nothing touches you." Her hand reaches slowly toward my face as though she's scared that I'm going to push her away. I want to. Seeing the soft look in her pretty greeny-gold eyes is too much for me to take. I like women who don't give a fuck. Broken women whose edges are as fractured as mine. When I rub up against them, they cut me as much as I cut them. We bleed like it's meant to be that way. All's fair.

But Sandy's not like that.

"Nothing touches me," I whisper as the warmth of her palm reaches the skin beneath my beard. My eyes drift closed on instinct.

"Nothing reaches you," she whispers as her other hand rests on my chest, above where my heart is banging against my ribs like it wants to break free.

"Nothing reaches me," I murmur, even though it's patently obvious that it isn't true. Sandy has touched me, and she has reached me more than I could have believed. Even through my flippancy, she's seen the truth of who I am.

When her lips find mine, I have to clench my hands

into fists just to feel some control in my body. I hear Able's breath hissing from his mouth. There he was, thinking he would be the first of us to kiss her, but Sandy had other ideas.

I'm not going to complain when she feels like satin and tastes of honey, even though a part of my hollowed-out chest suspects she's only this way with me out of pity. She's figured out that I laugh at everything to shield my shame, and now she's trying to prove she doesn't think less of me.

I wish I could resent her for it, but I can't. She feels too good, and I need this. I need her warmth and softness. I need to sink into her body and let the pleasure rock me to the core. I'll make her feel so good that there will be no pity left, just awe.

"Sandy, baby," I whisper when she pulls back to loosen the buckle on my belt. "Shall we go upstairs?"

She shakes her head gently, her pretty curls bouncing with the movement. "Here is good."

While she's undoing my jeans, she turns to Able and takes his hand, drawing him closer. They kiss, and I watch as her tongue licks out into his, and his hand grips her hair at her nape, holding her tightly. I help her with my jeans, and when they're open, I take her hand and shape it around my rigid cock. That's all it takes to get her attention back on me.

I know she knows what I've got going on. My triplet, Andrew, has already shown her. We're identical in most ways. That doesn't mean she's not impressed. A little puff of air leaves her lips as she gazes down, getting her first look. Her tongue flickers through her lips as though she's already thinking about tasting it. Andrew's not an asshole who kisses and tells usually, but he did share that Sandy can deep-throat even a cock as big as ours. I'd love to see her on her knees worshipping me.

And I know that Able would love it too. That's what

makes sharing so much fun.

"Take off your dress, princess," I say, stroking my hand over the white fabric currently blocking me from getting to see Sandy's peachy body. Damn, her thighs are going to look good. And that ass. Lord. Hitting that from behind would make my eyes water.

Sandy does as I ask, standing in front of me and undressing slowly. Able tugs off his shirt and unbuttons his pants, watching as our dessert is revealed.

Shit. She looks better than I imagined, with her cute, rounded belly and just a hint of dimpling across her thighs. Sandy is all woman.

"Get on your knees and spread your legs," I say, making my tone slow and lazy rather than bossy. I stroke the head of my cock, a shiver of anticipation running through me as she kneels, gazing up at me with wide eyes. "That's it." I cup her cheek and slide my fingers into her hair. It's soft as down and the prettiest color. She keeps her eyes on me as her tongue licks the tip of my dick. It feels like fire and ice runs down my spine, drawing up my balls. "You're gonna suck this cock, and my brother's gonna lick your pussy."

A tiny, breathy moan leaves Sandy's lips as her mouth sinks down my cock like the hottest, velvet. She bobs her head a few times, keeping it shallow, tongue teasing as I watch Able lie on the floor behind her. He tugs her hips until her pussy is over his mouth, and I know he's licked her clit because her lips tighten around my length and her moan vibrates as she takes me deep.

Shit. Able is good at eating out. So good, we've had girls knocking on the front door asking for him after a friend's recommendation. That shit has to be legendary to get passed around like that. And if he keeps Sandy satisfied, she's only going to give it to me better.

Although how she could get better, I have no idea. My hand is on the back of her neck, but it's just for effect. An intention to control, but this girl gives head like a pro. I guess Tyler trained her. Or maybe some other dude. Whoever it is, I'd shake their hand. Maybe buy them a Rolex or something.

"Fuck," I mutter as Sandy's hips start to roll against Able's face. He has one hand on her ass and fingers in her sweet pussy. It won't take him long to make her come, and when she does, I want to come too. Oh God, the feel of her tight throat makes my eyes roll. I don't think there is anything in life sweeter than this.

There's power here and surrender. Sandy might be in the submissive position, but it's me who is putty in her hands. There's pleasure, but there is also respect. Sandy groans again, losing her rhythm as the sensations build between her thick thighs. I slide my hand over her breast and tweak her nipple through the soft fabric of her bra. Just a little to help Able send her over into oblivion. Her fingers grip the denim stretched over my thighs, digging into the flesh and her eyes find mine, wild, pupils blown. Then her lids shut as she comes.

Sandy's moan is long and low, a kind of keening sound that vibrates between my legs and in my chest. Tyler wants this woman to be our mate. Our princess. To care for between us in all the ways that will bring her happiness. I thought he was crazy, but maybe he's the sanest of all of us. Nights like this, with my brothers—by blood and by choice—and a woman as perfect as Sandy would be a special kind of perfect.

And when I release into her mouth and she swallows me down, all the stresses that reverberate in my head slip away, if only for a moment.

25

ABLE

There is absolutely nothing hotter than feeling a woman's pussy contracting in waves around my fingers and my tongue. The smell of her arousal. The softness of her body. The sounds she makes.

My dick is like a baton, but I haven't even squeezed it for a little relief. I've been fixed on Sandy and making her feel good.

Somewhere behind me, Arden has come. He needed to go first. I love my brother, and I understand him through and through. His dyslexia has been like an open wound in his chest his whole life. It makes him feel less-than, and so I'm happy to step aside if it makes him feel better.

Sandy raises up, and I sit, taking in the overwhelmingly perfect view of her peachy ass as she rests her head on Arden's knee. He's sitting with his hand over his cock, and a glazed look on his face, like Sandy sucked the life out of him through the straw of his dick.

Sandy looks wrecked too. I gave her my best, and she

felt it. I reckon her legs are like jelly.

I move closer, running my hand down her smooth back, lingering where her waist tapers, tracing the dimples on her hips and the swell of her ass. She sighs gently as I kiss my way down her spine, reaching around to slide the strap of her bra down. When she turns, and our eyes meet, she's still dazed with pleasure.

"Use a condom," she says. There's one in my wallet on the couch, which I find quickly, and slide it over my length, shucking off my jeans and underwear. I don't want anything between us that isn't a necessity.

Sandy's panties slide easily over her hips, and she shuffles from side to side so I can remove them. We kiss softly, and her lips are still a little puffy, which feels good.

She touches my chest, following the line between my abs, over my navel and lower, gently rolling my balls in her hand. "You made me feel so good," she whispers. "Let me do that for you too."

"I'll make you feel good again," I say, my lips twitching as her lids drift closed at just the thought. "And Arden's going to watch."

As I take my place behind Sandy, my hands are jittery. Every bit of restraint I can muster tells me to go slow. This is our first time together and she's already been fucked by three of the men in this house. I don't want to hurt her. I want this to be good for both of us. There will never be another first time.

I know I've made her wet enough to take me, and when I notch at her entrance, it's Sandy who pushes back until I'm halfway in her tight, slick heat.

"Fuck," I hiss, as my balls draw high and tight. "Do you know how good you feel? Do you know how much I've wanted to do this since you first walked in the door?"

Sandy sighs, her hand reaching behind to seek mine. Our fingers dance over each other, linking and gripping as

I move slowly inside her. I curl over, kissing the back of Sandy's delicate neck and running my fingers down her spine. Just because I'm behind her doesn't mean this can't be intimate.

Her other hand is supporting her, resting on Arden's knee. He plays with her fingers, too, stroking them gently as he palms his cock, watching everything.

Maybe some men would find it uncomfortable to do this kind of thing in the presence of their brother, but it's never been like that for us. We've been together since the day our single cell split into three. We are each other in a strange way that I can't really ever explain to an outsider. When I look at my brothers, I see my own reflection.

Sometimes I describe that we're one bar of chocolate that has been snapped into three pieces—slightly different shapes but mostly the same.

"Does that feel good?" Arden asks Sandy, cupping her cheek. I think he's stroking over her bottom lip because it takes her a while to answer.

"So good," she murmurs.

"Is my brother fucking your sweet pussy?" he asks.

Sandy nods, her pussy squeezing around my cock from listening to Arden's dirty talk.

"One day…not today because we need to work you up to it…one day, we're both gonna fuck you in that pretty little pussy at the same time. Would you like that?"

I know she likes it before she moans. Her pussy contracts like a vice around me. We really would have to work up to that. She's so tight and good, and I'm starting to lose my rhythm from the pleasure beginning to pool.

I close my eyes, moving to shallower thrusts as I seek out her little clit. It's slick and swollen from my tongue, so I stroke around it gently, gauging her response. It must feel good because she wriggles her hips and gasps, so I carry on, beginning to tap just lightly at double time to my pumping hips.

I wish I could taste her again and fuck her at the same time. If that was anatomically possible, it would be awesome.

As though Arden has read my mind, he urges Sandy up, so her back is pressed against my front, both still kneeling. I cup her breast, supporting her against me with gentle squeezes as Arden drops to the floor and kneels in front of her.

I've never seen my brother get into this position when we've shared a girl. As he licks over her clit, in time to my thrusts, Sandy is gazing down at him in awe.

I know I'm not going to last much longer, and with Arden's clever tongue working on Sandy's clit, I doubt she is either. I go deep now, and Sandy's legs begin to quiver. "That's it," I croon, "that's it. Let go, baby."

We're slick between our bodies, a mixture of sweat and arousal, and I can smell the scent of her in the air that trips a switch in my brain. I wish I could mark this woman inside. I could fill her with my come and watch it drip from within her. That would be fucking amazing, but we're not there yet. In time she'll trust us, and it'll be worth the wait.

I want to show her that we can be what she needs because she is everything that is good for us.

The moment she comes is like the sun's rays bleeding through a cloud. She ripples inside like water disturbed by a falling stone, and my cock swells, balls pulling up so tight that my mouth drops open. I drag in deep fast breaths, pumping, pumping, pumping inside her, as pure white-hot pleasure surges through me.

She's limp in my arms as Arden rises to kiss her mouth.

We stay that way for a few minutes, hands roaming Sandy's warm body, mouths caressing her flesh.

Eventually, Arden finds a condom, sheathing himself

and pulling Sandy into his lap. She's limp and ruined, but he does all the work, pumping his hips against her from beneath.

There's a laziness to everything now, as though we're touching each other through a haze of sensation, a fog of lust. She shivers when I let my fingers roam between her ass cheeks, so I circle her taint, over and over, until her hips are bucking, and her back is arching, and she's coming all over again.

When Arden comes, he throws his head back, his Adam's apple bobbing as he swallows, and peace seems to settle in the room with the knowledge that we could do this all night, passing our girl between us and rocking her world.

We could do it tomorrow and the next day and never want anything else because Sandy's just what we need.

Tyler isn't crazy.

He's the one thinking the clearest in this house for a change.

26

SANDY

I wake up in a strange room, under a comforter that I don't recognize. Through my sleep-sticky eyes, I make out Arden's bearded face on my left and Able's smooth one on my right. Arden's arm is heavy on my stomach, and Able's hand is cupping my pussy as though he's possessive over me even in sleep. I blink a few times to shake away bleariness and stare up at the ceiling. My heart is full, the memories of the past few days settling inside me like a warm cup of hot chocolate with extra whipped cream.

Could I have asked for more?

Six men want to make me the center of their harem.

This is how it must have been for Connie and Natalie.

Overwhelming.

Filled with uncertainty.

Wanting all the good intentions to manifest into something that will work.

But maybe they had it easier. Their men were all new.

One of mine is someone I viewed as a mistake in my past. Tyler was a wound so open and raw that I couldn't let another man near me for fear he'd rip me open.

I need to talk to him. There are so many things we need to say. There I things I need to tell him, but I don't know how. Things big enough that they could splinter all these fragile feelings and intentions.

The truth of it is that I don't know who he is anymore. He's still my Tyler is some ways, but there's a hollowness about him that wasn't there when we were together.

There's a brittleness to him that makes me scared.

My secrets could break him.

Everything that he thinks about me is a lie. I know this because if he knew what happened when he left, he wouldn't bring me into his friendship group. He wouldn't be exposing his friends to the kind of woman I am. He'd be pushing me out the door, disgusted.

He'd be shouting after me with rage.

He'd never forgive me.

My car is ready today, but I don't know what to do. There are two parts of my life; this place that has become a refuge with six of the best men there are in the world, and my real life where things are going wrong all over again. I feel like I'm teetering between the two, not sure where to go or which version of myself to be.

I want to be *this* Sandy. The Sandy with security, who doesn't have to feel as though I'm floundering all the time. I want to be rooted and protected. I want all the things that I used to dream about having with Tyler and had to throw in the trash when he left without a trace.

But I also want the old me before Tyler left.

The one who didn't feel like a part of her is so damaged that she'll never fully heal.

The one who struggles to comprehend the shit that life

threw in her way.

I stare at these men who carried me to bed so tenderly last night and tucked me in like they were wrapping a precious package in the best quality giftwrap. Arden's face is so relaxed in sleep. The smirk that I'm so used to seeing playing at the edges of his mouth is gone. His beard is thick, and darker than his hair, but I know how soft it is. It tickled against my cheek and between my thighs. I see his vulnerability in a way that I don't fully understand.

And Able.

Able's jaw is shadowed with overnight growth, and he has a slight furrow in his brow as though he's holding troubles close. I wish I could hear their thoughts and see what's in their hearts. I wish that I could trust my instincts when it comes to all the men in this house, but my instincts have led me in the wrong direction before.

I've had hopes that have been dashed against the rocks so hard that there was nothing left of them.

I stumbled into this situation, wanting to dwell in a place where life was simple. But the way Tyler's been avoiding talking to me has me both relieved and worried in equal measure. We're both pretending that the present doesn't rest on the past, but it does.

Should I stay, or should I go?

As though Arden can feel my dilemma, he moves closer, his arm wrapping even more securely around me. His lips move, a sigh escaping.

I wish they'd wake up so that I can get lost in their bodies again. They're both already hard. It wouldn't take much to get started. After four years of no sex, these past few days have made me insatiable. But sex doesn't equal love when unspoken words rest beneath, threatening to spoil everything.

I'm about to caress Arden's arm with just the tips of my fingers when he stirs and says a word that brings the familiar burn of tears to the back of my throat.

"Stay," he says, gripping me tighter.

27

TYLER

It's done. Sandy's ours. She's been in the bed of every man in this house, and they've claimed her, not only for themselves but for all of us.

She's marked for us.

The Deep Six.

But there is still so much unsaid between us. I know it can't stay that way forever. Maybe in time I'll find a way to be open with the girl who's given me a bubble of hope in my chest. Maybe, if she loves us all, she'll find a way to see past my guilt.

All I know is that I can't risk telling her now.

I'm flipping pancakes in the kitchen when there's a knock on the front door. I glance at the clock, knowing that it's early, but I want to confirm the exact time. Seven-thirty am. Who the hell would be coming around at this time?

Greg slides off his chair and lumbers to open it. Maybe he's expecting a package or a visitor.

When I hear a woman's voice, I empty the pancake out of the pan so I can step away from the stove to see who it is.

Luna.

My sister, who I haven't spoken to for a long time. Almost as long as Sandy. I swear, the wind must be blowing in my direction because people from my past keep drifting back through. I'm so shocked to see her that I take a step back, bracing my hand on the counter.

Luna struts past Greg, who remains standing in the doorway, his eyebrows raised, and his mouth pulled to one side.. Behind her, a troop of men in black suits shuffles in. They look like the actors from *Men in Black,* but I know they're not secret service. They're her bodyguards.

"Tyler," she says curtly as soon as she steps over the threshold to the kitchen.

Damien glances up from his phone, his eyes practically bugging out of this head. All the boys know my sister from our childhood but none of them know this version of Luna from up close.

We've seen her on social media, all grown up and preened to fit in with the ideal teen pop star mold. It's too early for her to be in full makeup with her hair pulled into a slicked high ponytail, but that's how she's appeared. The outfit is out there too. A black catsuit that's tight all over, showing off her tiny waist and the womanly hips she's developed since we stopped communicating.

Two of the suited men stand on either side of her. One lurks in the hallway with Greg, and I can see at least another two outside. I don't know what's happened to her that she needs so much protection. Surely, a pop star on the brink of their first tour doesn't need this much security.

"Luna…" I don't know what to say to my sister. *Long time no see* would trivialize the reasons for the gap in our relationship. There are many buttons I could push that would explode all over again, and I don't want to do that. If Luna's here, maybe it's because she's forgiven me.

Greg takes a step closer to stand in the doorway, leaning on the doorjamb, crossing his arms, and staring at Luna's back as though he can't quite believe it's her. I'm in the same situation.

"I'm going on tour," she says, fully expecting me to be up to date with her career. I am, but I'm not going to tell her that I Google her at least once a week to make sure she's okay. How fucked up is that?

"Okay," I say.

Her head drops to the side as her eyes drift from me, scanning the kitchen, focusing momentarily on Damien before snapping back to me.

"I need you to take care of Mom."

"What?" The word whooshes out of my mouth like phlegm. Mom hasn't been in our lives since we were kids. The care system raised us, and when I was old enough, I took over.

Great job that I did too.

"I need you to take care of Mom. She's sober, but she won't be for long if I leave her behind with no one to force her to meetings and keep up with her recovery." Her green eyes scan me, waiting to see how I'm going to respond to this bombshell.

"You're in touch with Mom?"

"She's the only real family I have," Luna says. Her eyes narrow and just that look of resentment toward me makes my heart fall in the cavity of my chest. There was a time when Luna would say the same thing to Jake and me. We'd lie on the grass in the yard of our foster home, shoulder to shoulder as though pressing our bodies together would keep us fused as a unit. Sometimes Luna would slide her hand into mine, and we'd stare up at the sky. I don't know what my brother and sister were thinking, but I was praying that the universe would give us at least one adult to keep us safe and provide the security we needed to grow. That adult wasn't our mom or our dad. We were all we had in the world.

Now Jake is gone, and Luna has withdrawn from me.

And the woman who let us down, time and time again, has replaced both of us in Luna's life.

Jake would be devastated. I'm devastated. All I want is my brother and sister back.

But there is no way I can take on responsibility for Mom. She'd drag me into the hole she's been existing in since before we were born. I can't be pulled down again. I just can't.

"I'm sorry, Luna. Mom isn't my responsibility." I try to keep my voice even and calm. I try to convey that I'm sorry that I can't be the brother she needs in my tone, but she doesn't seem to get it.

"She gave us life. We owe it to her."

"We don't owe anybody anything," I say, inhaling a deep breath to push down the wave of anger that's bubbling in my chest.

"You owe me," Luna hisses. Her pretty face is so pinched that I have to look away. "You owe me a brother. The least you can do is take care of what I have left of a mother."

"Luna," Greg says in a low, warning tone.

She puts up her hand to silence him from saying anything else.

"I've tried..." she says, her shoulders slumping just slightly. "I've really tried to move past what happened. I'm trying to make things right. If you want to repair things between us, I need you to do this."

Damien twists his chair to face my sister, the scrape of

the wood on the tile loud enough to make me flinch. "Luna," he says in a soft but firm voice. "Tyler isn't going to take care of Kaylee. There isn't room in this house or space in his life for someone who only ever brings people down. We feel sorry for her, but we can't help."

As the words leave Damien's lips, there's movement from the hallway, and I turn to find Sandy dressed in just the sweet pajama set that Damien chose for her at the mall. Her hair is a riot of messy chestnut curls, and her lips are pink and plump. My eyes are drawn to her like she's magnetized, and all I'm constructed of is hastily swept together fragments of iron. By the time I register that Sandy is walking into the middle of a difficult conversation, Luna is already turned in her direction.

There's a moment of awkward silence.

A moment where the memory of the last time I was with Sandy before Jake's accident washes through my mind. There's so much contentment in that memory that it sticks my throat together with longing. I would give everything I have and everything I will ever be to go back to that moment and change what happened next. If I could lie in that bed with my arms wrapped around my sweet girl and her arms wrapped around me, I would. I'd erase the last four years in a heartbeat to get back to that moment.

"Who's this?" Luna asks, her nostrils flaring.

"I'm Sandy."

My eyelids drop as though they can shut out everything in front of me, and none of it will be there when they open. Except, when I force them open, everyone is still there, and now they're all looking at me.

"*The* Sandy?" Luna says with her head cocked to the side.

She never met Sandy back when we were dating, but she knew about her. She knew that I loved Sandy, and I was planning to ask her to marry me when I had enough saved to buy the kind of ring that she deserved to wear on her finger for life.

I nod, even though I don't want to. Exposing this fragile thing between us to Luna's anger and resentment is dangerous. I love my sister, but her tender little heart has become encased in steel since Jake died.

She's become something abrasive and razor-sharp.

"What the fuck is she doing here?"

A quick glance at Sandy reveals the confusion on her face. She takes a step back as though putting some distance between her and the rest of the room will calm the atmosphere. It won't.

"She's staying for a while," I say.

And as though the universe is conspiring to make things even more difficult, Arden chooses that moment to appear next to Sandy, sliding his hand over her belly and kissing her lazily on the cheek. All before he takes a look at what he's walking into.

Luna's lips part with shock at their intimacy, and when she turns to me, her eyes are wide. "She's with him?"

The bodyguard to Luna's right clears his throat. They've done a good job so far at remaining impassive behind their dark sunglasses. In their black suits, they can almost disappear into the background, but the conversation laced with tension must be getting to them.

"She is," I say.

"Working her way around you all, is she?" Luna spits. "I can't believe you put *her* before Jake...I can't believe that's what you sacrificed our brother for."

The green of her eyes has turned the color of clouds before a storm. They're fierce enough that I take another step back. I think it's that small step that sends Damien rising to his feet and Greg striding into the room until he's standing directly between Luna and me.

The bodyguards surge around her as though me and my boys are a threat to her safety. If anything, it's the other way around.

"Luna. I respect you as Tyler's sister, but you need to calm the fuck down and think about what you're letting leave that pretty mouth," Greg says.

"What the fuck has it got to do with you?" Luna hisses. "You're not family. You're just some ex-con who latched onto my brother when he was weak."

"LUNA!" Damien bellows. "JUST STOP."

"STOP?" She laughs as though his very suggestion is the most hilarious thing she's ever heard. She laughs as though she's manic, and all I want to do is pull my little sister into my arms and sing the lullaby that she used to love as a baby.

That sweet girl is still in there somewhere, buried amongst the ruins of our lives.

None of what happened is her fault, but she's the one who's most affected. "You want me to stop telling the truth? Life's too short for that." She takes a step forward, putting her close enough to Greg that he could kiss her if he leaned forward a couple of inches. "I'm done being the person who holds everything inside me until I feel crazy. I'm done pretending that everything is okay. I've got a mom who's always on the brink of killing herself with alcohol or drugs or just fucking neglect. I've got a brother in the ground before he had a chance to live. I've got a father who's been AWOL for longer than he's ever been a part of my life. And now I find out that the brother who should have been responsible for sorting all of this shit out so that it didn't happen is back with the woman he put ahead of his family. So excuse me if I don't keep my mouth shut about that."

I turn to Sandy, whose face has paled to the color of alabaster. Her eyes are on me, and she takes a step forward and then another until she's next to me. "Tyler," she says softly. "Are you okay?"

I don't get why she's asking me. I don't get why her expression is so worried. I don't get why she can't seem to take hold of my hand when she reaches out to it. Then I look down at my hand and find it shaking so violently it's almost a blur. Sound dulls around me like my head is underwater, and everything happening around me is above. Sandy's arms go to embrace me, but it doesn't feel good. It feels as though she's trying to hold me up, and that's not her job. I should be the one protecting her from the world. I need to be the one who's strong enough to keep it all together. I didn't do it for my family, but I can do it for her. I can do it for my boys.

"Tyler, sit," Sandy says gently. The press of the table against my legs prompts me to slump down. I can smell Sandy's scent on her soft skin, feel her fingers in my hair. My chest is rising and falling too rapidly, but I can't seem to get control over my breathing. Damien is standing behind Sandy, staring down at me like a father looking at his son. There are voices, but I can't make out what they're saying.

All I can do is close my eyes and hope it'll all go away.

28

GREG

When Luna walked into the house surrounded by bodyguards, I thought they were going to be a problem. As it turns out, they're the ones who see things going south and hustle her out of the front door. I'm close behind because there is no way I'm letting her leave without giving her a fucking huge piece of my mind.

"LUNA!" I shout as she's stumbling down the front path to her giant vehicle. She stops, and so does the suited dude who has his hand through her arm. For someone with a mouth on her the size of the Grand Canyon, she's actually really small and vulnerable looking now.

"What?"

"What you said to Tyler…it's wrong."

"Nothing I said was wrong. You just don't want to face the truth."

"The truth is that Jake was a grown man. The truth is that Tyler told him never to ride that motorcycle. He warned Jake in front of me how dangerous it was."

"He promised Jake that he would teach him to ride, but he never had time for us after he met Sandy."

"He was in love, Luna. For the first time in his life, he had someone who loved him the way he needed to be loved. I'm not trying to diminish you and Jake in his life...he loved you both more than anything else, but he'd been caring for you guys for so long...from when he was too young. He just wanted to have some time to himself. Jake shouldn't have taken the bike, but it wasn't Tyler's fault."

"Then why does he blame himself?" Luna spits as though she's proven her point right there.

"Because that's what big brothers do. That's what brothers who have had to step in to be mothers and fathers do. That's what anyone who's left behind after an accident does. We blame ourselves because there is no going back...there is no way to bring Jake back."

Luna stares at me, her bright green eyes swimming with unshed tears. The man at her side pushes at her arm to get her to move, but she resists. "He died," she mutters. "Jake died, and Tyler wasn't there, and I had no one."

"I know," I say, reaching out to touch her hand. It's so small that I could crush every bone without even trying. She's a force to be reconned with in a tiny, frail package. "But what happened broke Tyler, and you blaming him...you trying to heap more guilt onto him...it isn't going to make anything better. We're trying to bring him back. Sandy is here to try and bring him back."

I hear the rustle of clothes behind me and turn to find Sandy in the doorway. Her pretty eyes are glassy, and her head shakes from side to side as though she's in denial about whatever part of our conversation she heard. I scrunch my face in anticipation of some kind of confrontation. Luna is raw and resentful, and Sandy seems to be vulnerable, but angry. It's a dangerous combination.

"Luna." There's a hitch in Sandy's voice that stills Luna

immediately. Sandy pads outside, ignoring the fact that her feet are bare, and she's dressed more appropriately for indoors than out. I catch the heads of the bodyguards turning, and I don't think it's because they're concerned for Luna's safety. If this wasn't such a fucked-up situation, I'd be warning them off my girl.

"What?" Luna says, folding her arms.

I hold my breath, the tension enough to constrict my gut. Then Sandy throws her arms around Luna and holds her tight. "I'm so sorry about what happened to Jake," she whispers. "I'm so sorry that I was a distraction to Tyler when you needed him."

I'm so shocked. The rush of breath leaving my lips is loud enough to distract the bodyguard closest to me. Luna's spine is straight, her head held high, but after a few seconds, she crumples before my eyes, and I can't believe it.

Her arms slide from between her and Sandy, and she wraps them firmly around the girl who, five seconds ago, she was blaming. Tears trickle down her cheeks, and she buries her face into Sandy's hair, ashamed maybe, of her emotional response. At least, that's the way it seems.

It's an odd scene with Luna pristinely dressed and Sandy still bleary from sleep, both resting on the other as though their unity is the only thing keeping either of them standing. "You know that Tyler would do anything to go back and be there to tell Jake not to ride that motorcycle. You know that he'd give anything to have his brother back."

Luna nods and whispers yes.

"He needs you…he needs you in his life…he needs to know that you're with him."

"But he won't be there for Mom…she matters to me," Luna says.

"We'll work something out," Sandy says, although she

has no idea what she's promising. Tyler's mom has always been trouble of the kind that there's no saving.

"I just...I need to leave, but I can't if I don't know everything here is going to be okay."

"It will be. Just go inside and see Tyler before you go, and I'll deal with the rest."

They pull apart and face each other, eye to eye. An understanding passes between them. An understanding that maybe only women can grasp. These two women who love the same man can come together to make things right.

Luna nods and begins to make her way back inside, her shoulders slumped, still flanked by her black-suited protector.

I try to follow her, but Sandy grasps my elbow, holding me back.

"Tyler blames himself?" she asks me. "It was his bike?"

I nod, and another tear runs down her cheek.

"And he blames me?" she asks.

"No!" I rest my hand on her shoulder, the soft, warm skin so tantalizing in my palm. "He doesn't blame you."

"But he left, and he never came back. He blames me for distracting him. He blames me because he wasn't there to save his brother...to stop him from getting onto that bike?"

"No," I say again. She's not getting the truth of the situation. "He blames himself for Jake's death, and he doesn't believe that he can ever be a person who can love enough to keep you safe. He doesn't think you can trust him because he failed his brother...because one day, he'll fail you."

Sandy's lids close slowly, and she shakes her head gently from side to side.

"Trust," she whispers, blinking slowly again. When her pretty eyes meet mine, they're filled with sadness. "Maybe it's Tyler who shouldn't trust me."

29

SANDY

This whole thing is a disaster.

Even as Luna embraces Tyler, I can see how fractured he is by what happened. Four years is a long time, but it doesn't seem to have lessened the trauma of his brother's death or softened the way he feels about his role in it.

I understand why he blames himself, but I don't agree that it was his fault.

Jake was his own person. He made his own decision. He went against his big brother's advice and left nothing but devastation behind him.

It's so hard not to be angry with him. He's not here to defend himself, and he definitely didn't want to die. He was a risk-taker, just like Tyler was and still is.

The stupid racing.

The fast cars.

The fact he's pushed me into the arms of his friends because he doesn't trust himself with me.

I stand at Greg's side and wish he'd put his arm around me. I need his rock-like strength right now, just to get me through these next few minutes. I would have said anything to Luna to get her back in here so that Tyler wouldn't have that dead look in his eyes. And now I must find a solution to deal with their mom.

Tyler didn't share much about his family, but he did share what a disaster Kaylee is.

I can do that much for Luna and Tyler.

And then I need to break out of this crazy situation.

Nothing built on crumbling foundations can ever stand. These men don't know me. Not really. They don't know how weak I am or what I did when I was broken.

My secrets have no place here because Tyler could never handle knowing the truth. He has enough to blame himself for already. And I know he'd blame himself for what happened after he left me to go to be by his brother's deathbed.

I'm certain of all of this because, deep down, I know who he is.

Tyler's cocky exterior was just a front to cover everything beneath. His flippancy about life, his addiction to speed, are about pushing the boundaries, about tempting fate.

He didn't leave me behind because he didn't want me. He did it because he believed that I deserved more than a broken version of him.

What he doesn't know is that I would have done whatever it took to help him put himself back together again. I could have supported Luna too. They were too fractured to be there for each other.

Tyler's eyes find mine over Luna's shoulder. There's an ache in them that cuts my heart. An ache to turn back the clock to when everything was easier. When pain wasn't eating us all in some way or another.

Greg's hand envelopes mine. When I glance up at him, he's staring straight ahead, but his firm grasp helps me. It grounds me. He is what I need in the same way that I should be what Tyler needs. I wish I could be.

My throat tightens as I watch the other men in this house stand around, worried for their friend. Able steps forward as Luna draws back, moving closer to Tyler in case he needs support.

Luna's eyes search out the icy blue stare of her bodyguard. He gives her a curt nod, straightening as though he wants to make himself as tall as he can be. The earpiece he's wearing trails inside his black jacket, and he mutters something to communicate to the rest of his team that they're leaving. Luna's either in danger or has a load of over-enthusiastic fans to deserve this much security.

"Do you have her number?" I ask Greg. He nods stiffly in response. At least I have a way to get in touch with her if I need to. "Is my car ready?" I ask. This question prompts Greg to turn his head and look down at me with his inky black eyes. I think I must imagine the tick of his jaw before he speaks.

"Yes. Why? Are you going somewhere?"

"Just to run errands," I say.

"Well, before you run errands, I need to talk to you upstairs."

His palm tightens around my hand, squeezing the bridge of my knuckles enough to make me feel his coiled strength. I remember the way that huge rough palm gripped around my throat, and I'm instantly hot between my legs. I don't know how it is that each of these men, being so different, can push my buttons so perfectly. It's like they're a six-sided dice. Each time it tumbles, it brings up another number that is perfect for me.

But I'm not perfect for them.

This home is built on trust. These men have come

together to bring security and reliability into each other's lives because their families never have.

And as much as I would love to be a part of this, as much as I need these men in my life, I know I won't be able to live with myself if I become the reason this all falls apart.

Greg's need to talk is urgent enough that he takes my hand and leads me from the room. I pad upstairs, trailing behind him a step. He's silent until he's closed the door to his room behind us. Then his mouth is on mine, hungrier than any kiss I've ever had. The hand that squeezed mine is on my throat, keeping me pressed against the wall and totally in his control. His other hand shoves aside the silky fabric of my shorts, fingers slipping in my slickness and pushing deep inside me.

I gasp into his mouth and feel the twitch of a smile on his lips. His thumb grazes my clit lazily as he pumps deep, using his foot to kick my legs wider, and I'm on the precipice of coming before I've even properly registered what's happening.

Talking is obviously the last thing on Greg's mind.

I can feel the long bar of his hard cock against my hip. He nudges it into me, searching for friction, and it's the most demandingly erotic thing that anyone has ever done to me.

"I know what's on your mind," he whispers in my ear, lips seeking out my soft lobe, making me shiver. "I know what you're planning. You're going to take your car and drive out of here and leave us all behind."

I shake my head, even though it's true. Greg adds another finger, pumping so hard and deep into my pussy that I'm on my tiptoes, grunting with pleasure.

"You think that leaving will make Tyler better, but you're wrong. He needs you. We all need you. You're in our blood now. We've marked you. You don't get to drive off into the sunset without a backward look."

I shake my head again, a shiver running up my spine. Pleasure swells deep and low in my belly, spilling between my legs and into his palm. Warm liquid trickles down my thighs, and Greg smiles against my leg as I gasp, pussy clenching against his fingers in fast, tight ripples that I cannot control.

"You need us," Greg says, easing his hand from inside me, kissing my jaw as I wince. "Your body needs us. Your mind needs us." He draws back, his eyes lingering on mine, then dropping lower and lower over my peaked nipples and down to where my feet are wet from my orgasm. He made me squirt for the first time ever, and I'm so shocked at my body's response to him that my hands are trembling. "You think you know what it will be like to be our woman, but you don't. Not yet. We've gone easy on you, but we're just starting out. You want to leave this behind…all this potential…all this pleasure, for what?"

I close my eyes, the flutter of a sensation rushing up my spine is almost painful, and the tingles across my scalp make me drop my head.

Greg's seen me. He knows me. He's worked out my intentions and he's not going to let me leave without a fight. His possessiveness should piss me off. I'm a grown woman, and I can do what the hell I like. I don't need his permission or Tyler's or the approval of any of the other men in this house. But even though I shouldn't want him pressing his cock against me, raging with the intention to bend me over and break me, I do.

I don't need soft words and gentle intentions.

I need to feel exactly how much he wants me. I need to know he's never going to let me go, no matter what happens in our lives. No matter how weak I am or what selfish decisions I make.

Greg pushes me to my knees, freeing his cock from his black jeans, lifting his black shirt, so I get an eyeful of the ladder of his abs, stretching upward to the heaven of his gorgeous face. When I take him in my mouth, I taste arousal and the bite of his control. His hand in my hair forces what I would give willingly. My eyes water, my throat spasming around Greg's huge cock, and through it all, I can't take my eyes from his.

There's darkness there. So much darkness that I sense that he could swallow me so deep that I'd never find my way out. But there's also fear. The slight tremble to his hand and the hitch of his chest tell me how much he needs this. How much he wants me to stay.

Sex isn't just about two bodies moving against each other for pleasure. It's about power and control. It's about surrender and submission. Good sex is like opening your chest and letting another person root around inside you. At least, that's how it is for me.

I might have Greg's cock in my mouth, but he has his hand around my heart in a way that burns.

The tears leaking from my eyes aren't just caused by the thrust of his cock. They come from a deep place, stuffed down years before, at a time when I was so close to breaking, I knew I couldn't work through my grief.

When he shudders, coming deep in my throat, I swallow him down, relishing the deep groan that leaves his lungs. He's strong, I tell myself. He'll be okay. He'll find another woman to get on her knees for him. They all will. Maybe, when I'm gone, they'll come to their senses and realize that Tyler's idea was ridiculous. They'll each find their own woman to make it work.

They won't think of me then at all.

Tyler was fine without me. He built a life with his friends. They were all better off without me.

Just like Sophie.

30

ANDREW

Greg asks me to go get Sandy's car from the repair shop and bring it back to the house. I take it for a good run first, making sure that everything sounds right. When I'm certain that everything has been fixed, I head home, wondering what's going to happen.

Is Sandy going home to collect her things? She can't live out of a small suitcase and on a few gifts from the mall. She's going to need to bring her possessions so that she can settle in. We'll make her space in our closets and help her hang pictures if that's what she needs to feel at home.

There is a lot that can be done to the house to make it feel less like a bachelor pad. We keep it clean and tidy, but none of us has any great interior design skills.

I hope she's not going to stay away too long.

They say absences makes the heart grow fonder, but that saying comes with another part. *Too much absence, love no longer.* A big part of me worries that when Sandy steps out of our home and back into the real world that she'll realize that these past few days have been a blip in her otherwise perfectly ordinary life. A blip that she won't even consider returning to.

When I pull into our driveway, the front door is open. Sandy is standing at the window, and when she sees her car, she steps into the doorway, turning to look back into the house.

I throw the car into park and jump out, desperate to know what's going on.

Then I see Tyler holding Sandy's suitcase, and it's confirmed. She's leaving.

The rest of the boys gather behind. We should all be at Deep Repairs right now, but it's obvious that none of us gives a shit. I left a note on the door saying that we'll be opening late. Anyone who needs us can call the number on our sign.

"I'll be back soon," Sandy says breezily, her eyes wide as though she doesn't quite believe what she's saying. I pop the trunk, and Tyler rests Sandy's bag in the back, closing it with a thud that feels like punctuation at the end of a sentence.

A sentence at the end of a book.

Tyler is the first to pull Sandy into a hug. There's a tenderness to the way he enfolds her in his strong arms and a familiarity to his touch that speaks of their past relationship. When he draws back, he gazes down at her. Sandy meets his gaze with wide hazel eyes filled with uncertainty. "Drive carefully, okay. And call me when you get there." She nods, and her eyes flutter shut when he bends to press a gentle kiss to the corner of her mouth.

Even from a distance, I can see the sigh that leaves her lips when he pulls away.

Next, my brothers step forward, each hugging Sandy and kissing her goodbye. She touches Arden's beard and plays with the hair at the back of Able's neck in a way that feels as real to me as if she was caressing my own skin.

Damien is next. He bends to hug Sandy and lifts her off her feet, causing her to squeal. It's good that he's found a way to bring some lightness into this situation. When he puts her down, she swats his pec, and Damien grins broadly.

Greg is standing to the side, his big arms folded across his broad chest. He's watching everything like a bodyguard assessing the danger of a situation. There's a defensiveness to him too. He's a hard man, but he has a soft side. He's as needy of a woman's touch as we all are, and I've never seen him look at a woman the way he looks at Sandy. When Damien has stepped aside, Sandy looks around, knowing there are two of us left.

I make my way forward next, my heart beating hard against my ribs. I slide my hand into my jeans pocket and pull out the tiny building I took from my shelf. It's a model of The Shard from London, the building we spoke about. I didn't know what else to give her to remind her of her time with me. It's stupid, but maybe it'll be enough.

"Keep safe," I say, sliding the model into her hand as I hug her. When we draw apart, she looks down, and her face breaks into a smile. "I know it's not as good as the real thing, but one day..." I kiss her sweet rosy lips, and she rests her hand on my chest, most probably feeling the frantic beating of my heart.

Greg is the last, and Sandy has to seek him out. She looks like a child standing before a stern father. She touches his forearm, and his lids drop closed, then he takes her into his arms, crushing her against his chest. "I know," he says. "Don't pretend with me."

She buries her face in the fabric of his shirt, and when she pulls back, I can see the damp patches that her tears have left behind.

Sandy hurries to her car, tossing her purse onto the

passenger seat. She reaches for a pair of sunglasses, which she shoves onto her face to cover the tears in her eyes.

Tyler steps forward and pats the roof of the car. He seems happy, so I guess he really believes she'll be back soon.

Or maybe he's just kidding himself exactly like I'm trying to do.

31

SANDY

Packing up my apartment is so difficult. This place is where I set myself up after Tyler. This place was my hope for a better future, and now I have to put all of that behind me.

I fold the last of my sweaters and place them into the suitcase resting on the bare mattress. It takes a lot of effort to zip it closed, and I'm sweating by the time I'm done.

When I pull it off the bed, it drops to the floor with a thud.

I stare around at the almost empty space that I'm leaving behind. Everything that made it mine is now in boxes. It's a shell, ready for the new renter who will be here tomorrow.

I'm sure, they'll be happy here.

I have been.

A horn sounds outside, and then a car door slams. Suzanne is right on time. I hear her footsteps on the asphalt, and I shake my head, trying to bring some clarity back to my mind before she sees me.

I have to do this. There isn't a choice. There's no point in wallowing in what could have been or what should have been.

Sometimes life comes and takes away the future that you're expecting.

But when it does, there's always the option of another future. I learned that after Tyler.

The trouble is that even thinking about trying to build a future without Tyler and the boys tightens my throat and hollows my chest.

The door to the apartment is open, and Suzanne calls my name when she reaches the doorway.

"Sandy. Are you ready?"

"I'm in here," I call back, swallowing against the ache.

"Wow." She looks around and then shakes her head. "Not sure everything's gonna fit in the truck."

"We'll have to make it fit," I say. "The agent is coming to pick up the key."

"Well, we'd better get a move on then," she says.

I leave the suitcase where it is and focus on taking the heaviest boxes down to the truck with Suzanne. It's a struggle, but we manage the best we can, huffing and puffing and working up a sweat.

We pack my comforter, blankets, and pillows next, filling every available space in the vehicle. I concentrate on the practicalities and push my emotions down. It's what I've learned to do.

The suitcase rests in the backseat along with my potted plants, a mirror, and some photo frames that could shatter if something lands on them while in transit.

And I fill my car too. Just opening the trunk reminds me of Tyler and saying goodbye. He placed my things in my car with so much care and kissed me with tenderness that hurt rather than soothed.

Everything reminds me of the boys I left behind.

When the agent arrives, I fish for the keys in my purse and unhook them from my key ring.

"I'm sure there's going to be no problem releasing the deposit," he says after taking a quick look around the apartment. "You've kept it perfectly."

"Thanks." I'm relieved that all my effort rubbing the damage from the walls has paid off. "I could do with getting the money back as quickly as possible."

"I'm sure that won't be a problem," he says, but he's not really focused on me. He's already swiping through his phone, looking in his calendar for his next appointment.

Walking out of the apartment feels surreal.

This place was my roots, and now I'm left moving into Suzanne's home with the ghost of Tyler and the boys aching inside me.

I wish I knew what to do. I wish there was an easy answer.

I wish that I could tell Tyler what I did and not break his heart.

As I follow my sister back to the house, I'm filled with a mix of trepidation and excitement. It's been three weeks since I saw my niece's pretty face. Three weeks since she gave me a cuddle and kissed my cheek and told me how much she loves me.

Three weeks is too long to be apart from her.

Suzanne has my room all ready for me to settle into. It's in the basement, but it's not gloomy. There is some natural light coming from two high-up windows, and there is even a door that opens to a steep flight of steps into the yard.

There's a bathroom down here, too, so I can keep some privacy. I mean, I love Suzanne's husband, Vernon, but it's still weird to have to see him in a towel or vice versa.

But even though I kind of have my own space, I still feel like a teenager again.

"I'm not going to unpack everything," I say to Suzanne.

"Whatever you want to do," she says patiently but with a small furrow of worry between her brows.

"I'm not going to be here for long," I say. "I need to sort myself out, get another job as quickly as possible so I won't be under your feet."

"There's no rush." Suzanne glances around at the room, which was tidy but now looks like a storage unit. "I want you to try to find something that you think is going to be really good for you. Don't rush into a job too quickly and then regret it after a couple of months."

I know she thinks that's what I did with my last job. There's no way I could tell her what happened with the principal. She'd be marching me up to the school to make a formal complaint to the board. She'd want me to report that asshole to the police, but I just don't have the strength to go through with that. It might be a coward's way out but leaving quietly and trying to pick up the pieces of my life seems a whole lot easier.

"Maybe." I say, then to change the subject, I ask, "What time are we collecting Sophie from kindergarten?

"Three o'clock," Suzanne replies. "We have time for a coffee."

I follow my sister up the stairs and make my way into the hallway that's lined with photos of Suzanne, her husband, and Sophie. In the kitchen, a bunch of beautiful flowers stands in a vase on the counter. Suzanne's husband buys them for her each week. She's so blessed to have such a happy marriage and great family life. I smile, even though my heart aches for the gaps in my own experiences.

A rack of delicious-looking muffins sits cooling under a

net umbrella. "Can I get you a muffin?" Suzanne asks before I have a chance to ask.

"Sure," I say as she readies a plate and sets the coffee pot going.

I perch at the counter, looking around this place that my sister calls home. There is so much that is familiar here.

"So, how was Connie's wedding?" Suzanne asks. "You haven't told me about what happened."

"It was lovely," I say. "Perfect, really. There was so much love there." I break a section of the muffin top away and pop it in my mouth, relishing the tart blueberry and soft, sweet cake. "I didn't make it for the ceremony. Just for the reception."

"Well, it's good you made it for that much," Suzanne says. "Breaking down in the middle of nowhere…anything could have happened. I was so worried about you."

"It was lucky that I ran into Tyler," I say. Suzanne's body freezes, her shoulders bunching as the coffee pot slowly lowers back to the counter.

She turns to face me, and I try to keep my face impassive. "You ran into Tyler?"

"Yeah. He has a repair shop now. He was the one who came to collect me in the recovery vehicle."

"Tyler, your ex-boyfriend, Tyler?"

"Yes," I say. We don't know any other Tyler but I get why Suzanne is making extra sure.

Suzanne's hand flutters to her chest, letting me know just how much the news has affected her. While Tyler was out of the picture, she could forget.

"So, what happened?"

"He took my car back to his repair shop, and then he volunteered to drive me to Connie's wedding."

"So that's how you made it?"

I fiddle with the ridged side of the plate. "Yes. I would

have missed it all if it wasn't for him. I guess fate had a plan."

"And how was he?"

I get the feeling that Suzanne's question is less about Tyler's health and wellbeing and more about what happened between us.

"Okay," I tell her. "He looks good. He's doing well for himself; he has his own business and a really nice house."

"You went to his house?"

I nod, and Suzanne inhales a quick surprised breath before she turns to finish the coffee, giving herself a moment to think without showing me her expression. I can read my sister so well.

"And how was it for you? It must have been hard to see him after all these years."

"It was," I say. "At first, I didn't know how to be. But then it was like no time had passed. It was so strange. Some things about him were the same, and some things were very different."

"That's what time does," Suzanne says, her voice light and wistful. "It changes us in ways we don't necessarily notice until something forces us to look back on the person we were before."

She's right. That moment, when I recognized Tyler, it was as though a magnifying glass shone back on the girl I was when we were together. Seeing her and feeling her again made me feel old and bruised.

Suzanne turns with a mug of coffee in her hand. "What did Carmella think when she saw him at the wedding?" She eyes me, trying to read my expression, wanting to know more than I'm sharing.

I laugh, trying to bring some lightness to the mood to the mood. "She looked like her head was about to explode. She didn't know whether to punch him in the face or hug him. It was really awkward."

"I'm surprised she didn't punch him," Suzanne says. "I would have been tempted."

"He had a reason for leaving," I say softly. "His brother was in an accident. He died."

Suzanne gasps, her hand flying to her mouth. "He was younger, wasn't he?"

I nod, feeling the burn of tears in my throat.

"So what happened to Tyler? Why did he pull away like that?"

"He blamed himself," I say. "He was grieving, and he didn't know how to do that and be with me."

"Is that what he told you?" Suzanne pulls out a stool to sit next to me. Her hand reaches out to clasp mine.

"No. He didn't speak about it. He just…his friends told me."

"So he still doesn't feel able to communicate with you," she says. "That must have been tough."

"I understand it, though." I pull my hand away and distract myself with my coffee.

"Did you tell him about you?" Suzanne asks, finally getting around to asking me the question that I know must have been burning on her tongue.

"How could I?" I say. "Tyler already blames himself for what happened to Jake. He'd never forgive himself if I told him what happened when he left."

Suzanne nods, and she inhales a deep breath, which slightly flares her nostrils. "Do you think you'll ever tell him?"

"I don't know. Before, when I didn't know where he was, it didn't seem like something I'd ever have to think about, but now…"

"Now you feel that not telling him isn't fair?" Suzanne guesses.

"Kind of. I mean, he deserves to know. But I feel like

holding this all inside me is protecting everyone. As soon as I let it out, it could be like a bomb going off. I don't want to drag everyone down."

"I understand what you're saying." Suzanne takes a bite of her muffin and chews it with a frown playing between her eyebrows. "I can't say I haven't thought about what might happen if Tyler ever came back on the scene. It's a scenario that's been with me for the past few years. I've even dreamed about it a couple of times."

"You have?"

Suzanne tucks a strand of chestnut hair behind her ear. It's the first time I've noticed that she's wearing Mom's pearl earrings. I guess she must be feeling less resentful than she used to. Maybe she's right. Time does change us. "How could I not?" she says. "So much of our lives have been wrapped up in what happened between you and Tyler. It's not just about you, is it?"

"No. It isn't."

"So, what are you planning to do?"

I don't know what to tell my sister because I have no idea. I'm a piece of driftwood, bouncing on tumultuous waves in the middle of the ocean. I can tell Suzanne wants to probe more, but she knows me well. I'll tell her in my own time. We don't usually keep secrets from one another.

Except, I don't think she'd react well to finding out what I've been doing for the past few days. She already thinks I have an innate need to self-sabotage. Maybe she's right. Feeling happiness can hurt when it's layered over unresolved pain. Maybe that's why Greg's bruising hands are those that settle me the most.

"I'm planning to try to get my life in order," I tell her.

It is my plan.

Take the easy way out.

Leave everything behind and pretend it never happened. Pretend I can wipe the slate clean and be a new

Sandy. A Sandy without baggage.

It's what I've been good at. I'm a pro at pretending.

And I think they'll let me walk away, even though what we had together was so good. Tyler will let me because he doesn't believe he deserves me, and the rest will do it out of loyalty to the man who brought us together in the first place.

32

DAMIEN

I knew that when Sandy drove away, she wasn't planning to come back. There were tears in her eyes that she tried to hide, and a hunch to her shoulders that only comes with sadness.

Since then, I've had hunched shoulders too. The memories of our time together are too sweet for me to think about without wanting to punch something, and I'm not the only one. The whole house is seething with angry, frustrated men who've had a taste of paradise and have been tossed back down to earth with a thud.

Tyler hasn't said a word about it, and none of us have discussed it in front of him. We're all treading on eggshells, wondering if he's going to change again.

There's a race tonight, and I'm worried. It shouldn't be Tyler's turn, but he's racing anyway. I'm not going to tell him he can't, and neither are the rest of the boys. If this is what he needs to do to burn out his frustration, then so be it.

I can think of worse ways.

Drugs, alcohol, gambling, women; there are other vices more dangerous for the soul than racing.

But with his mind out of the game, he's going to be more prone to making mistakes. The cars we race are kitted out for the worst, but people are fleshy, and cars, roads, and walls are hard. There is only so much you can do to prevent injury when you're traveling at such high speeds.

"What are we going to do?" Able asks me as we're bent over an engine, trying to work out where the oil is leaking from.

"Fuck knows," I say.

"One of us should go find her. Bring her back," he says.

"We don't know where she's gone," I say. "Tyler trusted her to go and come back. He wasn't planning on having to drag her back."

"I don't think that planning is one of Tyler's strongest characteristics," Able mutters. "Anyway, finding someone is easy. She's a teacher, right? A simple Google search will find her school district."

"That's not exactly narrowing it down, is it?"

"Well, it's better than nothing." He sighs, rubbing his jaw. "Wanna help me start to search?"

"I don't know," I say. "If she wanted us, she would have called. She wouldn't have driven off into the sunset without a backward glance. Even if we find her, what can we say that will change her mind. We did our best to show her how good life could be. We know she's open to the idea of a group relationship because it's her friends who are already living that way. Don't they say 'If you want someone, set them free?'"

"Yeah, they do, but this doesn't feel like we've set her free. We've let her go. There's a difference."

"You're speaking like we had a choice. We couldn't keep her at our house against her will. That shit would be kidnapping."

"I know that." Able rolls his eyes. "That's not what I'm suggesting. I guess I just wonder if we'd talked more about what we wanted. If we'd shown her more of how it could be if we were all together at the same time…"

"You think a gang bang would have solved things?" I laugh.

"Don't make it into something disgusting," Able says softly. "I mean, if we'd worshipped her the way she deserves at the very center of our group, and showed her that we are a real group, not just a house of individuals, then maybe she would have understood the possibilities more."

"Is that how this shit works?" I ask, straightening up and wiping my hands on a rag. This conversation needs focus, and I can't think when my head is close to an engine.

"I did some reading on polyamory. It depends. Some people keep the sex separate…you know…have different nights for different people. Others do everything together. I think those are the ones with more of a chance of success. There's less opportunity for jealousy or feeling left out."

I shake my head, pursing my lips. "I've never fucked in front of anyone before."

"There's nothing to it," Able says. "So long as you trust all the people involved. It's actually fucking sexy to watch and then be able to join in."

"Is that how it was with you and Arden?"

"Yeah. It was mind-blowing."

"Shit." I lean against the car, folding my arms as I realize that Able isn't talking shit. Maybe we did go wrong in keeping things so separate. We were trying not to scare

Sandy, but with hindsight, she really doesn't seem like the kind of woman who'd scare easily. Her friends are already living this life, and I know what women are like. They share a lot of information about sex, especially when it's good.

"I think we should find her. We need to at least try to bring her back," Able says.

"Okay. I'll help you try."

Later, Tyler and Arden drive the cars to race. Arden has a hard-on to win tonight, and so does Tyler. The problem is that Arden's eyes are alert, and Tyler looks dead. There are purple smudges beneath his eyes which tell me he hasn't been sleeping. No one should race if they're not one hundred percent engaged.

"He's fucked," I whisper to Greg.

"I know," Greg says, crossing his arm and shaking his head as Tyler slumps low over the steering wheel. "As soon as I saw that girl, I knew this was coming."

"You think Sandy's trouble?"

He shakes his head, his jaw ticking as he grits his teeth. "She's not trouble. She's what he needs. She's what we all need. Except Tyler's too messed up to be with anyone, let alone someone who was in his life before Jake."

"He feels like he's fucked things up twice," I say.

Behind us, some douchebags crank up their music loud. Hardcore rap isn't my thing, but it fits with the atmosphere tonight. I'm already wound tight, and the music just makes the tension in my spine worse.

I know what would make everything better. Pushing my cock inside Sandy's sweet pussy. Spilling my seed inside her and watching her come apart with pleasure. I swear her body was made for mine. Soft in all the places that I'm hard. Curvy in the places I'm tapered.

Why doesn't she see that?

"Tyler's up," Greg says, stepping forward and leaning closer to the car.

"Ty, you got this?" he asks.

Tyler nods, his eyes fixed to the dark road ahead. "I've got this," he says, but I don't believe him. His fingers twitch on the steering wheel, and his foot presses the accelerator, revving the engine so hard it screams. Fumes fill the air as he grits his teeth.

He's doing this because he needs to win at something. He needs something to go his way.

He needs to not feel guilty, even if it's for a minute of rubber-burning speed.

"You sure, Ty?" I say.

He turns his head slowly, and when his eyes meet mine, a shiver runs through me. I haven't seen him look this dark since the night Jake died. All the color in his eyes has been obliterated by the storm cloud of emotions in his heart.

"I've got nothing to lose," he says.

"That's not fucking true," Greg hisses. "You've got a whole fucking lot to lose, you hear me? You better tell me that the last statement was a fucking joke, or I'm going to yank you out of that car so fast you'll fly."

Tyler blinks slowly. "Let me do what I need to do."

Before Greg has a chance to do anything, Tyler is pulling forward, taking his place next to the asshole he's racing.

Greg swears under his breath. "I know he's a grown man, but hell, sometimes I feel like I'm taking care of a younger brother."

"I know what you mean," I say. A flash of my brother's face fills my mind. I pray for him every morning, though I don't know who I'm asking to keep him safe.

I say the same prayer now for Tyler, and when I'm

done, I turn away from the road. My heart can't take watching what feels like a race of self-sabotage. "Able thinks we should go after Sandy. He thinks we should try and find her and convince her to come back. What do you think?" I ask Greg.

"That woman has a secret. You've gotta find out what's keeping her buttoned up so tight and what's stopping her from loving like I know she wants to."

"A secret."

Greg nods, and I don't question how he knows. That man has more instinct than anyone I've ever met.

The sounds of tires spinning make me jump. Tyler's and his rival's cars screech into the distance, leaving dust and exhaust fumes and a whole bundle of worry behind them.

Andrew and Able are at the finish. They'll be the first to know if anything goes wrong. I count in my head the seconds it will take for Tyler to make it safely over the line. I count as my heart races double-time, the anticipation that his tiredness and hopelessness might damage his concentration clenching my stomach. Greg stands next to me, facing Tyler's wake. Maybe Greg has more courage than me to face up to the darkness in life. He's seen a whole lot more of the worst of humanity than all of us, and sometimes I wonder if it's permanently damaged his ability to feel.

When cheering sounds at the other end, and a message flashes on my phone from Andrew that Tyler is safe and sound, Greg turns to me. "We've got to get Sandy back," he says. "There's no alternative. There's no going back to what it was like before. Not for Tyler. Not for me."

"Not for any of us," I say, remembering Andrew's pained face at breakfast and Arden's jittery leg at lunch. We all need Sandy more than is good for us.

But isn't that what the best relationships are built on?

33

SANDY

My first night sleeping at Suzanne's, I have strange dreams of cars racing toward me with headlights so bright that it's impossible for me to make out the driver. Each time, I brace myself for impact, but the car disappears before it reaches me, and I'm left reeling from shock. I wake with sweat on my chest and a racing heart, completely unsettled.

I remember the street race that Greg and Tyler took part in. Is that where this dream has come from? Is it just a strange recollection, or is it something more? I didn't like the jittery way Tyler was when he was racing. Now I know what happened to Jake, I wonder why this is even something that Tyler is considering doing?

Doesn't he worry about losing his life as his brother did?

Is he testing fate by throwing himself down the exact pathway that ended Jake?

The thought makes me sick.

Suzanne is at work, and Sophie's at kindergarten by the time I stumble into the kitchen. I make myself a coffee and a bowl of sugary cereal and perch at the counter, trying not to let my mind wander back to another morning where I did the exact same thing.

I have two important tasks to do today. One is to polish my résumé so that I can send it out to as many recruiters and websites as possible. The other is to call Luna so that I can find out what she needs. I may have walked away from Tyler, but that doesn't mean I'll forget my promise. If this is the one thing that I can do to help Tyler and his sister, then it's what I'm going to do.

After breakfast, I shower and dress quickly, determined to keep busy while I'm alone in the house without the distraction of other people. My résumé doesn't take me long. All I need to do is add my last employer. When I type the school's name, I shudder, remembering hands on my flesh that I didn't ask to be there and the odor of stale coffee breath and breath mint that haunts my nightmares. But it's the recall of that asshole's smirk as he told me I wouldn't be coming back next year that makes me want to cry. I really loved my colleagues, and the kids at the school were awesome.

It isn't fair that I'm the one who got punished when it was him who acted inappropriately.

When I'm done sending the résumés, I tab through my phone for Luna's number. I'm not expecting her to answer immediately. She must be ridiculously busy planning and rehearsing for her tour. Maybe I'll catch her mail service, and I can leave a message. When her crystal-clear voice answers with a bright "Hello," I'm momentarily paralyzed.

"Hello?" she repeats, sounding uncertain, then before I have a chance to reply she yells, "Listen, you asshole. Stop calling me. Stop messaging me. Stop the harassment. You've already been reported to the police, and if my bodyguards catch you, they're going to tear you limb from limb, do you understand me?"

"LUNA," I yell over the end of her tirade. "It's me, Sandy."

The phone is quiet for a moment, and then she mumbles, "Sorry…I…uh…I just get fed up with assholes finding out my personal number and calling me at all hours of the day and night."

"Does that really happen?"

"You have no idea." I can imagine her grimacing on the end of the line, her little nose scrunching. It's funny how we all look at the celebrity lifestyle as something awesome when there must be so many downsides to being in the public eye.

"Well, I was calling to see what I can do to help you with your mom."

Luna sighs softly. "You're such a sweetheart, and I feel so terrible for railing on you at Tyler's. It just caught me off guard, and I'm so stressed with everything that's happening. I just feel like my life isn't in my hands anymore."

"I get that," I say.

"But you know what? Tyler called me last night. He said he's going to deal with Mom. It's a big relief."

"Are you sure Tyler is up to it?" I say, remembering his face when Luna asked him the first time.

"He said he is. I mean, there really isn't so much to do, and Mom is a lot better than she was before."

"Well, if you're sure."

"I am. I think it will be good for Ty. He's been so withdrawn since Jake. He blames himself, but he also blames our parents. I guess if they weren't such fuck-ups, we might have all been living different lives. Jake was the youngest. He didn't get the support he needed."

"Tyler didn't either. He was the oldest, and the

responsibility was a lot for him."

"He never showed it," Luna says. "It always seemed as though he enjoyed being the one to make the big decisions."

"Those decisions weigh heavy on someone so young."

She doesn't know how much I'm speaking from experience. How I fumbled my way through my challenges four years ago, I'll never know.

"Well, I think he'll be okay. Maybe you can support him?" She sounds hopeful, and it puts a sharp, round lump into my throat.

"I think Tyler is better off without me," I say.

"I think you're crazy." I can hear rustling on the other end of the line and then voices. For a while, Luna's attention is drawn away from our conversation, and I dig my nails into my palm, waiting. Eventually, she clears her throat. "I know how happy Tyler was when you guys were together. It was like someone stuck a megawatt bulb up his ass. He was always smiling."

"But it wouldn't be the same now," I say. "Too much has happened."

"He still loves you," she says. "He never stopped."

"He doesn't know me anymore." The hitch in my voice is loud enough for Luna to hear, and she's quiet for a while.

"I always had this idea in my mind about what love is," she says softly. "I don't know where I got it from because I certainly didn't see it at home. The kind of love that I want is the love that sees all the good and all the bad and exists anyway. A forgiving love. An accepting love. I know my brother, and that's the kind of man he is. Whatever is making you think that he won't love the person you are now…maybe you should just tell him and let him decide."

"But what if knowing will hurt him?" I ask. "What if it could change everything?"

"What have you got to lose?"

I rub my forehead, the stress of the conversation starting to bring on a headache. "It's not only me that has something to lose," I say. "That's the problem."

There's more talking in the background at Luna's end, and more shuffling noises. "I've got to go," she says. "I'm sorry. I wish I could say something that would make things easier. I guess you're the only one who can decide what's best. It just seems sad to let love go."

"Thanks, Luna, and good luck on your tour."

"Thanks, Sandy."

When she hangs up, I place the phone on my desk, her words ringing in my ears. It is a terrible thing to let love go, but sometimes, we have to hurt ourselves to do what's best for the people we love. Tyler deserves that from me.

At least, I thought he did.

I thought he was too damaged to deal with his mom, but it seems he's had a change of heart.

Could he be strong enough to hear my secrets and not allow them to cause irreparable damage?

The only way I'll know is to go back but it's been days and I haven't called. They'll be mad as hell.

I miss them all so much. I wish I knew what to do.

After everything that's happened, maybe they won't want me back.

34

GREG

Tyler is fucked.

I don't mean he's sitting around crying or lying in bed depressed.

He did plenty of that after Jake, and I knew how to deal with it, but this, I'm not so sure.

On the outside, he seems fine. He's working. He's speaking to customers and dealing with work issues. I heard him on the phone to Luna last night agreeing to take care of their mom while Luna's on tour. To the untrained eye, he's functioning fine.

But I know Tyler. His eyes are dark, like the bright green of them has been swamped by his internal troubles. His hands are too quick, and his leg jitters when he's sitting. He's wired in a way I've never seen him before, wound tight with the stress of Sandy leaving.

It's because of Tyler that I have no qualms about doing what I'm doing.

Chasing a woman who's walked away isn't my style. If

I've treated her right and she doesn't want what I've got to offer, then I'd rather she walked away.

But this isn't just about me.

Tyler needs Sandy.

We all do.

And Sandy needs us too.

I know it. I feel it in a part of my chest that has been quiet for so long.

"I called the school," Able says. "The receptionist said most of the teachers are on vacation, but some of the senior team are around."

"You really think they're going to tell us anything about Sandy? There's got to be a whole lot of privacy regulations, hasn't there."

"I guess I'm hoping that between my charm and your menacing stare, we might get something out of someone. Maybe a colleague?"

"I reckon we're going to leave this place with nothing, but we've got to try," I say.

When we pull into the parking lot, I'm filled with a sense of unease that I can't explain. We stroll toward the large double doors at the front entrance, and I'm glancing from side to side, scanning for trouble. It's just instinct that comes from too many bad experiences, even though we're in a place that's supposed to be safe for kids.

Able doesn't seem to be worried. He walks ahead of me with his eyes fixed on the entrance. With around twenty steps still to go, a woman emerges from the building, struggling to balance a box and push the doors open with her back.

"Here, let me help you," Able says, speeding up into a jog and grabbing the door. The woman who must be in her fifties smiles at him with wide, appreciative eyes.

"Oh, thank you," she says. "I knew this box was too heavy for me, but I didn't want to make two trips."

"That's okay." Able shoots her a panty-melting grin, his blue eyes sparkling in the sunshine. He's pulling out all the stops to charm her. "Actually, you might be able to help us. We're looking for Sandy Dawson. Is she in today?"

The smile drops from the woman's face, and her arms falter. Able is there to grab the box before it falls, and I'm immediately filled with unease. "She's not here," the woman says. She glances back into the school and then around the yard as though she's worried about being overheard. "Could you help me to my car?" She begins to walk to the right without waiting for Able to agree, and we follow closely. She has a large burgundy people carrier. The trunk creaks when it's opened. It needs some lubricant, but I don't have any in the car, or I'd offer to help her out too.

Again, she glances around furtively as Able loads the box into the car. "Are you friends of Sandy's?"

"Yeah. We're friends of Sandy and her sister Suzanne," Able says smoothly. Clever to add the reassuring mention of Sandy's family. The woman's shoulders relax a little, taken in by Able's easy manner, but she glances at me as though she's unsure whether she should be speaking in front of such a tattooed brute. I smile awkwardly, trying to be reassuring even though it's doubtful I'll achieve it. My look was designed to scare people away, not encourage them to open up with their secrets. But then she takes a deep breath and talks, and I realize that I haven't totally fucked things up.

"I'm so upset about what happened to Sandy," she whispers, even though there is nobody around to overhear us. "If I could manage without this job, I would have walked out of here with her, but things are difficult at home. My husband hasn't worked for a while. I'm the only one bringing in any money right now." Able nods as though he knows what she's talking about, even we have no idea. "There have been rumors about Principal Gregory for a while, but I always thought they were stirred up by people who were jealous of his success. Then, when I found Sandy crying in the hallway after he groped her, well, I knew the rumors were true. Sandy isn't the kind to lie about something like that. She was distraught."

What the fuck? My fingers flex into tightly held fists, and my whole body goes rigid with fury. The principal groped Sandy, and she was crying. I want to tear the asshole's head from his neck.

"That must have been hard," Able says, and I can tell from the tight sound to his voice that he's holding back his own anger in order to find out more.

"It was so hard. I told her she needed to report him to the police. I told her I'd go with her for support, you know…but she wouldn't hear it. She just…she told me that she didn't want to make any trouble. That girl… she's just too sweet for her own good."

"So she didn't report him?"

The woman shakes her head, her short red curls bouncing. Her round face is tinged with pink, maybe from the excitement of telling her story or her frustration about what happened to Sandy. "She just went home. The next thing I heard is that her contract wasn't being renewed. I knew it was that asshole getting his own back because she rejected his advances."

"He fired her because she wouldn't let him touch her?" I growl. Able stares at me, his eyes widening in a warning.

"Exactly." The woman shakes her shoulders as though she's getting worked up. "That asshole is on holiday right now enjoying himself, and poor Sandy has to look for another job. She even had to move out of her apartment."

"That was going to be our next question," Able says, picking up on the opportunity. "We went past her place, but there was someone else living there." It's a lie but plausible and adds to our credibility.

"Well, she's over on Hanover Street at her sister's."

"It's been a while since we visited, and we wanted it to be a surprise…you know…to cheer Sandy up. What was the door number again?"

"It's sixteen," the woman says without hesitation or concern. "I hope you'll manage to cheer her up. It must be so hard for her to try to find another job with all of this hanging over her."

"We'll do our best," Able says, shooting her another megawatt grin. "Now, is there anything else we can help you with?"

"You're such a sweetheart," the woman says with a blush. "But no. I struggled to bring everything out in one go. Thank goodness you were here to help."

"Well, ma'am, thank you for all your help," he says with a bow of his head. When he turns to face me, he mouths, *let's get out of here*, so that's what we do. When we're back in the truck, Able exhales and shakes his head. "I can't believe Sandy's been going through all of this, and she never said a thing."

"She didn't want to burden us," I say. "She's that kind of person who feels like sharing anything less than sunshine and roses is overstepping."

"She's gotten used to dealing with her trouble on her own," Able says. "Haven't we all."

I nod because he's right. The more we suffer and look around for help and find none available, the less we ever want to rely on others in the future. Maybe Tyler is responsible for this trait in Sandy. Maybe, if we can show her that we'll help her deal with her troubles, she'll come around to needing us.

"What should we do now?" I ask him.

"I think we should head over there. I think we need

to *really* talk to Sandy."

"I think you're right." In my chest, my heart thuds faster at the thought of seeing her again. Yes, it might be awkward. Yes, it might take a lot of work to change her mind. Yes, we have a lot to prove, but I'm going to make damned sure that we give it our all.

Sandy's sister lives ten minutes from the school. It's getting on to lunchtime, and my stomach rumbles. As we get closer, my nerves seem to buzz, like she's a magnet, and my body is beginning to feel her tug. "We're doing the right thing, right?" Able says as though he's feeling it too.

"What have we got to lose?" It's what I keep telling myself. It's what's driven me to come on this wild-goose chase. The greatest risk is that she tells us to fuck off. Or maybe something else. Maybe she has a boyfriend she didn't disclose. Maybe she sees everything that happened as a big mistake. My confidence falters over the last few minutes of the journey, which isn't like me at all. It tells me everything I need to know about how I feel about Sandy.

Able drives slow so we can find Suzanne's house. It's a nice, whitewashed place with a wrap-around porch and swing. There are some children's toys in a basket. Sandy must be an auntie. Able parks up on the opposite side of the road and exhales long and deep as he drops his hands from the wheel. "I have no idea how this is going to go," he says.

"Neither do I, but we gotta do it." I throw the door open, stepping into the midday sunshine. I roll my shoulders and flex my hands like I'm getting ready for a fight. It's an unconscious thing, which I stop as soon as I start to bounce on the balls of my feet. I guess this is how I exhibit nerves. Able locks up and then joins me to cross the road.

We both stare up at the house, wondering if Sandy's in one of the upstairs windows looking down on us. Will she pretend she's not home even though her car's out front? If nothing else, I'm happy to confirm that the repairs we made to it got her home safely.

The front door is painted a bluey-green color and there's a black metal knocker that I leave Able to use. I don't trust myself not to be too rough.

We wait for a few seconds, ears craning to hear what's going on inside. "I'm coming," a voice rings out, and there are thuds from inside, which sound like someone running up the stairs. The front door opens, and there is Sandy, dressed in yoga pants and my old band shirt, her hair in a messy bun. It's like stepping from a dark cave into desert sunshine. My heart feels warm at the sight of her, but as soon as she sees us, her face drops, and so does all of my hope.

35

TYLER

I'm doing something I never thought I'd do, and I don't know how to feel about it. Parked up in front of the address my mom now calls home, I'm taking a few deep breaths before I head on in there to fulfill my promise to my sister.

This is more about Luna than it is about Kaylee. People say that family is important, and it is, to a certain extent. When you have amazing relatives who you can rely on, family should be the center of your universe. Jake and Luna were always that for me. Mom and Dad, not so much.

Adults should be responsible. They should put their kids first. They should care enough about the impact they have to try their best to overcome their difficulties. That was the problem with my parents. They were selfish. They didn't give a thought to what their addictions were doing to our childhoods, and I can't forgive that lack of care.

I could forgive the weakness.

We all have it in our souls in one way or another. None of us is perfect. Like Achilles had his heel, we all nurse the soft parts of us that don't cope well with life.

Men aren't supposed to admit to things like that. We're taught that any kind of weakness makes us lesser. Tears are feminine. Depression is something for weaklings, not real men. I believed it for a long time, too. My grief consumed me, and I hated myself for allowing it. In a way, dwelling in my darkness became a way to escape the reality of everything Jake's death had cost me. I was never going to have another brother. I was never going to have another girl like Sandy in my life. I was never going to forget the guilt that came with an older brother's responsibility when there are no parents.

It made me hate my mom even more than I already did.

If she'd been around, if she'd chosen a better man and held our family together, then nothing would be as it is.

The thing is, over time, I've realized that the knocks we have—the potholes on our road—make us who we are. There's no joy without sorrow. There's no wisdom without learning hard lessons. I'll always miss my brother, but there's no going back. Greg told me that Jake would be pissed at me. He was a young man who loved life, and he'd be mad as hell to watch me wasting mine. Seeing Luna again and making peace with her has made me realize that there are still people in my life whom I love and who love me. I may have lost my blood brother, but I have five of the best-acquired brothers a man could ever have.

The only thing I can't get back is Sandy.

It's not fair to ask. I did my best to try to keep her. I gave her the most important people in my life, but it didn't work. The pain in her eyes was so evident when she stared into mine. Putting pressure on her just isn't the right thing to do.

DEEP 6

I fling open the door to my truck, my big black boots hitting the ground with a loud purposeful thud. Sandy has her reasons, and the best thing I can do is leave her in peace.

From inside the house, I can hear loud music. The song is familiar. Something my mom has been playing since my childhood. Something that used to accompany her worst binges. Luna's only been gone a day. Has she already relapsed in that time?

I bang my fist on the door decisively. Whatever is inside, I'm going to deal with it. I'm not the disappointed little boy anymore. I'm a man who can look at the situation without emotion.

At first, there is no response. I bang again, and a man's voice grumbles from inside. Then I hear an expletive, and I try the handle. The door swings on its hinges with too much ease and the smell from inside hits me in the face.

Cigarettes, alcohol, stale bodies, and old food. It smells like a dorm after a party, except this house is where a middle-aged woman lives. I take a step inside, glancing around. In the den, I can see a man's feet sticking out from behind a couch. To the right is the kitchen and two more steps tells me it's empty apart from the discarded beer bottles on the floor. The stairs rise to the first floor, and I take them two at a time, not caring who I might discover or what they might be engaged in. I made a promise to my sister, and I'll handle whatever I find.

There are two doors at the top. Luna secured the lease on this place, and it would be nice if anyone else was living here. Mom is too busy fucking up her life to deal with chores. I peek into the room on the left, but it's empty. In the room on the right, I find mom face down on her bed. For a moment, I think she's dead. She's finally taken things too far. She still has the same emaciated frame and lank hair, and everything about her screams addict. But then her chest rises, and I know she's just sleeping.

I don't go any closer. Instead, I turn, jog down the stairs and out into the front yard, drawing in lungfuls of fresh air.

Pulling out my phone, I dial Damien's number. It doesn't take me long to explain what I need. When he hangs up, I lean against my truck.

I can't save my mom, but what I can do is bring in some cleaners to sort out the house and some good food to fill her fridge. I can get my boys down here to help me remove whoever the swearing scumbag is in the den. I can toss out all the drugs I can find and spend half an hour trying to persuade Mom not to go back to her dealer.

And after that, I'll go home and get on with my life. Until Luna's back, I'll check in on her weekly as I promised. Kaylee's lasted this long. She'll probably outlast us all.

I may not be the best son in the world, but I'll try to do what I can.

36

SANDY

I don't know who I was expecting to find standing on my doorstep in the middle of the day, but it sure wasn't Able and Greg. Well, if I'd had to guess which of the six boys from Deep Repairs would have come after me, Able would have been top of my list. Greg would have been bottom, and yet he's here, looking at me with his intense black eyes, turning my heart inside out.

"What are you doing here?" I ask. It tumbles out of my mouth on a wave of shock and embarrassment. I left thinking I wouldn't have to face them again.

Nothing in my life ever goes to plan.

Greg takes a step forward, and I automatically take a step back. That carries on until he's through the front door, and I'm almost backed against the stair rail, my hands hanging limply at my sides. Able follows and closes the door behind him softly. "Did something happen to Tyler?" I gasp. That has to be why they've come. I left, knowing he was low. Did I push him to do something stupid?

"Tyler's fine," Able says. "Well, not fine, but alive."

I grasp the handrail behind me, the bottom falling out of my world. "Is he hurt? Did something happen at the race?"

"He's fine," Greg growls. "You fucked up his heart, but that's it."

Fucked up his heart. It's said with a menace that chills me to the bone. It's not that I fear these men, far from it. I know they'd lay down their lives for me if they had to. It's just that hearing the impact of me leaving is so hard.

"I'm sorry," I blurt.

"Sorry?" Greg takes a step closer. He's so close that I can smell the washing power smell that clings to his shirt and sense the power coiled inside his body. I can't look at him, so I keep my eyes at the level of his throat. He doesn't like that, though. When his finger rests gently under my chin so that he can tip my face up, everything in me seems to still. He's like a conductor, waving his stick to control the orchestra of my soul.

When our eyes meet, it brings back the moment he slid his cock inside me. His stare penetrates in a way that is raw and explicit, and I feel bare before him.

"Why did you leave?" he asks huskily. "Was it something we did?"

I shake my head, and he lowers his lids, his nostrils flaring slightly as he draws in a breath.

"Was it something we didn't do?" he asks. When I shake my head, his brow furrows. "Then what was it?"

I'm so taken up by Greg's intensity that I haven't noticed Able has turned to look at the photos on the wall in the hall. It's not until he gasps that I realize what's happened.

The very thing I didn't want to happen.

DEEP 6

He knows.

Greg turns to his friend, wondering what the fuss is about. Able turns from the most recent picture of Sophie taken at kindergarten. The photo that stabbed me in the heart when Sophie bought it home because there's no hiding it.

Sophie might be a little girl, but she's the image of her daddy, cat-green eyes and all.

It takes Greg a little longer to figure out what Able is seeing, and by the time they both turn to me, my hands are shaking. The strength seems to leave my legs, and I fall back, landing on the stairs. They're there in a second—Able next to me and Greg kneeling in front of me—expressions genuinely concerned.

Greg's hand on my shoulder is there to make sure I don't fall. Able takes my hand in his warm palm. "Are you okay?" he asks. "Do you feel dizzy?" Dizzy is not the right word. Overwhelmed is better. Filled with dread too. What's going to happen now? When I shake my head, Greg sighs. I can't tell if it's from relief or frustration.

"She's Tyler's?" he murmurs, and my instinct is to press my face into my palm.

"Yes," I whisper.

"You came back because of her?"

I want to say yes. I wish I could tell him that I'm her momma and I needed to come back to care for her, but it wouldn't be true. I'm Auntie Sandy. Sophie has a mom and a dad, and they aren't Tyler or me.

Able squeezes the hand he's still clutching. "You could have told him," he says softly. "It would have been a shock, but he'd have been happy."

"Happy?" I spit. "Happy? Nothing about this situation is going to bring any of us happiness."

"What do you mean?" Greg says. "You think Tyler won't want his daughter? You guys come as a package deal.

We get that. Tyler will get that. He'll be over the moon, Sandy."

"Over the moon..." I shake my head, and a tear leaks from my eye, dropping onto my yoga pants, leaving a dark stain of my sorrow. "You shouldn't have come here," I whisper. "You don't know what you're stirring up. You have no idea."

"SO TELL US," Greg growls. It's the first time he's raised his voice in front of me, and Able gives him a warning look.

"MY SISTER ADOPTED HER!" I shout, then I grit my teeth, knowing that I'm going to have to explain without breaking down. "When Tyler left, I didn't have a way of supporting us. I was still at college. My heart was broken. I just couldn't deal with what was happening to me...and my sister can't have kids, so she offered to take Sophie. It was the best solution at the time, but now..."

"Now you've found Tyler again..." Able says softly.

"I've found Tyler, but nothing's changed. He's not ready for this. Finding out that he walked out on me when I was pregnant is going to kill him. Finding out his daughter was adopted and now calls another man Dad...what do you think that's going to do to him?"

The hall is silent. Able and Greg sit in what I'm assuming is shock, and I feel like a weight has been lifted from my shoulders. I'm not carrying this burden of knowledge by myself anymore. I don't have to make this huge decision in isolation. Now they know they're going to have to help me.

"Where is she now?" Able asks eventually.

"At kindergarten. She won't be back until later."

He nods and then puts his arm around my shoulders, pulling me into his chest and kissing me on the top of my head. Greg rests his big hand with HATE on the knuckles on my knee, but there is no hate in his gesture. Just care.

"You should have told us," Greg murmurs eventually. "Even if you felt like you couldn't tell Tyler, you should have told one of us. You just left and didn't come back." His thumb moves back and forth over my knee as though he's trying to soothe me, and it's too much. Greg's hands are about power and control. They're about toughness and safety, not about tenderness. The lump that burns in my throat comes from the realization that I've hurt him.

I never imagined that was a possibility.

"I couldn't," I whisper, resting my hand over his. "Your loyalties lie with Tyler, not with me. This connection between us was all new. I couldn't risk dumping such a massive thing into the midst of your lives, especially when Tyler was still so volatile."

"You could," Able says. "We would have done our best to help you in whatever you decided."

"You would never have kept it a secret from Tyler, though, would you? I couldn't have asked that of you."

"And now we know…" Greg looks back at the photo as though he needs to confirm that what he saw is real.

"Now you know, Tyler will have to know too." Saying the words brings it all crashing down on me. This isn't just about Tyler and me and our past, this is about Suzanne and her husband, and most importantly, it's about Sophie. Little Sophie, who looks so much like her daddy that it's uncanny.

"It'll be okay," Able is quick to say. "Tyler's not as bad as you think. He's gone to take care of his mom today."

"I never thought I'd see the day," Greg says, shaking his head.

"I know," I tell them. "Luna told me."

"So you know he's facing up to his challenges…"

I sigh, taking my hand from Greg's and worry at the hangnail on my thumb. "This isn't a challenge. It's the lives of five people.

"Ten," Greg says softly. When I meet his eyes, it's like looking into a child's room at night. There's darkness there, but softness and comfort too.

"Will he want to get to know her?" I ask, even though I know the answer. Of course he will. How could he resist the gorgeous little girl we made when we were young and in love before all the hurt and grief caught us in its ugly web.

"Of course he will," Able says.

"Will he be angry with me?"

Greg shakes his head. "He'll be angry with himself, but that will pass because he'll have her to spend time with."

"I feel like there is so much that has happened. So much that has broken both our hearts."

Able squeezes my shoulders. "You know, Sandy, over your life, your heart is going to break so many times. That's just how it is. But you can't sit around sifting through the shards. You have to realize that in the end, it's all of the broken and whole pieces that make up the beautiful mosaic of our lives."

I turn to him, so in awe of the lovely truth that pours out of him, and I know what I have to do. "I need to talk to my sister, and then I'll come back and tell Tyler everything. It's the only way we have a chance of being together."

"And that's what you want?" Greg asks, the hopefulness a vulnerable edge to his usually gruff voice.

"It is," I say. "It really is."

His hand touches my cheek before he presses his lips against mine. It's a gentle kiss. Gentler than any we've shared before, and I slide into it like slipping into warm water. When Greg pulls back, I turn to Able and reach for him, hooking my hand around his neck. His kiss is as sweet as fairground candy, and with it, some of the ache drifts from my heart.

DEEP 6

And although this decision is only one small step in the difficulties to come, I feel as though a huge weight has already been lifted from my shoulders.

37

TYLER

Greg and Able have been gone all day. Andrew and Arden made excuses for them that were thin and implausible, but I didn't dig too deep. Wherever they are and whatever they're doing, I trust them with my life.

It's after dark, and I'm sitting at the kitchen counter with a beer, decompressing after finally settling Mom into her cleaned house. I don't have the energy to call Luna, and to be honest, I don't want to share the state I found Mom in. Luna's tour is taking her far and wide, and wherever she is, she's too remote to make any kind of difference here. I don't want to worry her unnecessarily.

I hear the sound of a truck in the driveway and then the rumble of a smaller engine—big heavy feet crunch on the driveway as well as some smaller, lighter ones. I don't want to hope that maybe it's Sandy outside because the disappointment would be too great if it wasn't. Still, a little part of me will always hold out that she'll come back to me again.

When the front door clicks, I glance up, finding Greg and Able coming through the door, and then it's held open for another person.

The sight of Sandy in the doorway is like the sun rising on a clear day. My eyes seem to need a moment to adjust before my brain really accepts the truth. She's here. They've brought her back.

I'm happy until I take in her expression. She's worried. Nervous. Her hands are clasped in front of her, and she's twisting them. I search Greg and Able's faces, and they both look as though they're holding secrets; tight-lipped, eyes slightly wider than normal. I don't know what's going on but after the day I've had, I hope it's nothing serious.

Standing, I cross the room, and rather than speak, I wrap my arms around the only girl who's ever held my heart. She's as stiff as a board for a couple of seconds, then Sandy relaxes against me and wraps her arms tightly around my back. My eyes meet Greg's, and he nods. I've done the right thing, and so has he. He went to fetch my girl back, and she's here.

I want to feel happy, but this isn't a gushing reunion. There's something weighing on Sandy. Something that has her trembling in my arms, and when Able and Greg motion to Andrew, Arden, and Damien to leave the room, I know I'm about to find out what it is.

Drawing away from Sandy, I clutch her upper arms in my hands, searching her face. "You came back."

She nods, only maintaining fleeting eye contact, then she takes a step back and makes her way over to the couch. She slumps down, so she's perched on the edge, clasping her hands again. "I need to talk to you," she says softly. "I've been psyching myself up for it the entire journey, playing out a million conversations in my head, trying to find the right way to tell you something."

"You don't need to do that," I say, moving to sit next to her but leaving a space between us. "You don't need to worry about how to talk to me. Just tell me…whatever it is."

Her shoulders rise as she takes in a deep breath. Her fingers twist, wrapping themselves around each other, then untwist again. A sense of panic bubbles in my chest. Is she sick? Is that why she left and didn't come back? If she thinks I wouldn't love her…or that she'd be a burden to us if she's not in full health, she's wrong. This thing between us can't just be about good times. It has to be about all the times; happy and sad, easy and difficult.

Sandy's eyes stay low, but if that's what it takes to help her speak, then so be it. "When you left, I didn't know where you'd gone. I tried calling you, but you never picked up. I was so worried."

"I'm sorry," I say. "I just, I wasn't thinking…I was out of my mind."

"I know that now," she says softly. "But at the time, it broke my heart. I didn't get out of bed for weeks. My sister…she came and got me and took me to stay with her. She helped me through it."

Reaching out, I touch her knee. "I'm sorry."

"You don't have to keep saying that," she says. "I'm not here because I'm searching for an apology. I'm here to tell you what happened after."

"Okay," I say.

"By the time I began to function again, I realized that I had missed my period. I thought it was because I was so heartbroken…you know, things like that can mess with a woman's body, but…"

Sandy trails off, her fingers knotting again, and my heart clenches because I think I know what she's going to say. She was pregnant and she had an abortion. Fuck.

I don't think I could deal with my part in that. Jake died, and I left…I was responsible.

"…but Suzanne, she made me take a pregnancy test,

and it was positive."

I feel like my heart has dropped into my stomach. "I left you to deal with this alone. I…If I'd known."

"I know that now," she says quickly, "but at the time, I thought you didn't love me."

"That wasn't it," I snap, needing her to know. "I loved you. I still love you, Sandy. Nothing will change that. Nothing you can say will make it different…"

"You can't know that," Sandy says, shaking her head, but she continues regardless as though she wound herself up like an old-fashioned toy, and now she's going to speak until the end of her planned speech. "I didn't know what I was going to do, and then Suzanne asked me if I'd consider letting her adopt the baby."

"Adopt?" I shake my head, trying to let everything sink in. "You had the baby? You didn't terminate it?"

Sandy turns to me, blinking slowly. "That's what you thought? No, I didn't have a termination. I had the baby…a little girl…and I let my sister adopt and raise her."

"You had a little girl. I'm a father?" My hand reaches out to touch Sandy's knee. It's an automatic reaction…a need for connection to the woman delivering such overwhelming news.

Sandy nods, and then her face falls, and she shakes her head. "Sophie has a father…my sister's husband. She has a mother…my sister Suzanne. I'm her fun Auntie San San…" Her body seems to crumple, and a tear runs down her cheek. "I gave her up, and I know…I know you're not going to be able to forgive me."

"Forgive?" The word drops out of my mouth with shock. Is that what she's worried about? Me blaming her for doing what she had to because I wasn't there to support her? If I need to forgive someone, it's going to be me. "I have a child, Sandy. We have a child." My voice is breathy and filled with awe and it's enough to make her turn and stare at me. "You don't hate me?"

"For what?"

"For not being there for you?"

Sandy's brow forms a deep frown. "I can't hate you for that. You didn't leave willingly or maliciously. You left because of something terrible. I could never hate you for that."

The tight feeling in my chest seems to ease a little, but I still have so many questions. "What does Sophie look like?"

Sandy reaches for her purse that fell to the floor when she sat. She opens her wallet, and inside is a small picture of a little green-eyed girl who looks like me. I don't consciously snatch it from Sandy's fingers. It's the deep fascination within me that drives my hand to seize the wallet so I can bring it closer and take in this little flesh and blood part of me that I didn't realize existed all these years. Although she looks like my double, there is also very clearly something Sandy-ish about her too. Her smile, maybe, but her eyes, her hair, and the rest of her face are mine.

A small sound of amazement leaves my lips. "She's perfect," I say with awe. "Absolutely perfect."

"She is," Sandy says. "She's such a good girl and really smart."

"She's smart?"

"Yeah…she's reading already and counting well. I think she's at least a year ahead of expectations."

"Wow…she definitely takes that from you," I say, smiling.

Sandy blinks, her eyes still watery. "I spoke to my sister about telling you. She is obviously worried about what is going to happen next…if you're going to want to meet Sophie…what that might look like…what your expectations are, you know?"

"I'd love to meet her," I say. "But I understand that she's been adopted, and she's only little. There will come a time for us to be transparent with her, but it isn't yet."

"She knows she grew in my tummy because her mommy can't grow a baby," Sandy says. "I guess we can explain that you put your seed in my belly to help. It's the truth, at least. The rest can come later. If that's okay with you?"

"Will your sister be okay with that?" I ask. It's more than I could have hoped for under the circumstances.

"She will. She's nervous, understandably. She doesn't want anything to hurt Sophie, but I know you won't want that either. We just have to do whatever it takes so that she's not unsettled."

"Definitely," I say. I bring the picture closer to me again and use my finger to trace the little face I see there. There is something in her sparkling eyes that reminds me of Jake, too, and that fills my heart. "You know she was growing in your belly before Jake died," I say. "When he passed, I thought I'd lost everything, but now I see that something else just as precious came into my life. I just didn't know it then."

Sandy's eyes are wet with tears, and one spills over, tricking down her pretty cheek. Her eyes are wide and sad, and I bring my hand to her cheek, tracing her beautiful face the way I just did with our daughter's. "Thank you," I say softly. "For being so strong when I was weak. For giving our daughter the best start in life that you could."

A sob leaves Sandy's lips, and I quickly bring her into my arms, holding her trembling body against mine. I kiss the side of her head and breathe in the sweet scent of her hair, and it feels like coming home. "Don't cry, baby," I say. "We're here. We made it through everything, and we're here, together. And whatever comes our way, we'll make it through that too. But this time, we'll be together."

Sandy's arms come around me, and her face tips up to

mine, and I kiss her sweet lips so tenderly, it's like the brush of a feather.

And I know that this is it. Sandy's come back to me. She's come back to us.

I have a daughter and the most perfect woman and the best friends a man could ever hope for, and we can be one big happy family in whatever form that takes.

I might never fully forgive myself for Jake's death. If I didn't buy the bike and I didn't leave the keys somewhere he could find them, he never would have died. But I also know for sure that he wouldn't want me to dwell on his death for the rest of my life. Jake was everything that was good and brave and fun about life. And maybe a part of him lives on in my daughter.

One day at a time.

One step in front of the other, and we'll get there.

I hope, from the bottom of my heart, that we'll find a way.

38

ANDREW

Damien couldn't rest, so he's standing in the doorway with his ear craned to where Tyler and Sandy are talking. My eyes are watching him for any kind of response. Greg filled us in on what he and Able found out, and it's big. Tyler and Sandy have a daughter together.

It changes so much and, at the same time, nothing at all.

We still want her in our lives. We want to make her the center of our world if she has a kid, all the better because we all want kids if Sandy is up for making some more.

When Damien turns and puts his thumb up, I breathe a huge sigh of relief. Tyler's okay, and Sandy's okay. She's told him everything, and there hasn't been an implosion or explosion: no breakdown or shouting, just calm discussion, and affection. The affection is making Damien smile, and I'm certain because it doesn't just mean Tyler is cool with the news. It means that Sandy is back for good.

Damien suddenly darts back into the den as quickly as

his lumbering form can move, and then Tyler appears in the kitchen doorway, holding Sandy like he's a groom carrying his bride over the threshold. He walks slowly down the hallway toward the stairs with Sandy's face buried into his chest and her hand on his neck. He jerks his head to indicate that we should follow, and my heart and cock kick at the same time.

This is what I've been waiting for.

This is the moment we're going to seal our relationship.

It's the moment that everything will fall into place.

Sandy will become our lover, and not just one-on-one but as the very center of our group.

There's no scuffle to follow Tyler, just an orderly procession of men who know something big is about to happen. There's anticipation in the air and something that feels strangely ceremonial and sacred.

At the top of the stairs, Tyler takes Sandy to Greg's room. It's the biggest and definitely the tidiest. He kisses Sandy's forehead and lowers her gently onto the crisp white sheets.

There is something so vulnerable about her, like all her emotions have been laid bare, but when her eyes meet mine across the room, there's a fire burning in them too.

Sandy wants this as much as we do. She's put aside what took her away from us and now we're all free to be what we want.

Tyler kneels on the floor in front of her, gently slipping her shoes from her feet. Her toenails are painted hot pink, and he runs his thumb over her foot, discovering her all over again. The blue shirt dress she's wearing has buttons down the front, and he unfastens it from the bottom. It's a slow process, and each second that ticks past just increases the static in the room. It's as though he's unwrapping a precious parcel, and he wants to savor the surprise that is beneath.

I want to savor this moment too. It'll be etched into my memory for life.

"Are you okay?" Tyler asks, cupping Sandy's cheeks. She gazes at him in a moment of intimacy that is just between the two of them.

"I'm okay now I'm with you all," she says, and then her eyes trail over us, meeting the gaze of each man in the room. When she looks into my baby blues, I feel as though she's staring into my soul. She's reassuring me of the connection between us that is going to build and build from here on in.

"We'll be gentle," Tyler says. He looks around to make sure each of us has heard, but Sandy shakes her head.

"I want you to be exactly as you are. True to yourselves and true to me."

My God this girl is perfect. She gets what we need, and I hope that between us, we can deliver what she needs too.

Sandy's the one to shimmy out of her dress and unfasten her pretty black lace bra. The sight of her rounded breasts tipped with soft pink nipples sends blood surging to my cock. I want to wrap my mouth around those nipples so badly. I want to feel them come to life against my tongue, stiffening with arousal. I want to feel her shake and shiver and maybe even beg for more.

But I'm not the only one in the room.

I've shared girls with Able and Arden before. And some of the others have with each other too, but we've never been with one girl all at the same time. Somehow, six on one feels very different than three. With three, there is space for everyone to be involved. Here, at least some of us will be bystanders. But maybe that will be sexy. Maybe watching Sandy's pleasure and waiting my turn will increase the buzz. I cup my dick with my palm, pressing it against my body to relieve some of the pressure.

Tyler is the first to lick Sandy's nipple, and that feels

right. This girl was his once, and now he's sharing her with us.

I don't think there is a greater gift a man could give to another than the woman he loves.

Sandy runs her fingers over Tyler's scalp, gazing down at him with awe. Greg doesn't wait to be invited to join. He tugs off his shirt with one strong-armed flourish, shoves off his jeans, and climbs onto the bed behind Sandy. He touches the bare skin across her shoulders as Tyler worships her breasts. She's sandwiched between two of my best friends, and it's the horniest thing I've ever seen.

As Tyler drops lower, kissing Sandy's stomach and bending until his face is between her legs, Greg uses his huge palm to cup her throat, tipping up her chin and whispering in her ear. I can't hear what he says, but whatever it is, it makes her whimper.

Damien is next to strip down to his boxers, and when he kneels on the bed, the mattress bows under his weight. "Lay down, princess," he says. "Let us worship you."

Greg supports her as she does as Damien instructed, and then Arden and Able are stripping off too. I watch my brothers surround Sandy, their hands caressing her soft peachy skin and their mouths tasting her lust-peaked nipples. I want to pull off my shirt, but I don't want to miss a second of the ecstasy on Sandy's face as Tyler licks between her thighs. That, and there's no space for me right now.

I watch as Greg pulls out his cock and fist it hard once, twice, three times, all while Sandy's eyes fix on it. Her bottom lip folds into her mouth as though she's hungry, and Greg shifts closer until he can run the tip of his cock across her lips. Sandy opens for him like it's the most natural thing in the world to her, licking out to taste him, then allowing him to push deep into her mouth. I remember burying myself in her sweet, wet throat. I remember how well she took me and the rush of sensation, and she takes Greg just as well. His hand fists her hair, but he's careful not to be too rough because of the angle. Arden's hands trail Sandy's flesh as he fists his cock. Damien has one of her rounded breasts beneath his huge hand.

Sandy groans as Tyler's tongue players harder between her legs. The memory of the taste of her fills my mouth, and I'm desperate to take his place and give her an orgasm she won't forget.

I guess I'm the only one thinking clearly because no one has produced a condom, and Sandy has been very clear that they're required. Luckily, I have six in my pocket, ready to go. When I toss them onto the bed, Sandy turns from Greg's cock, letting it slap up against his stomach. Her eyes meet mine, and she smiles.

"Andrew first," she says softly, and my heart skips.

"Why Andrew?" Arden says petulantly. I swear he's always been terrible at sharing, but he's going to have to learn to get better.

"Because he's the only one who hasn't been inside me yet."

It's true. I am the only one that didn't get to fuck Sandy in the fullest sense. In a way, I'm happy we had those moments of intimacy together. I never feel like there's a rush to move things forward. Increasing the build-up only increases the intensity.

"Better get undressed then," Greg grunts, nodding at my still-clothed body. It doesn't take me long to strip, and by then, Tyler has stepped aside, and Sandy's legs are splayed open, ready for me.

Oh God, I don't think there is a sweeter sight than a woman waiting for my cock. Tearing the foil and sliding the condom over my length is like torture, but while I'm doing it, Sandy shimmies out of her panties and lets her legs fall wide, showing me her pretty pink pussy.

Damn.

I bend to lick her, coating my tongue in her arousal. She's slick and warm, the perfect place for my cock.

When I climb over her, she smiles, and her eyes seem to dance with amusement. "Time to claim me as yours," she says softly.

"Oh, you were mine from the moment I saw you."

"From the moment I told you that you could have her," Tyler corrects, and I guess he's right. I would never have gotten myself into this position with Sandy without Tyler's okay.

They might have a past, but we're making a future here today.

I don't hold my cock to find Sandy's entrance. I let it slide between her slick sex until it notches where it needs to be. The first push is like heaven. She's so tight that it takes effort to stretch her open. Her eyes flutter shut as she concentrates on the shallow cant of my hips. I make it in an inch and rest there, letting her body accommodate me. My body thrums for this woman. Between my legs, my balls tighten with the anticipation of the release.

Then I can't wait anymore.

I need to be deep inside her. As deep as I can be, buried to the hilt, surrounded by this woman. The need to claim her is so primal. I feel out of control in a way that I'm not used to at all.

"That's it," Arden says. "Fuck her like you mean it."

And I do. With every thrust, I tell her she's mine. With every grind of my hips, I tell her she'll always be my priority in life as well as in the bedroom. With every kiss, I show her just how much I need her. Even though there are five other men surrounding us, the sex is intimate.

But I want more. I want to see Sandy overwhelmed by

the pleasure we can all give her. I want to see her drown in our bodies and scream from sensation. I want to blow her body and mind so intensely that she won't be able to walk tomorrow and, most of all, so that she'll never want to leave us again.

39

SANDY

Andrew is inside me, and it feels so good.

When he stares into my eyes with his crystal-clear baby blues, I feel like I'm sliding into the warm ocean as the sun sets. And when his brothers start to touch me too, I drift away into the stratosphere.

I know what it's like to be with two men. Arden and Able rocked my world, showing me that pleasure is indefinable. But that was two. What will six men show me?

Arden's mouth latches onto my breast, and he sucks my nipple hard before nipping it with his teeth. I jump and moan simultaneously, and he grins as though he enjoys having so much control over my body's reactions.

Able's fingers slide over my shoulder and down the soft skin of the inside of my arm, caressing until shivers pass up my neck and into my scalp. His fingers intertwine with mine, and I grasp onto him as Andrew's thrusts become harder. Rocking my hips is hard in this position, but I try. I can chase my orgasm from beneath, and I do…

Greg tips my face gently, searching for my mouth to return to his cock and I let him slide it over my tongue and into my throat. Tyler takes my free hand, wrapping it tightly around his rock-hard length, slicking my palm with his arousal and working into my grip more fiercely than I would have thought was pleasurable. Damien is somewhere here behind me, and when fingers start to stroke my hair, I know it's him. He's found a way, amongst all of these men, to make me feel treasured.

When I was lost, they came to find me. When I needed support, they were my rocks, and now, they're showing me what it takes for us to be together.

Six men and just one of me.

My Deep Six.

Deep because of our connection.

Deep because of their love for each other.

My eyes find Andrew's, and it's like a jolt of electricity zaps my body from within. My pussy draws tight, and then I'm coming and coming, muscles convulsing around the stiff rod of his dick.

"That's it," Greg croons as he pulls back, giving me breathing space to soak up my pleasure. Andrew rocks into me slowly while the orgasm has my body in its throes, and then faster, chasing his own release. It aches when he empties high up inside me, rooting so deep I feel a cramp, but then he's withdrawing carefully and kissing my lips, telling me that I'm beautiful and that he's so happy that we're together. And I am too. So happy I can barely think straight.

"Get her onto her knees," Greg orders, assuming the role of director to the group. Tyler and Damien take my hands, pulling me into a seated position, and then I clamber onto my hands and knees and look up at Greg.

He's staring down at me, his dark eyes unfathomable. His big hand cups my throat, tipping up that chin. "Can you take two of us?" he asks.

"She can," Arden says quickly.

"Three," I say. This might be the first time that I'm sharing a bed with so many men, but I'm not a group-sex novice. Since Connie and Natalie hooked up with their harems, I've watched a fair bit of porn with three or more men. I know the positions that I think I can deal with. I want my men to know that I've got what it takes to keep them satisfied because they've already shown me that they've got what it takes to rock my world.

There's an audible inhalation of shock at my response, or maybe it's arousal.

Andrew has worked hard to spread me open, now two of his brothers will get to reap the benefits.

"Able, lay on your back," I say softly. He's there in a flash, his bright blue eyes open wide as I straddle his muscular body and settle my pussy over his sheathed cock. He holds it at the root as I work him inside me, thick inch by thick inch until I'm gasping, and he's buried deep. I roll my hips a few times, accommodating to the position, resting on my arms, so I'm leaning low over him.

He leans up to rub his nose against mine, and I kiss his soft lips, loving how gentle he is with me.

"Arden," I whisper. "Do you think you can find space too?"

"Hell yeah."

I knew he'd handle this part with enthusiasm. When he's behind me, he kisses the base of my spine, the heat of his breath sending a cascade of shivers over my skin. When he notches at my entrance, alongside his brother, I wonder if I've made a huge mistake.

Their cocks are so big.

I'm filled with one, so how will they squeeze in two?

They'll tear me open and make soup of my insides. The

girls in the porn movies must have trained for this, but I'm just an ordinary girl, who up until a few weeks ago, had only slept with one man.

Now look at me.

"Just breathe," Able says, stroking my damp hair from my face and holding my cheeks so I have to look into his eyes. "Arden will go slow. You've got this."

And Arden does as his brother says, easing his cock over his brother's, stretching my entrance, and then deeper...deeper. I have to close my eyes as his body presses against me. The sensation is overwhelmingly good, but my heart is skittering in my chest with panic as much as anticipation.

What will it be like when they move? I want it to feel good, not to hurt.

"Slowly," Able says again. Maybe he feels my nerves. Maybe Arden does, too, because he slides his hand down my side and over my ass, keeping totally still inside me.

They know how to bring me into the moment and keep me there, and when Arden begins to move, all that exists is deep rolling pleasure that makes me gasp.

"Open that pretty mouth for me," Greg says, tipping my face to him. I gaze up, over his broad tattooed chest to his coal-dark eyes. When I obey, the flicker of pleasure on his lips fills me with warmth. This huge, terrifying man came to find me. He held me close and told me that everything would be okay, and I want to show him the same thing.

I keep my eyes on him as I take him deep into my mouth.

My body isn't my own anymore. I'm a vessel of desire and pleasure for these men, and they're going to fill all the places in me that need security and love. Tyler's hand strokes over my breast, and his lips nip my earlobe.

"That's it, baby," he says. "You look so good. You

taste so good. All I want to do is wrap you in my arms and hold you tight."

I moan, and Greg grips my jaw as though the vibrations are too much for him.

They definitely are because when I do it again, he groans and releases into my mouth as Able begins to thrust from beneath me.

I swallow quickly and gasp as the slip of pleasure builds between my legs, my clit grazing against Able with every move they make.

"That's it," Arden says, and he slaps my ass enough to sting and trip a little sex-switch that I didn't know I had.

My pussy bears down, rippling as I come, my eyes scrunch closed and mouth opens with a moan that seems to go on and on and on. Able grunts beneath me, pulling me down against his body, his heavy arm anchoring me, so I don't float into oblivion. The stretch when Able and Arden come has my pussy thrumming, but knowing how much pleasure they're feeling sends my head spinning.

When Arden withdraws first, and then Able, I'm left feeling ravaged and empty, but not for long.

It's as though Damien has grown tired of waiting, and he tugs me off Able's sweat-slicked chest and into his waiting lap. I'm still panting, but he kisses my mouth, capturing my ecstatic breaths with lips that feel too soft to belong to such a tough man.

"I've been waiting to do this with you again," he says, palming my breasts and then running his rough hands over my sides, mapping the curves of my body like he did when we fucked in his truck.

"You don't want to try a different position?" I ask, running my hands over his scruff-covered jaw, smiling when he quickly shakes his head.

"If it ain't broke," he says, taking his cock and sliding it inside me, throwing his head back in ecstasy when he's buried to the hilt.

I move against him as I did in the parking lot, rolling my hips and grinding my pleasure-ravaged clit against his rock-hard body. His hands grip me hard enough to feel it but not so hard it hurts. There's care in his touch, and then the way he kisses me, and care in Tyler's hands as he strokes over my back and kisses my neck.

I turn to face Tyler, the man who made me a woman, the man who made me a mother, the man who gave me a group of men who want to build a life with me. In this moment, it's like all the time when we were apart disappears, and time stitches our lives back together.

"I love you," I whisper to him. It's right that he should hear it first. I'll tell the rest of them when the days we spend together weave enough of a bond that it'll feel real. Until then, they can feel our connection in my touch and my kisses, in the movement of my body, and the care I will take of them as we live together in this house.

"I love you too," he says, dipping to kiss my lips. He tastes of the past when we were just kids finding our way in the world, but also like the greatest of life's possibilities.

My life that was so closed down with feelings shuttered and secrets buried now feels wide open with potential.

I'm high on it.

High on these men who surround me like lions around a lioness.

"That's it," Damien says, his teeth gritted as he gets closer. I hook my arms around his neck, bringing our bodies close.

"You feel so big," I tell him, nipping on his bottom lip. "I love sitting on your big cock."

"Yeah, you do," he huffs. His hands clamp against my ass, forcing my hips to thud against his body, and I gasp with every pass because it shouldn't be possible for me to come again, but I am. I am. I am.

Tears prickle my eyes as Damien swells inside me, his arms wrapping around my back so tightly that I struggle to breathe. "Baby," he whispers, his breath coming fast, his chest heaving and heart thudding against me.

I stroke his hair, loving how small I feel in his enveloping embrace.

But he doesn't hold me for too long. He knows there's one more man who needs to take his turn.

Tyler's waited so patiently, and it feels right that he's last to seal this relationship that came from his idea for how he wanted his life to be.

He didn't trust himself to be enough for me, but he underestimated us both. Tyler would have been enough for the Sandy that broke down by the side of the road, with a shattered heart and secrets that weighed heavy. He would have been enough if he'd only opened up.

But we had to come on this journey to find a way back to each other again, and in the process, he made me a bigger, better, brighter version of the girl I was.

I'm enough for these men.

I can see it in their eyes and feel it in their bodies.

And they're everything to me.

"Lay with me," Tyler says softly as I slip from Damien's lap.

Greg and the triplets have moved to give us space and are seated around the edges of the huge bed.

I lie facing Tyler and close my eyes as he plays with my hair. "I love you," he whispers again, and I snuggle closer to him, burying my face in his neck and breathing him in.

The way he touches me isn't new. We've traveled this path so many times before, and even though it was a long time ago, we both remember the ways to please each other. The slow build of caresses and kisses is intimate, despite the fact that five other men surround us.

Tyler is showing them how to love me his way.

He hooks my top leg over his arm, opening me enough that he can push inside me. We're on our sides but face to face, so I can watch every moment of pleasure that passes over his face, and he can see the effect of every move he makes on mine.

I used to love this position because it's so lazy and slow. We used to fuck like this in the morning, and after, I'd be humming happily for the rest of the day.

We kiss long and deep, and as Tyler's thrusts get faster, the bed shifts, and hands begin to caress my skin. "That's it," Greg murmurs close to my ear. His fingers slide over my breasts, tweaking my nipple then passing with a feather light touch over my side. Damien is there too, stroking my hair from my face. Arden runs the side of his hand between the cheeks of my ass, and I shudder with arousal. Andrew and Able are with me, too, caressing my thighs and my calves.

And in amongst all of this attention, the impossible happens. Another orgasm grips me, sending my mind tumbling further and faster than it ever has before. Soft words are whispered, but I can't make them out. My mind is scrambled, and all I feel is deep, primal pleasure.

I'm aware of Tyler swelling inside me and his body seizing, but it all happens in a haze, almost as though I'm outside of myself.

"Sandy," someone whispers.

"Leave her," another voice says. "It's a lot for her to take. You've had one orgasm, she's had four."

"Let her rest," someone else says, and I moan my agreement. All I want to do is slip into a sex coma of sleep.

"Here." A blanket is wrapped around me, and the bed shifts as my men take their places around me.

This bed isn't big enough for all of us to sleep. We can work on that another day, but for now, I'm at peace, and it's the best feeling ever.

40

TYLER

Sandy's sister's house is big and pretty. It's the kind of house that anyone would want to raise their child in and I'm happy to see that Sophie's growing up in a good place.

As soon as we pull up in the driveway, the front door opens. Suzanne doesn't look so different after four years. Maybe her shorter hair gives her more maturity. She's wearing practical jeans and a blue sweater, and her hand is gripping the edge of the door tight enough that her knuckles are whitened.

I inhale a deep breath, gripping the steering wheel the same way. Sandy's warm palm covers my closest hand, and she squeezes it gently. "It's going to be fine," she says.

"It's me who should be reassuring you," I tell her. When our eyes meet, the warmth of our connection seeps into my nervous stomach.

"I know Sophie, and I know my sister. I have an advantage." She grins, trying to make light of the situation.

"I just...I want her to like me," I say. It's tough to

expose the most vulnerable sides of ourselves, especially as men. We're taught that we have to be impenetrable rocks and show no feelings. But I do feel so much in this moment, and I want Sandy to know.

This is the biggest, most important moment of my life.

Most men get to meet their children on the day of their birth. My daughter is already a fully formed little person who can speak. I've got some catching up to do.

I glance away from Sandy to the doorway, and my heart skips a beat. She's there. My little girl, standing holding onto Suzanne's leg and resting her head against her jeans. She's not smiling, but I can see she's not worried. There's a serene look to her sweet expression. And it's uncanny how much she looks like me.

"There she is," Sandy says, her voice tinged with a breathy whisper that I take to be wistful. We've spoken a lot about how she feels not to be raising Sophie, and there is a lot to unpack. I think it's inevitable that Sandy will hold some regrets. If she'd been older and if I had been around, she never would have agreed to Suzanne adopting our baby. But that wasn't the circumstance, and she knows she's given our little girl the best start and given her sister the greatest blessing. There is comfort in that, and a sense of pride too. I think the burden is easier now we've talked about what family life might look like for us in the future. Kids are very much a part of that. However many Sandy is prepared to have.

"You ready?" she asks.

"As I'll ever be." With a deep breath, I throw open the door and emerge into the morning sunshine. I walk side by side with Sandy up the driveway, and when we get closer, Sophie leaves Suzanne's side and runs to her as fast as her little legs will carry her.

"Auntie San San," she says as Sandy bends to give her the kind of cuddle that squeezes tight. Sandy's eyes are closed, and so are Sophie's, and the ache in my heart is great. Then Sophie pulls away and looks up at me.

"You look like me," she says, a little furrow appearing between her eyebrows. I laugh in a big bubbling way that feels like light streaming out of my chest.

"I know. How awesome is that."

"We have the same eyes." She presses a hand over one closed lid like a pirate's patch.

"Eyes like emeralds," I say. I hold my right hand out. "I'm Tyler. Pleased to meet you."

Sophie takes my hand gently, her soft little hand so small in mine that I'm scared to squeeze it in case I hurt her. This is the first time I've touched my daughter. The first time I've felt the warmth of her living skin against mine, and it's beautiful.

"Mommy told me you gave Auntie San San your seed so that she could make me in her tummy," she says, cocking her head to one side. I'm so surprised by her frankness that I laugh again.

"Yes, I did." Glancing at Sandy, I can see amusement dancing in her eyes. "Auntie San San is just awesome at growing seeds, isn't she?"

Sophie puts her hand on Sandy's tummy. "I think your seed must be strong too," Sophie says. "That's why I look like you so much."

Sandy snorts with laughter and ruffles Sophie's hair. "What do you know about strong seeds?" she asks.

"I grew a sunflower at kindergarten. It was the tallest in class, and my teacher told me it must have been a strong seed."

"Well, your teacher sounds very wise," I say. I glance up to where Suzanne is standing and find her husband there too, with his arm around her. This is the part I've been most nervous about, funnily. I've tried to imagine what Vernon will be feeling as a man who's being faced with the real father of his adopted daughter. There must be an element of territorialism. If the situation was reversed, I'd feel it, for sure. I want him to know that it's not my intention to tread on anyone's toes. I don't want to disrupt Sophie in any way. Suzanne and Vernon are quite obviously doing an amazing job, and Sophie seems really happy.

"Can I show you my strong seed?" Sophie says.

"Of course. Where is it?"

"It's in the backyard. Come." She holds her hand out, and I reach for it. It's so strange to be led by this little girl who's half of me mixed with half of Sandy. We don't need to go through the house to get to the backyard. I simply follow Sophie down the side of the house and into a beautiful yard with a treehouse, a swing set, and a sandpit; all the things I would have loved as a child. "There it is," Sophie says, dropping my hand and breaking into a cute little trot that has her hair flying in the breeze. The sunflower is over six feet tall, with a head so heavy that it's had to be propped up with a cane.

"Wow," I say. "It's as tall as me!"

"It is," she says.

Suzanne and Vernon appear on the back deck, watching us closely. I get down to Sophie's level by resting on one knee. "How did you feel when you heard I was coming to see you today?" I ask.

"Mommy showed me a picture of you. I wanted to see the person who looks like me," she says.

"Auntie San San showed me a picture of you, and I was excited to meet you too."

"Do you like muffins? Mommy makes the best banana and chocolate chip."

I smile at her quick change of subject, watching as her eyes dart around for what is going to interest her next. She's so sharp and inquisitive, two traits that will serve her well. "I love muffins," I say.

"Can you push me on the swing?"

"Sure."

Sophie's running across the yard before I get back on my feet. I find Sandy next to me, and I take her hand as we both gaze across at the miracle of our child. Suzanne and Vernon find their way next to us too. "She's amazing," I say.

"Yes, she is," Vernon says. I turn and hold my hand out to him to shake but instead, he pulls me into a short sharp hug. "Thank you," he says, and by the time he pulls back, my throat is burning with tears that I fight hard not to shed. This isn't the time for emotion, so when he slaps me on the shoulder and asks me if I want a beer, I say a grateful yes.

"Come on, Uncle Tyler," Sophie shouts. She's holding onto the chains and trying to jump onto the swing, but she isn't tall enough.

"You'd better go," Suzanne says. "Little miss doesn't like to be kept waiting."

I smile, shaking my head at the emotions running through me.

When I think about what my life was like a few weeks ago, I hardly recognize where I am. Before I saw Sandy all dressed up by the side of the road, I was trapped in the shadow of sadness. My brother had died, and I had lost the love of my life. I hadn't managed to find a way to deal with either of those events. My friends had dragged me out of the worst, but I felt as though I was treading water rather than living. I kept trying to find ways to make myself feel alive again. Ways that didn't involve me slipping into addiction like my parents.

And then, there she was. An angel who needed rescuing, and that's what I tried to do. I tried to find a way to resurrect the love we had in a way I could manage, and, in the process, I built a new life not only for Sandy and me but for my friends too.

Then there's Sophie. This amazing reminder of the past and a way for us all to look into the future. A blessing I don't deserve and could never have expected.

As I jog across the grass, not wanting to keep my daughter waiting, I'm filled with a rush of love for Sandy, for Sophie, for my friends, and for life.

When circumstances drag us deep into times of trouble, it is possible to find a way out and back into a place of love.

Deeper love.

EPILOGUE

SANDY

Greg pours me a cup of steaming hot, freshly ground coffee while Arden butters my toast. I'm sitting with my feet upon Damien's lap, and he's massaging the arch so perfectly, I could purr. Across the table, Andrew is studying the most recent accounts for the repair shop, and Able is writing a list for the grocery store.

It's absolute domestic bliss, and I can't stop smiling.

When the key turns in the front door, I know it's about to get even better.

Little feet sound on the hardwood first. "Auntie San San," Sophie calls. Behind her, Tyler appears with the hugest smile and the softest green eyes. His expression is always like that when he's looking at our daughter. It's like something inside him melts at the sight of her.

Damien releases my feet, and I swing my legs down to enjoy the warm hug that Sophie is desperate to give me. She smells of strawberry shampoo and blueberry muffins which she probably had for breakfast. She's going to be with us for the whole weekend while Suzanne and Vernon head to a work social event. It's a good time for them to have a break and for us to have some quality time with Sophie.

"She sang the whole way over," Tyler says.

"And Uncle Ty did too," Sophie grins, then leans in, cupping her hand around my ear. "He's not a good singer," she whispers, and I snort with laughter.

"What's she saying?" he asks, bending down to tickle Sophie's ribs. "Is she telling you that I should become a pop star like my sister instead of a dirty old mechanic?"

"No..." Sophie squeals, wriggling and laughing as the rest of my boys watch the scene with smiles on their faces.

Sophie loves spending time here. What girl wouldn't? She has six uncles who love her to bits. Six uncles who are willing to throw her in the air a million times. Six uncles to build her the coolest princess house in the yard. The last time she came to stay, I found her painting Greg's fingernails baby blue.

He will absolutely never live that down.

"So, what are we going to do today?" I ask everyone.

"Uncle Ty said we could have a picnic in the park?"

Sophie's eyes are wide and hopeful, and she clasps her little hands together in front of her. In her denim shorts and Marvel shirt, she's just the cutest thing I've ever seen. "Well, I think Uncle Ty has the best ideas," I smile.

"By the way, Suzanne said you need to check out the local newspaper online," Tyler says.

"Why?"

He shrugs. "She didn't say. Just told me you need to see the headline and she'll talk to you about it when she gets back."

Intrigued, I grab my phone from the table and search. The headline and image that appear on the homepage send a terrible shiver through me. The principal of my old school has been arrested after a report of sexual assault. Another two women have come forward with allegations of sexual harassment too.

I wasn't the only one.

Being careful not to show Sophie, I hold the phone out so the boys can see. It's been tough over the past few months to keep them from going to rip that man's asshole through his mouth. The idea that a man would touch their girl without her permission has been a difficult one for them to deal with. In the end, though, they understood why I didn't want to put myself through the stress of reporting him, but now?

Now I feel like I need to. I feel like I can because I know my six men have my back, whatever happens.

"On Monday, I'm going to the police station," I say. "It's time to deal with this situation once and for all."

"Good," Greg says, folding his arms menacingly across his chest. I always get hot between my legs when he does that. It's something primal that trips a switch in my head.

Big strong man, in a big strong stance.

It would be pathetic if it didn't feel so awesome.

"We'll be right there with you," Able says.

Turning my attention back to Sophie, I pull her onto my knee. "So, missy, you want a picnic. What kind of food shall we make, and will you help me?"

"YES!" she says excitedly. "I want mini sandwiches and cupcakes."

"Well, that sounds easy enough." I lean close to whisper in her ear. "Can I make big sandwiches for big uncles?"

She giggles, her hands resting on my arms that encircle her little body. Those same hands that held my fingers the day I gave birth to her. "I think that would be a good idea."

We laugh together as my men look on, bemused.

Later, in the park, I'm lying on a blanket on the grass next to an empty picnic basket. My head is resting on Tyler's stomach, and he's stroking my hair, watching Sophie play catch with Arden, Able, and Andrew.

Greg and Damien are close too, talking shop.

"She's just the most adorable thing," Tyler says wistfully.

"I know," I say, gazing with awe at the beautiful child we created.

"Do you feel ready to make another adorable thing?"

Turning to him, I find his emerald eyes a little wider than usual, and his dark eyebrows raised hopefully. "I might," I say, smiling.

A growl rumbles in his throat, drawing the attention of Greg and Damien.

"What?" Greg asks.

"It's on," Tyler says, cocking an eyebrow. A couple of seconds pass as Greg and Damien work out what Tyler is talking about, and then it's raised eyebrows all around. They must have already discussed this between them.

"You sure?" Damien asks.

"It's a big decision," Greg says.

"I'm sure," I say. "Let's make pretty babies."

There's a collective sigh around the group that makes me giggle from deep in my belly. Who would have thought it'd be the six guys in this relationship who are so desperate to procreate? I always thought it was women who had to do the convincing.

Later that night, when we're certain Sophie is settled

and sleeping deeply, we converge in Greg's room. There have been some changes in here, mainly the addition of another huge bed so that there is just about enough room for all of us to sleep together some of the time. I have to admit that being sandwiched between so many roasting hot men can be a challenge. I'm not good with spooning while I'm asleep or finding myself covered in heavy arms and legs from all sides. Plus, it's nice for me to have moments of alone time with each of my men. It's during those nights that I've found out so much about each of them. About Arden's struggles with dyslexia, which I'm helping him to overcome, and about Greg's time in jail. Andrew has shared some of their childhood and Able details about their time in foster homes. Damien has told me about his brother, who he practically raised, and how worried he is about him being stationed overseas.

And Tyler? Well, we've been open about everything in our past and found a way to leave it all behind. It will forever be a part of our story, but it isn't the chapter we are writing now. But if we have a baby boy, we've already decided that we'll call him Jake.

"So, how are we going to do this," Able whispers. "Like, are we going to draw straws to decide the order, or mix up our cum like a potion to be inserted with a turkey baster?"

"Fuck the turkey baster idea. I say we leave it up to nature," Tyler says.

"But who will we put on the birth certificate?" Andrew asks.

"Shall we cross that bridge another time when we don't have a needy girl half-naked on the bed?" Arden laughs. "The legalities of paternity don't exactly constitute dirty talk."

"I say we ask Sandy. It's her body that's going to be doing the hard work," Greg says.

Six sets of hungry and confused eyes land on me. This

is a whole lot of pressure.

"Well, we won't just have to do this once," I say. "Conceiving can take a lot of work."

"We're willing to do whatever it takes," Damien says seriously, and Tyler slaps him on the back with a grin.

"So, maybe we try six times over the next six days. Each time, you rotate once in order. That way, you'll all get a turn in each position."

"I don't care what position I'm in as long as I get between those pretty legs..." Arden says, rubbing his beard.

"So, Arden can go last." Andrew rolls his eyes.

"Anyway, isn't it like these guys are getting three times the chances?" Damien asks. "I mean, they're genetically the same."

"My cock is my own," Arden says, grabbing it for effect.

"Not wanting to hurry anyone but..." I let my legs flop open so they can see the hot pink lacy underwear I have under my short bed shirt.

Greg is on the bed in a flash, his face buried between my thighs, his hot tongue rubbing over my clit through the lace.

I don't think I've ever seen my boys strip faster.

The sex is great, but different. For a change, they all want it in missionary position, which is fine by me. I love being pinned underneath their huge muscular bodies, feeling them work to bring me pleasure. And this time, there're no condoms. By the time Arden slides inside me, I'm full to the brim with their strong seeds.

Who knows which one of them will be the father of my next child? To be honest, I don't really care because they will all make the best dads in the world. Of that, I am sure.

When I packed my small bag and jumped into my car

to attend Connie's wedding, I was grateful for the distraction from my disaster of a life. Who could have predicted that I'd run into the man who broke my heart or that I'd find six men to mend it?

I found six friends who'd become family to each other in a way, and they wanted me to become part of their lives. And now, as our love grows deeper, we're making a family of our own.

ABOUT THE AUTHOR

Stephanie Brother writes scintillating stories with bad boys and step-siblings as their main romantic focus. She's always been curious about the forbidden, and this is her way of exploring such complex relationships that threaten to keep her couples apart. As she writes her way to her dream job, Ms. Brother hopes that her readers will enjoy the full emotional and romantic experience as much as she's enjoyed writing them.

Printed in Great Britain
by Amazon